THREE
SMALL
BONES

BOOKS BY JENNIFER CHASE

First Watch

Never Forgotten

JENNIFER CHASE

THREE SMALL BONES

bookouture

Published by Bookouture in 2022

An imprint of Storyfire Ltd.
Carmelite House
50 Victoria Embankment
London EC4Y 0DZ

www.bookouture.com

ISBN: 978-1-80314-594-5
eBook ISBN: 978-1-80314-593-8

For Eric

PROLOGUE

FOUR YEARS AGO

The heat was even more scorching than usual. It wasn't a surprise to the special army team whose mission it was to find bombs and insurgents in Afghanistan while keeping civilians safe. It was late afternoon, barely 1700 hours. Still, the temperature raged at one hundred ten degrees and wasn't showing any remorse.

The assignment was to enter a small village, search it, and maintain a presence while waiting for further orders. They had intelligence information that the enemy had possibly used the village for storing bomb-making paraphernalia. The inhabitants were not known hostiles, merely farmers, and would not pose any type of danger.

Katie Scott took point, which meant she was holding the most exposed position leading her unit. She trudged forward, feeling every muscle ache in her body. Her gear seemed heavier than it had only two hours ago. She adjusted her helmet and, keeping her weapon poised and ready, watched the black German shepherd pad along the roadway. The dog's posture was almost regal and he was on high alert, ears perked forward as his head moved from side to side catching scents from the open area. Cisco was Katie's constant companion and partner, one who had alerted her team to danger on several occasions. The dog was invaluable in so many ways, thwarting multiple potential dangers and keeping the team safe.

They finally entered the village. A couple of elderly towns-people acknowledged the American soldiers with a subtle nod but stopped what they were doing immediately to take refuge in their small, makeshift homes. There were supposed to be fami-lies with children in the village, but now Katie could only see two young men out and about.

It seemed strange.

Something was out of place.

Katie slowed her pace and her sergeant caught up with her.

"What's up, Scotty?" he said quietly, still keeping his eyes on any movement around the village.

"I don't know..." she said softly. "But something is wrong."

They stopped.

The rest of the team spread out and kept a watchful eye around them.

Cisco stopped too. He stood completely still, taking in the sights and sounds as the hot breeze ruffled his black fur. He growled and turned his attention ahead toward a group of buildings.

"He senses something," she whispered to her sergeant.

The sergeant gestured for the rest to follow in that direction.

The company moved out. Each soldier had their position, watching for any movement as they covered each other's backs.

Katie could feel her heart beating hard. She shivered even though the temperature was blistering. Moving cautiously in the direction that Cisco had headed, she brought the dog close by her side. She was ready to return fire or take cover. She took a deep breath to steady her nerves and keep focus. They continued to advance.

A building made of mud bricks and concrete with blocked up windows sat silent. It didn't appear to be the same structure type as the family homes around it. On one side of the dwelling the windows were crumbling, appearing more ancient than the rest.

Katie watched Cisco slow his pace. His fur bristled down his spine.

The team stopped just before the entrance. There was no visibility as to what was inside.

Under the direction of the sergeant, two team members opened the door and then cleared the entrance, heading farther inside.

Katie heard gasps from her group. She cautiously entered behind them, directing her weapon in front of her. The musty stench hit her first—it was an unmistakable odor. As her vision slowly became accustomed to the dim, dusty lighting, she saw what her teammates had seen. Death.

At first, it appeared to be a large pile of clothes. Katie saw shoes and various materials, but she then realized that the clothes were covering bodies that were by now mostly bones but there were some that were in the first stages of decomposition. There were smaller bones that had been children.

She gulped and took a few steps back. Her mouth went dry and her heart hammered. Her team searched and cleared the building before moving out in formation.

Cisco kept close to her side as Katie tried hard to erase the horrific spectacle from her mind. It had been a massacre. Parents had still had their arms wrapped around their children. She had seen tiny shoes and part of a toy.

Without warning, gunfire bombarded them, peppering off the old clay walls. Smoke filled the air. The team took their positions and returned fire. Katie tucked into a safe place with Cisco next to her. She began to help hold off the ambush attack by firing in the direction of the threat.

Later on, Katie realized that it had been the longest gun battle she had been in, lasting nearly thirty minutes. But the worst part wasn't the shooting. It was that now she could never forget the image of the town whose inhabitants had been systematically murdered just to keep the enemy's weapons safe. Something had changed in her perspective that day. The incident fused into her soul, and she would always now carry it with her.

ONE

PRESENT DAY

Wednesday 0755 hours

A low rumble followed by a crackling snap caused the small, intricate device to ignite a single flame. A low flame at first, as if it were a cigarette lighter, but soon growing exponentially, fueled by accelerant expertly placed on and around the back of the garage. It was also cleverly placed at the far back corner of the house, where the electricity meter was attached, conveniently out of the view of any neighbors. It proved to be a seamless plan as the fire rapidly increased. It only took moments for the house to become immersed in an all-out blaze.

The flames quickly engulfed the empty two-story home, escaping with searing fire tentacles through broken windows. Smoke spiraled fiercely as the intense heat reached the rooftop. Any windows that were intact exploded. Trim around the frames melted. Plants near the front door were scorched and disintegrated. What was once a modest home was now only a burning reminder—blackened and collapsing.

Sirens blared suddenly, overpowering the sound of the blaze and gaining momentum as emergency vehicles barreled down the otherwise quiet street to 717 Maple Road. Two fire trucks pulled up along the curb in front of the burning home and several firefighters jumped out. Each moved effortlessly to their duties. A hydrant was attached to the oversized hoses and two firefighters began to douse the structure from each corner to contain it. Water sprayed out in an arc, shooting directly into the inferno as the men held firm and battled the blaze.

Two neighbors hesitantly stepped from their driveways, one with a cell phone in hand, daring to move into the street to gain a better view.

"Take the back fence area!" yelled Captain Steve Landers. His concern was making sure the fire didn't ignite the fence or any large pine trees, or jump to any nearby homes.

"Sir, radio from dispatch," said one of the firefighters, approaching him with a radio.

Captain Landers took it. "Landers." He paused. "I see. Thank you." He handed the radio back. He had been informed that the house was empty and had been for several months. It raised some red flags for him—could this be a homeowner's attempt to collect insurance?

He noticed two Pine Valley Sheriff's Department cruisers had been dispatched and had pulled up a few houses down. This was the usual procedure as a precaution to help with the perimeter detail or keep bystanders back until the blaze was under control.

The wind changed direction and black smoke began to waft down the street, causing any curious neighbors to retreat back inside the safety of their homes.

The flames were finally settling down and the fire crew had it under control—it would soon be safe for them to enter the premises to continue the fire protocol.

Captain Landers had a gut feeling, which made him want to accompany two of his firefighters into what remained of the house. He had been with Pine Valley Fire Department for twenty-four years and in that time had seen quite a variety of "accidents" that ended up being covers for intentionally set fires.

Once the blaze had been extinguished enough, his firefighters moved to enter the house to search and continue to smother any new flames that popped up.

Carrying an ax, Landers stepped over the broken window glass and then over the threshold, which had once been the front door but now was just a burned-out opening. He immediately scanned left to right as his crew tended to various small fires. There was nothing left. No signs of furniture, personal items, and most importantly—no bodies. It was just as he had been told—an empty rental house waiting for new tenants.

Moving throughout the structure with his mask on, he eyed anything that might represent where the fire had started. No signs of accelerants. No obvious loose wiring. Or a problem with the incoming gas line in the kitchen. Nothing caught his attention.

One of his men approached him. "Sir," he said, his voice muffled through his face mask, "you need to see something."

"What is it?"

"I just... you just need to see..."

"Where is it?"

"Down in the basement." The firefighter turned and led the captain toward the far end of the house.

The captain stepped over burned-down beams and pieces of hot wreckage. Thoughts of how the fire had started still propelled through his mind; some type of clever incendiary device, or a dozen burning candles set up with a pack of matches?

He reached the basement entrance. The door had burned away almost completely and the remaining hinges lay on the charred floor, but the steps were mostly intact and the fire hadn't ravaged the area as much as the rest of the house.

He went down the stairs behind his colleague. When he reached the bottom, he saw there were several support beams barely affected by the intense heat and flames. Some of the small windows looking out at the ground level were still intact. Obviously, the basement wasn't the origin of the fire. The floor was mostly packed dirt with some cement blocks around the perimeter. There were strange vertical gouges along one of the wood-faced walls.

He was curious as to why he had been summoned to the basement. He soon got his answer as the firefighter pointed at the floor area in the farthest corner.

"What's up?" the captain asked.

"I came down to inspect the support beams and to look for any signs of how the fire might have originated... and... I saw... this..."

Captain Landers focused his attention on the floor. There was still smoke in the air, obscuring his vision. He took a moment to focus and gain his bearings. There was an area where the packed dirt had been disturbed—he was unable to tell if it was recent or not. The surrounding cinderblocks weren't charred and appeared to be in their appropriate places. A wall nearby had some structural damage not caused by the fire.

The dirt of the floor had been trampled by numerous footprints. Some were recent and some had been made over time, muddling the impressions into almost a hieroglyphic pattern. More tracks were to be seen in the area nearest the wall and in the far corner.

In the area of question there was a slight rise to the ground, a mound that caught his attention. It appeared to be some strange rocks or dried driftwood protruding straight up from the earth.

The captain bent over and gently brushed some of the loose soil with his heavy glove. He still wasn't sure what he was seeing—he continued to clear away the loose dirt. The more he saw, the faster he wiped the dirt away. Until he saw a single bony finger poking up, almost as if it were trying to capture someone's attention. It was an eerie summons from the dead.

The firefighter that had brought this to his attention stood quietly—watching.

The captain stood up straight, sucked in a breath, unable to tear his eyes away from those three small bones. He had seen his fair share of burned bodies, limbs curled beyond recognition, but nothing like this. He slowly bent down again and continued to dust away some more of the loose dirt, his hand shaking. He still hoped that there was some logical explanation and he had been mistaken. He spent another minute slowly uncovering a skeletal arm, which had the badly decomposed remains of a navy shirt. His heart sank. His pulse quickened. His mind raced.

He stood up abruptly. "Step away from this area—carefully. It's now a crime scene. We need to call the police and detectives now—and alert the arson investigator on duty."

The firefighter immediately retraced his path to the stairs and took the basement steps two at a time before disappearing.

Captain Landers remained for a moment standing over the remains, unable to pry his eyes away—giving his respects. He stared at a plain gold wedding band that still remained on the skeleton's ring finger.

TWO

"Cisco! Bring that back!" said Detective Katie Scott as she watched her retired military K9 steal a dry paintbrush from a bucket and take off running through the house like a streak. She couldn't help but laugh as the jet-black German shepherd playfully ran back and forth with the brush between his teeth.

Katie set down the paint tray and roller, and stepped down from the ladder. Her loose T-shirt and jeans were now speckled with light gray paint and she had a long streak of it through her dark hair. She walked carefully around the drop cloths and the plastic coverings protecting her furniture and belongings.

She went into the hallway to take a break and looked back at her handiwork. It was coming together nicely. She had already painted two bedrooms and the hallway. The interior was beginning to look fresh and new—it had been long overdue. There was also an underlying reason she was painting the house —she might be selling it so that she and Chad, her fiancé, could buy a new house together after they got married. Truthfully, she wasn't sure if she wanted to sell the only home she had ever known. Memories always filtered through the house. Even though she lived alone, these remembrances kept her company.

Katie walked into the master bedroom and stood for a moment. The three-bedroom farmhouse had been where Katie had grown up. She had inherited it after her parents had been killed in a car accident when she was only a teen. Being an only child and with no other family, bar her Uncle Wayne, made life feel sometimes a bit lonely. She was glad that she had her work to fill the gap. Getting married would begin a new part of her life.

Picking up a water bottle, she downed several gulps.

Cisco returned and dropped the paintbrush at her feet.

"Oh, really?" she said.

Cisco let out a high-pitch whine and wagged his tail in anticipation.

Katie retrieved the brush.

Cisco barked, clearly wanting to play.

"I don't think so," she said. "Go get one of your toys."

The dog bolted to the other room, where she heard him searching his toy basket for just the right toy. Fast squeaks and rustlings resounded.

As she stood in the master bedroom scrutinizing her painting of the corners and around the trim, her gaze took in the photos in frames that sat on her bureau under the plastic. A photo of her army team with Cisco produced so many memories —some positive and some horrific, the latter meant she had carried home with her the effects of PTSD. But her team had been her family. Two tours in Afghanistan did that to a person. She and Cisco had been the K9 explosives team. After her uncle called in some well-placed favors, she had been allowed to bring Cisco home, retired so that he could live with her permanently.

She perused again the photos that she had already looked at a million times. It always made her proud to see the picture of her graduation from the police academy—and now she headed up the cold-case unit for the Pine Valley Sheriff's Department. What an amazing journey her career had been so far.

Cisco returned and dropped a toy at her feet that used to resemble a squeaky squirrel.

"Now that's more like it," she said, picking up the toy and tossing it.

Cisco disappeared down the hallway and then began barking incessantly.

The doorbell rang, explaining Cisco's excitement.

Katie sighed and tried to wipe her hands on a rag. "Coming." She watched Cisco spin in circles, suggesting it was someone he knew.

She opened the door. Outside her partner, Detective Sean McGaven, stood patiently waiting. His six-foot-six-and-a-half height filled the doorway. He was smiling broadly with his fair good looks as if he had an amazing secret.

"Hey," she said. "What are you doing here?" She was surprised but happy to see him.

"You need to come with me," he said with dramatic flair.

"What?" She opened the door wider as he stepped inside.

McGaven looked around. "What happened? Is this what goes on when you take some time off?"

"Very funny. I'm in the middle of redecorating."

"I see," he said still looking around. He seemed to agree with her color choice.

"What do you mean, I need to come with you?" she asked.

"The sheriff needs you to work a crime scene."

"Tell me more," she said immediately. All thoughts of painting evaporated.

"Got anything to drink?" he asked.

Cisco dropped the slobbery toy at McGaven's feet.

"Yeah, sure," said Katie. She went to the kitchen and filled two glasses with the iced tea she'd made fresh that day. Walking back to the living room, she handed her partner one of them. "What case?"

"A grave."

"A grave?"

"Of sorts," he said, taking a couple of gulps.

"I have three more days off. Why call me in?"

He chuckled. "You're not going to want to skip a crime scene. Besides, the sheriff specifically told me to come here to get you right now." He bent down to retrieve the toy and tossed it for Cisco.

"Right now?" she said.

"Yep."

"Can I at least change first?" She suddenly became conscious of what a mess she must've looked like painting for the past two hours.

"I think that would be a good idea." He smiled.

She hurried to her bedroom and quickly shed her clothes. Pulling on a pair of jeans, a shirt, and shoes, she was just about to leave when she caught her image in the mirror. "Ugh." She tried to clean the paint out of her hair and then secured it in a long ponytail. She grabbed a hand towel from her bathroom and vigorously cleaned her face with soap and water.

Katie got in shotgun next to McGaven as he started up the unmarked police car. He backed out of her driveway and headed northeast.

"So are you going to tell me what this is all about?" she asked, watching her partner closely. "C'mon. Give something."

"All I know is the sheriff called me and said to bring you."

"What's the crime scene?"

"A fire. It was called in by a neighbor around 8 a.m."

"House? Car? Commercial building?"

"It was a house fire on Maple Road near the old Snyder Subdivision."

Katie knew this was a modest middle-income area. Nice homes. Low crime rate. "Couldn't Hamilton handle it?" There had been some friction between her and Detective Hamilton from a homicide investigation in the past, mostly due to the hierarchy of the police department and her being the sheriff's niece, but she had managed to smooth it over with time. She still wasn't entirely sure if their disagreements were over for good, though.

"Hamilton was called in."

"And?"

"It was suggested—rather *highly* suggested—that we take lead on this particular investigation."

Katie tried to read her partner. It was clear he wasn't telling her everything. Her thoughts jumped around—serial killer, someone with celebrity status murdered, or... She let out a noisy breath. "That means that Hamilton gets bumped from another homicide investigation and we're taking the lead. But we're the cold-case unit." She frowned as she thought about the possible consequences.

McGaven sighed. "The only thing I know it was a house fire and a body was found buried in the basement. That's a cold case, isn't it?"

"Any ID yet? Was it recent? Was it a missing person?"

"Slow down," he said, taking a corner with considerable speed. "I don't know anything else yet. That's why the sheriff wants us to work this. We'll find out *all* the answers to your questions shortly—and more." He smiled and glanced at his partner.

Katie leaned back, impatiently tapping her index finger on the armrest. She watched the neighborhoods vary slightly as they sped past until they reached the area that included the Snyder Subdivision. She remembered her parents had had good friends who lived in the area and that they had visited them on several occasions.

As McGaven turned down Maple Road, there were all types of emergency vehicles lined up, barely leaving enough room for access through the neighborhood.

"Wow," she said. "Is every emergency response vehicle in town parked here?"

McGaven squeezed the sedan through and then drove farther down the road until there was a space.

Katie craned her neck as they drove past. She saw that her uncle, Sheriff Scott, was already there with his command SUV. John, the forensic supervisor for the Pine Valley Sheriff's Department's CSI, was there. The was a large fire truck and a few firefighters still extinguishing small fires and making sure flames didn't stoke up again. There was the arson investigator's SUV and three more patrol vehicles parked farther down the street.

"Kind of a circus," said McGaven.

Katie nodded in agreement.

He parked the car next to a tree. "You ready?" he said.

"Definitely." Katie grabbed protective gloves and booties for both of them from the back seat.

They left the vehicle and walked toward the house. There were no sidewalks or curbs, so front yards ended at the street area, making the surface uneven. Most were neat and tidy, but a few were overgrown, raggedy, and in need of maintenance.

Katie slowed her pace. She was concentrating on her senses —the air cool against her face and the hints of smoke in the breeze. The morning sun wasn't all the way above them yet and shadows still fell against the ground. While she had visited this area as a child once or twice, she wasn't familiar with this exact neighborhood, so she wanted to give it a once-over.

The first thing she thought about was the fact that the fire had happened around 8 a.m. She knew that fires could happen anytime—but according to statistics on previous fires in Sequoia County, more than half occurred in the evening or nighttime. The three leading causes of home fires were cooking, heating, and faulty wiring. When all of those sources were dismissed, then investigators looked into other causes: such as arson, accident, or covering up a crime.

She scanned the houses on the street and noticed they were varied in style and uniquely situated on their lots. The house across the street wasn't directly opposite the burned home—it was slightly south, meaning it would have been difficult to see if someone had entered the home unless you had been looking for it. The rest of the houses' views were partially obscured by pine trees, fences, and overgrown bushes. She doubted anyone had seen anything unusual at the house unless they had happened to be driving by or been out for an early morning walk. But she remained hopeful.

The smoke was still visible and the smell lingered in the air like a burned barbecue.

Katie saw that the forensic van's doors were open. John was nowhere to be seen. She wondered what he could already be documenting at the crime scene before the police had had a chance to perform the first search.

Detective Hamilton was talking with two firefighters and making notes as he did so. He didn't notice Katie and McGaven approaching the area—or he purposely ignored their presence.

Several uniformed officers were moving about, keeping the process flowing and any curious neighbors at bay.

Sheriff Wayne Scott emerged from the house. He was dressed casually in jeans, sweatshirt, and sheriff's jacket. His salt-and-pepper cropped hair and clean-shaven face made him look serious and intelligent—there was no doubt he was in charge. He caught sight of Katie and McGaven heading toward him.

"Detectives," he said approaching. There was no small talk. He seemed troubled by what was under the house.

Katie saw that her uncle seemed more stressed than usual. His jaw was clenched and his upper body seemed rigid. "What do we have?" she said, trying not to let her anxiety surface.

"They found skeletal remains in the basement. This place is a rental residence, but has been vacant for two months. Since it's an unusual scene and circumstances, I'm assigning this case to you both. Patrol is canvassing around the neighborhood to see if anyone saw or heard anything."

"I see," she said. Her mind immediately went through a few possible scenarios.

"We saw Detective Hamilton," said McGaven, a questioning note in his voice.

"He was originally called out here, but I'm reassigning him to a commercial burglary case and as backup if needed. I have a feeling that this case will take some serious manpower." The sheriff turned and walked back toward the house. It was clear he expected the detectives to follow. "The scene has been secured. I had them cordon off the whole area including the backyard. It's ready for you. I don't have to remind you that I want full detailed reports—daily. No exceptions."

"Yes, sir." She nodded to the sheriff and entered the main front door area, McGaven following.

Katie moved quickly through the shell of the house, studying the damage. The structure was still secure, but the interior was something else.

The two-by-fours of the original construction were still standing. Mostly everything had burned except for a wall between the kitchen and living room. They walked on a blackened cement slab. Katie noticed small pieces of what appeared to be carpet around what was once a hallway and kitchen that hadn't completely disintegrated.

"Detectives," said a firefighter. "This way." He gestured to an area where steps led down to the basement.

"Thanks," she said. "By the way, what's left of this house is now an official crime scene until we know more what we're dealing with."

The firefighter nodded, took the hint, and left the area.

Katie and McGaven donned their gloves and slipped on booties over their shoes.

She began to descend the stairs. They were sturdy and didn't squeak underfoot. It was curious to Katie that they'd be in such good condition. The smoke from the house seemed to lift in the basement, leaving behind the usual musty-smelling air beneath the house. Going further into the depths below, she began to feel lightheaded and claustrophobic, as if the walls were closing in on her. She put out her hand to steady herself, then took a couple of deep breaths and tried to focus on the job in hand—the symptoms never completely go away but she pushed herself to move forward. It was what her therapist had taught her under stressful conditions—stop momentarily, step back, and rethink your actions. Her anxious thoughts were not going to dominate her, she told herself. Her PTSD, the lasting symptom of her two tours, was going to stay on the sidelines—at least for today.

As she reached the bottom, the dirt beneath her feet felt solid and sufficiently packed after years of settling. The main floor above was low, barely six feet over their heads. "Watch the low ceiling," she said over her shoulder to McGaven.

"Got it. Thanks for the heads-up," said McGaven as he hunched over.

The basement walls appeared to have been resurfaced and painted recently, but the strange vertical scratch marks that marred one of them from floor to ceiling stopped Katie. What could have made those marks? She pondered. Construction repair? Moving storage cabinets? She could see that McGaven noticed them too as he stepped closer to scrutinize.

Katie surveyed the basement, which went the entire length of the house. At the far end, it was illuminated by two lights propped up on heavy tripods. The artificial glow cast strange shadows around the rest of the room. Several yellow markers outlined an area at the back. There was a plain wooden door leading outside to a small, enclosed backyard. The door stood wide open, showing a reinforced metal frame within. It was miraculously unscathed by the fire. She assumed John must've set up the lighting and markers to help with the search.

"I'll be right here," said McGaven as he carefully squeezed and ducked through the door to the yard. "I don't want to contaminate anything by hovering around. And I can stand upright." He leaned against the doorframe, still able to see inside while Katie conducted her search.

"Okay."

"Tell me what you see," he said.

Katie purposely hadn't looked for the skeletal remains when she first entered the basement. She'd wanted to look at the surroundings as a way of grounding her observations. But now, she didn't have any other choice, so she went across and looked down to where the skeleton's hand was poking through the dirt. Memories from Afghanistan flooded her mind. Bodies. The image of the remains of families flickered across her memory, bodies huddled together in one last-ditch effort to protect their children in a rural, poverty-stricken village. She pushed the memory away with difficulty, determined to stay focused.

She knelt down carefully and moved closer to the hand. There was no skin or tissue left. It had most likely been stripped clean by rodents and decomposition. Looking closer, she saw that the hand was relaxed upward from the carpal bones at the wrist, and the fingers were gently curled in. She studied all the finger bones: the proximal, middle, and distal phalanges seemed to be intact. A small gold band rested on the ring finger.

Katie leaned back. The memories of the bodies of war—the sights, the sounds, and smells of the hot dusty days swirled around her again. She took a deep breath and forced her concentration back on to her immediate surroundings and the bones currently in front of her.

"What's up?" said McGaven, leaning into the basement as far as he could without touching anything.

Katie gently dusted some of the dirt from the hand and wrist to reveal more of a disintegrated shirtsleeve. "I'm not sure."

"Male or female?"

"I can't say for sure, but the ring appears to be a woman's, by its small size."

"What do we do now?"

"Where's John?"

"Right here," said a voice from the yard area.

Katie got up and moved carefully away from the body toward the door. She stepped out into the fresher air of the yard.

John Blackburn, forensic supervisor for the Pine Valley Sheriff's Department, walked up to her, his dark eyes focused on her. He was dressed in jeans and a dark T-shirt, his Navy Seal tattoos visible. She spoke to him without preamble.

"We need to unearth the rest of the remains to see what we're dealing with and if it's indeed a complete body... and find out if there's anything else that can give us clues to the identity and what happened."

"Absolutely," he said.

"You ever dig up a complete skeleton before?" she asked.

"Yes, several times."

"I know I don't have to tell you... but we really need to keep and protect any potential evidence."

"Say no more," he said, raising his right hand. "I have some specialized tools, and I'll be extra careful. We'll see what we have and take it from there."

Katie smiled. "I sometimes forget who I'm talking to."

John grabbed his satchel and made his way back into the basement. Katie and McGaven watched him disappear into the shadowy gloom beyond the reinforced doorway and turned to look out across the yard. The air was already getting warmer.

"How do you want to handle this?" said McGaven.

"We'll wait to see what John initially uncovers. In the meantime, let's take a look around at the rest of the property."

"And you'll be reporting to me," said a familiar voice.

"What?" said Katie, turning round to see her fiancé walking towards them.

"This is my first official arson investigation," said Chad, smiling. His intense blue eyes watched her reaction. Instead of being dressed as a firefighter, he was in slacks and a jacket that identified him as a fire investigator. "And for now, at least, I'm overseeing this investigation to determine if the fire was indeed arson."

"Wow," said McGaven. He chuckled and looked between Katie and Chad.

"Okay. The sheriff hasn't advised me of this. We have a potential homicide here and I'm overseeing that investigation."

"That's fine," he said, still smiling. "Except now, our departments will be working together on this case. We share information."

Katie's stomach dropped, leaving her a bit off balance, but she tried to seem calm and collected. The last thing she wanted to do was work with Chad. They had so far managed to keep their professional lives separate from their personal ones. In Katie's mind, it was what made their relationship continue to work, without getting muddled up with their demanding professions. With this news, the arson case now meant complications.

"This is going to be fun," said McGaven.

"Do you have anything yet?" asked Chad.

"Not yet. We're working on it."

"Glad to hear it," he said, clearly amused by the situation as he walked away.

"Detective Scott?" interrupted John, leaning out the door. "You need to see this."

Katie turned immediately towards him, relieved to focus back on the body and the crime scene.

"What is it?"

"Come look for yourself. I've just done a preliminary search and..."

Katie and McGaven hurried back into the basement and went over to where John had removed some of the dirt. More of the skeleton was revealed. The skull had been uncovered. Some remnants of skin were still visible, along with strands of dark hair. But the most unsettling aspect was the hole on the side of the skull that could only have been caused by some type of blunt-force trauma with something heavy.

"Looks like we might be dealing with a homicide," she said. "It still could be accidental, but I don't think so."

"And..." said John. "Look there." He pointed, directing her attention to the upper body.

"What is it?" said McGaven.

Katie turned her attention to the torso. She could see something underneath the skeleton.

Looking up at her partner, she said softly, "There are two bodies."

THREE

"Stop," Katie said.

John ceased what he was doing and stared at her. "What's wrong?"

"We don't get another chance at uncovering this body and the one underneath. We can see already that there was blunt-force trauma... whether accidental or a homicide is yet to be determined by the medical examiner. But we need to proceed as if it is a homicide."

"Of course. But is there something else bothering you?"

Katie looked at the location and positions of the bodies as they related to the house. "Doesn't it seem strange to you that there are two bodies, one on top of the other, this close to a load-bearing wall?"

McGaven looked around the basement door. "It looks like at some stage there was some type of trench or pipes that ran along the back of the house to the fence."

"Water?" she said.

"That usually comes from the street and not through the backyard," said McGaven.

Katie stood up to study the area better. "I'm wondering if there was some type of renovation... one that created a trench and the perfect opportunity to bury bodies. And I think that where there are two bodies..."

"There might be more..." said McGaven, finishing her sentence in a whisper.

"We need to check from here," she said, pointing to the ground at her feet, "in a straight line through the backyard to the fence."

"I'm in agreement with you both," said John. "Moving forward with extra precautions here."

The thought of more bodies buried in the yard made Katie's stomach drop.

"I can have one of the forensic techs run the ground-penetrating radar to see if there's anything to your theory," said John as he retrieved his cell phone.

Katie stepped back out into the yard. It was a relief to feel the sunshine again instead of the musty air of the basement.

"You really think there could be more?" said McGaven.

"It's better to rule it out," she said. "Has anyone contacted the owner of the property?"

"Hamilton. He's getting all his information together right now and forwarding it to us." He referred to his notes. "The owner's name is Travis Stone."

"Okay," she said. "We need a list of the previous tenants. Also, the names of people who applied for this house and didn't get it. Set up a meeting with the owner ASAP." She thought for a moment while looking back at what was left of the house. "Hopefully one of the neighbors might have seen something. We need to find out all of the information on any building or renovations done to this property."

"I'll start with the building and planning departments for

any permits pulled," said McGaven. He headed back to the car to access information from his phone and to call the records division.

Sheriff Scott approached. "What's the progress?"

"There's another body buried beneath the first skeleton. We're having a forensic tech run a GPR on the property. Basically down this line," said Katie gesturing to the yard area.

"Reasoning?"

"It seems that the two bodies are in an old trench or maybe some type of old water line. It seems odd how they are buried—could indicate who put them there or at least where to start. I want to make sure there aren't more bodies."

"That's going to take a while," he said.

"I was wondering if we could get a more dependable barrier to secure this property until we're done searching?"

"Consider it done."

John walked up to them. "Sir, it might be helpful if we had an expert look at the bones—and maybe assist in recovering them."

Katie thought it was a smart idea. At this point, they didn't know if the bodies were buried a month ago or when the house was built.

"Did you have someone in mind?" asked Sheriff Scott.

"Yes," said John. "I went to a couple of crime scene and forensic conferences where a renowned forensic anthropologist who is an expert in forensic osteology gave amazing talks. His name is Dr. Sal Rimini and he's a professor at the university."

"That would be helpful. He'll presumably have more in-depth knowledge about the condition and typing of the remains. That could only help us in the investigation," said Katie.

"Would he be available to help with the recovery?" said the sheriff.

"I'll call him," said John.

"Make sure he understands the confidentiality of the investigation."

John nodded.

"Katie, you need to take point and coordinate all of this, which means working with the arson investigator," said the sheriff. He eyed her curiously.

"Of course." She knew what her uncle really meant: was she okay working with her fiancé?

Sheriff Scott studied her for a moment. "I'm looking forward to your reports. I'll approve the reinforcements to guard and secure this property for as long as needed." He started to walk away. "Oh," he said. "I'll check on Cisco if you want. This could be a long day for you."

"Thank you." Katie was relieved, hating to leave Cisco too long. She walked back over to the car to see if McGaven was having any luck on his searches.

"Hey," said Chad from where he stood near the street.

"Hi." Katie stopped to talk to him. She tried to seem natural but felt conspicuous, as if everyone else was staring at them to see if they could work together as professionals.

"I wanted to let you know first before I file the preliminary reports."

Katie sucked in a breath in anticipation. "And?"

"We found traces of common accelerants, flammable agents, and some pieces of what appears to be some type of creative incendiary device. It was supposed to completely burn, but we found some fragments near the back corner of the house. Everything will be going to the state lab for examination and full testing."

"So it's officially arson?"

Chad nodded. "No doubt. It's arson."

"Now we have to not only figure out who burned down the house, but if they burned the house to cover up a crime—or expose it."

FOUR

Wednesday 1350 hours

The low, steady beeping kept rhythm as the ground-penetrating radar machine carefully moved along the backyard in a strip-grid pattern. A screen connected to the apparatus showed images from different depths underground. The machine itself was similar to a metal detector, but had a larger rectangular piece of machinery that ran along the ground. To the untrained eye the display appeared like blobs on the screen in different dark greens and blues, but to the trained operator it revealed any mass underground. Everything was recorded and would be used as evidence if needed.

Forensic technician Jimmy Turner held the equipment steady as he studied the screen. He had been with the Pine Valley Sheriff's Department for two years and was a great asset, not only to the department, but to John as well. The sun beat down on the technician's dark red hair, causing sweat to run down his neck and soak his T-shirt, but he was so focused he barely seemed to notice.

Suddenly the machine made a high-pitched sound.

"Have something?" said Katie as she waited in anticipation.

"No, it's just a deep zone. That's normal for this area due to the terrain of the region," said the technician. He kept moving, slow and steady.

Katie paced back and forth beside the wreckage of the house. Her mind raced, thoughts bouncing among experiences she'd had in the army—usually terrible and unsettling ones. Taking a couple of conscious breaths, she pushed those images aside for the thousandth time and tried to concentrate on the events unfolding in front of her. She hoped that there would be no more bodies, but her instincts said otherwise. She had left McGaven setting up an appointment to meet with the property owner, Travis Stone, and John had halted the excavation of the two bodies in the basement until the professor from the university arrived.

Her anxious energy made her stomach churn and she realized that she hadn't eaten anything that morning except for a piece of raisin toast and a strong cup of coffee.

McGaven joined her. "Anything yet?"

"No, but the professor will be arriving any moment."

"Wow. You sure that's not overkill? It's not like we're uncovering an ancient mummy or something."

"Maybe. It depends upon when the bodies were buried—he could really be helpful for us. There could be important evidence that hasn't yet deteriorated. He should be able to give us a basic overview of the remains."

"I got a hold of the landlord, Travis Stone. We have a meeting later, at around 5 p.m. He should have lists of tenants and applicants for us."

"Okay," she said and glanced at her watch. Sheriff Scott had been right: it was going to be a long day.

"I'm having Denise track down any records or permits on this property as well as the insurance. That should be telling," he said. Denise was McGaven's girlfriend and supervisor in the records division of the sheriff's department. She often helped out on cases.

"Good. Let's do a walkthrough of the area."

"What's left of it," said McGaven.

They headed over to the front of the house where officers were barricading the perimeter of the property and rolling out chain-link fencing. There would be two officers guarding the area twenty-four hours a day until the search was over and the property was released from being a crime scene.

"Chad said that they recovered some pieces of an incendiary device and samples of the accelerant that was used. I want to look around the area."

The detectives walked across the front yard. It was almost barren, with unkempt grass that was in desperate need of watering. There were some empty planter pots next to the house, but nothing except weeds and two scorched bushes anywhere else.

Katie led the way to the far corner of the garage where she guessed the electrical box leading into the house would be located. Very little of that part of the structure remained. The section of the garage suspected of being the likely point of origin for the fire was now securely taped off, the evidence collected marked by red tape with identifying numbers. Samples had been taken and already sent to the state lab to be tested for types of accelerants.

The backyard itself was small and narrow, laid out in grass mixed with weeds about five inches tall. Along the back side against the fence were the remains of a few flowerbeds. The wooden border had partially disintegrated, but was still visible.

Katie stood for a moment pondering. The yard was mostly level, but the back fence dipped in places. She looked around near where the garage was and, slipping her search gloves back on, found a piece of rebar. She walked along the fence line, stopping every now and again to inspect areas that didn't resemble the rest.

"What are you looking for?" asked McGaven.

"Notice how the yard is flat, but it looks like someone had been digging here recently—or not that long ago."

"It's in need of some maintenance."

"It's pretty common for rental properties not to have land-scaping. Tenants don't want to take care of the yard, and the owner doesn't much care as long as the rent is paid." She frowned. Dropping to her knees, she took the metal rebar and began digging where the soil looked to be not as compacted as the rest of the area.

McGaven joined her and began moving dirt.

Nothing could be seen at first, but as the dirt was so loose Katie and McGaven kept going. Eventually Katie scraped something that wasn't earth. Gradually they uncovered a folded tattered blue tarp nearly a foot down.

Katie stopped and looked at McGaven.

"Maybe it's a pet that has been buried?" he suggested.

"I don't know, it's flat." Katie hoped it wasn't the remains of the family cat or dog. She kept moving forward and found a corner where she could carefully bend it back. Underneath were clothes, neatly folded. The first thing she saw was a pink hoodie and then below it a small pair of jeans.

Katie gasped, realizing they were children's clothes. "That's a child's hoodie, jeans, and..." She pointed to a small white purse with a keychain attached to the strap. On the chain was a single key—a house key. She thought a moment as to why there would be children's clothes buried here. *Who would do that? To cover up a crime? To get rid of evidence?*

"Found something!" yelled Jimmy suddenly from the side yard.

Katie stood up, looking in that direction. Could it be? Dread filled her. She stopped and carefully left the potential evidence as she had found it.

"Let's find out," he said.

Katie and McGaven hurried from the backyard, joining John and the technician.

"Here." Jimmy gestured to the computer screen. He was jittery and excited at the same time, making it difficult for him to stay in one place.

When Katie looked at the display in Jimmy's hands she felt a hammer hit her gut. The ground-penetrating radar monitor showed a distinct, dark-blue outline resembling not just one body, but two, laid out head to toe along the property lines from the basement to the fence. She couldn't respond to Jimmy at first. Her first thought was it couldn't possibly be correct what she was seeing, but the facts were staring her in the face. There was no other possibility.

Everyone around her was quiet, making the scene even more uncomfortable.

Katie was the first to speak. "Those are bodies, but..." She looked at the graph and measurement lines on the screen display. She swallowed hard, still staring at the images. "Are they small?" The words barely escaped her lips as she knew what it meant if he said yes.

Jimmy moved the image and clicked on a few icons. "They're less than four feet long and about four and a half feet deep."

"Less than four feet each—that's roughly the size of a child," said Katie. Her stomach became queasy and it was all she could do to keep from crying. Horrifying. Two children had been buried in a yard in a quiet neighborhood without anyone knowing. Had they been buried alive? Were their last moments terrifying? Did they know their killer? So many scenarios rolled through her mind. She quickly tried to push these thoughts aside until she had real facts and hard evidence. There could be a plausible explanation—no matter how remote. Still staring at the small blue rectangular representations of bodies on the computer screen, she managed to say, "We just found some children's clothing and a house key buried in the flowerbed just behind the house. They need to be documented and collected... we need to search every area of the yard for anything else."

"We're on it," said John.

An alert activated on McGaven's cell phone. "McGaven," he answered. Listening for about a minute, he hung up.

"Anything?" said Katie.

"Denise located the names of the previous tenants. William and Heather Cross. There's no forwarding address."

"Kids?"

McGaven nodded. "One. Eight-year-old girl. Raven."

The name Raven kept replaying over in her mind. Was she looking at the grave for eight-year-old Raven?

A family... Two adult bodies. Two children...

Glancing at her watch, Katie said, "We'll have to see what the owner of the property has to say later." She was starting to feel the familiar sense that a fuse had been lit and they only had so much time before it burned to the end and exploded.

"In the meantime, I'm going to see what they've uncovered from the canvass of the neighborhood and check in with Hamilton," said McGaven.

"Okay," she said as she watched John and Jimmy begin to peel layers of dirt away from the area identified by the radar, making a trench. The process was going to take a while to do properly.

Katie needed a moment to let the thought soak in that there could be a family under the burned house and in the ground of the yard. She began mentally going through her checklists of what had to happen next, as well as listing any potential stumbling blocks. It was essential for her to make all the right decisions.

She needed to clear her mind of anything unnecessary. She decided to take another walk around the area, in case they had missed anything first time round and to help her keep her mind alert. But out of the corner of her eye she spotted a man wandering into their cordoned-off area. Dressed in tan baggy cargo pants and a loose fitting T-shirt, the fair-haired man with gold-rimmed glasses looked strangely out of place. He seemed very relaxed. Could he be more than just a curious neighbor?

"Excuse me," said Katie approaching him. "This is a restricted area. You're going to have to leave."

"I was told to come here," he said.

"This is a crime scene."

"I'm Sal Rimini."

"Dr. Rimini?"

"Yes, but I prefer Sal," he said, smiling. "Dr. Rimini sounds more like my dad."

Katie was surprised that he was so young. She'd expected someone with graying hair and in his fifties. This guy was barely a day over thirty.

"And... you are?"

"Detective Katie Scott. I'm overseeing this investigation."

"Oh, *you're* Detective Scott."

Katie didn't quite understand his tone. "Yes."

"Nice to meet you. If you can point me in the direction of where I can find John Blackburn, I'll get out of your way."

"Of course. Follow me," she said and led him to the side yard next to the entrance to the basement.

"Sal," said John coming up to greet him. He shook his hand. "Thank you for coming out so quickly."

"How could I not? This definitely gets a solid ten on the curiosity scale."

"No big lectures today?"

"No. I had my TA take over my classes this afternoon."

"Great." Turning to Katie, John said, "You've met Detective Scott?"

"Yes," he said, nodding.

"Great. Let's get to work," said John. "Detective, I'll have some news for you soon."

Katie watched the two men disappear into the basement while behind her Jimmy was still stripping back layers of dirt along the trench. She knew that she couldn't do anything with the crime scene until the bodies were completely uncovered. As much as she wanted to stay and watch, scrutinizing what took place, she and McGaven needed to keep the other parts of the investigation moving.

FIVE

Wednesday 1640 hours

Katie and McGaven drove to Travis Stone's house which turned out to be located in a swanky neighborhood. The houses were large and had almost perfectly landscaped yards, with many having black wrought-iron fences outlining the properties. Green grass and various beds of plants and flowers made each estate look unique. Shady trees were expertly placed and flocks of birds enjoyed the canopy.

"You're extremely quiet," said McGaven.

Katie watched the huge houses pass by her window, each more ornate than the last. "Just thinking..."

"About?"

"How could those bodies in the basement not have been discovered sooner? It looked as if someone might have already dug up that first body, by accident, or so that it would be found." Katie kept flashing through mental images of the property, yard, and the burned-out house. "It doesn't make any sense."

"If that's true—that would mean that someone wanted us to

find them. Did they know about the body beneath, or the two other bodies in the yard?"

"Exactly," she said.

"Here we are," said McGaven parking in the driveway. "1617 Grand Avenue. The home of Mr. Travis Stone."

"Wow," she said as she scoped out the estate. "Being a landlord pays well. What's his bio?"

"He's the owner of various properties around Pine Valley, but that's just a small slice of a portfolio of many other investments."

Katie stepped out, taking in the glorious landscape with its perfectly manicured bushes and trees. A huge lawn with a path of stepping stones led up to the grand porch. Normally she would pause, to take in her surroundings, but she was too anxious to get on with the investigation. She couldn't get a feel yet of what to expect from meeting Travis Stone.

The detectives stood on the porch and Katie pressed the doorbell button, causing a pleasant chime to ring in a few different octaves. The massive front door was opened by a thin older man dressed in a type of butler's uniform with a white dress shirt and tan slacks. He forced a smile and said, "Yes, may I help you?"

"I'm Detective Scott and this is Detective McGaven. We're here to speak with Travis Stone. He's expecting us," said Katie.

The man hesitated as if he didn't recognize the name. "Of course. Come with me."

Katie stepped inside into the marble floor foyer. It reminded her of a museum or a set for a movie. Huge oil paintings hung on the walls, marble statues stood around, and gaudy furniture with gold accents rounded out the décor. She had never been inside a home like this before and it made her uneasy. She eyed McGaven who had a look on his face of exactly what she felt.

They walked down a long hallway, through stained-glass double doors into a study and then through another door, which led to a solarium. It was in the middle of the home, enclosed in a glass dome, which sheltered a full-sized swimming pool. Tall palms and various large plants gave the area a vacation vibe, added to by the increased humidity. Katie felt a slight breeze against her face and realized that air was being piped in to add to the tropical atmosphere.

The butler stopped and slightly bowed as he left Katie and McGaven.

"Okay," said McGaven, rolling his eyes.

Katie held back a laugh.

A man was swimming in the pool. It was difficult to see what he looked like as he was doing freestyle with his head down as he neared the edge. Taking a gasping breath to end his lap, the man, presumably Travis Stone himself, took the steps out from the shallow end, exiting the pool and walking toward a lounge chair set with a towel carefully laid out in front of him.

Katie remained silent and couldn't help but notice that Mr. Stone was fit, muscular, and around his mid-forties. His dark hair was longer than most men's, but the style seemed to fit him —even as it was now, wet and slicked back. It wasn't until he picked up the white towel, drying his hair off with it and then wrapping it around his waist, that he acknowledged the detectives.

"Mr. Stone?" said Katie. "Travis Stone?"

"Yes? And I assume you're the detectives assigned to my case."

"I'm Detective Scott and this is my partner Detective McGaven."

"Nice to meet you both," he said, walking closer, glancing at McGaven. "Can I get you anything to drink?"

"No, thank you. We would like to ask you a few questions," said Katie, keeping eye contact with him.

Mr. Stone gestured to the chairs at a small outdoor table. "Ask anything you like."

Katie took a seat while McGaven remained standing. It was usual protocol between the detectives: Katie would take lead asking questions, while McGaven subtly took a look around while listening and would interject questions.

"Mr. Stone—" began Katie.

"Please, call me Travis."

"Okay, Travis. How long have you owned the house on Maple Road?"

"I assume you mean 717? I own three houses on Maple Road."

Katie hadn't received this information, but didn't let it put her off. "Yes, 717."

"For the past seven years."

"Has it always been a rental home?"

"Yes, I buy older homes that no one else wants, make sure they're up to code and then rent them out. But I'm more than a landlord. I invest in many ventures. Oh, I'm sure you've already found out, or will find out, that I have an insurance policy worth eight hundred thousand dollars on the home. Take from that what you will. I wouldn't have all this," he said, gesturing to his surroundings, "if I made the wrong investments."

Katie watched Travis. She wasn't surprised that he told them immediately how much he had insured the rental for—he seemed proud of the success of his acquisitions. "The last tenants were William and Heather Cross?"

"Yes, they signed a contract for two years. That's a wonderful way to keep the rent the same—a win-win for both parties." He smiled, showing his perfectly straight, professionally whitened teeth.

"Were they good tenants?"

"Yes. Paid their rent on time. No complaints."

"Did you ever get any complaints from the neighbors?"

"No."

"Have you spoken to them since they vacated?"

"No."

"Would you know how to contact them?"

"No."

"How did they get back their deposit?"

"I sent them a check to their post office box they left."

"Can you give us that address?"

"Of course. I'll have everything made available for you, Detective."

"The house seems to have been empty for a while. Why is that?"

"I was in the middle of negotiations with a contractor to update the kitchen and to install a new heating and air-conditioning system. Obviously it's too late since everything is gone now." His voice had an almost gleeful tone to it.

"We're going to have to interview the contractor as soon as possible."

"Seth Randall—Randall Construction. He does all my renovations on the rentals."

Katie glanced at McGaven as he made a note of the contractor's name. "Is there anything else you can tell me about the property?"

"Like what?" he said. It was clear that he was getting bored with the questioning, so Katie wanted to turn up the heat.

"Like why there are bodies buried beneath it."

"What do you mean, bodies?"

"What would you say if we told you that multiple bodies had been found buried on the property?"

Travis sighed. "I thought this interview was about the fire?"

"Actually, we're not investigating the fire. We're investigating the bodies found on your property," she said.

"I see." He shrugged and didn't seem to be shocked or interested.

McGaven watched him closely but remained hovering in the background.

"Do you have anything to say? Comments? Questions?" she asked.

"How would I know if there were bodies buried on my property? Just because I own it, doesn't mean that I know what's buried underground. It's of no interest to me. It's not like the land has mineral rights."

Katie thought that was a strange way to answer. She wasn't sure if it suggested some type of guilt or just his high-minded attitude.

Travis leaned forward in his chair as if he had a secret to tell. "You've come here for some leads, correct?"

"We work through every lead by starting from the beginning." Katie gritted her teeth. She was becoming weary of dealing with this man.

"Simon?" he said, speaking to his butler and assistant. "Please bring the detectives the list of all tenants and applications for all my properties."

Simon had been waiting near the door, but disappeared for a moment and shortly returned. He set several folders down on the table in front of Katie.

"That should be everything you need," said Travis. "It includes all my properties, when I bought them, and from whom. Since I have a suspicion you'll be asking me for all the details at a later date, I saved you the trouble." In a whisper, he said, "My personal cell phone number is in there in case you need to call me—anytime." He raised his eyebrows in a suggestive manner.

Katie hid her dislike for the man and tried to ignore his smarmy sneer. "Thank you, Mr. Stone. This will be very helpful." She dropped a business card on the table.

"Aw, we're back to Mr. Stone again? Pity." He rose and dropped his towel, waiting a moment so that Katie could see his fit body before jumping back into the pool, sending water everywhere.

Katie grabbed the bundle of folders, which was thicker than she had expected, and rose from the table. She glanced at McGaven as they began to retrace their steps toward the front door. She could hear the splashing in the pool as Mr. Stone continued his workout. The creepy butler-assistant was nowhere to be found, but instincts told Katie that he was near or had some way of keeping tabs on guests.

When they stepped into the office, it was instantly cooler, a relief from the humidity of the solarium. Glancing at the desk and accessories, she realized that this wasn't Travis's working office but only an impression of it, most likely one kept for visitors. Things were too neat and lacking in items that would be found in an investor's office—messages, notebooks, laptop computer, and the like. It was almost as if it were a showroom for an expensive furniture store—merely a facade.

Katie paused as she looked at the wall of photos. It was only thing in the room that appeared genuine. There were myriad images ranging from black-and-white personal vintage photos to glossy color photographs of various properties. She assumed they were his investments, but it was strange to mix everything up. Looking closer at a smaller photo, she saw a tall man with a stern expression in a business suit with a teenage boy dressed in a suit too. The boy had a mischievous look upon his face and failed to fill out the clothing, which was two sizes too big.

"Stone? My guess," said McGaven.

"It appears to be," she said.

McGaven glanced at each photo. "Interesting."

Katie headed to the door and walked back towards the massive entrance. Still no one appeared. The detectives exited the house and got in the car.

McGaven was the first to speak. "What the hell was that all about?"

Katie laughed. "What? You haven't met many rich jerks in your life?"

"I have... but still, that was weird."

"I don't know who was weirder, Stone or the manservant," she said.

"The servant for sure. I'm surprised that the eyes in the paintings weren't watching us." McGaven started the engine and slowly drove out of the driveway. "He was right out of a horror movie."

"I think it goes without saying. We need a complete background on Travis Stone—types of business associates, girlfriends, family, and any construction work on the properties. Pull up everything about his properties. He's a person of interest already, but maybe something in his background might steer us in new directions."

"I'll have Denise pull up some information from the database and we can dig for the rest. Then we can see a better picture of this guy."

As McGaven drove, Katie flipped open the files Stone had given her. Everything looked to be in order. The file for the most recent tenants of 717 Maple Road were on top, showing the details of William and Heather Cross.

"Anything?" he said.

"Their previous address in Arizona and their employment record. He worked for an architect and she was a receptionist for a high-end spa." Katie kept reading.

"There's still some time before we need to get back," he said.

"Let's pay the contractor Seth Randall a visit. It seems like the next logical step, to see what the construction company has to say. They've recently been in the house and on the property."

"On it," he said as he entered the name of the company into GPS. "Hopefully they haven't left for the day already."

"Oh and..."

"Yeah?"

"Let's stop at the Sandwich Shack first—I'm starving."

SIX

After eating a sandwich in record time, Katie and McGaven headed to Randall Construction. It was located out in the industrial part of the county, surrounded by businesses from automotive and machine repair to landscaping and other construction companies.

"I remember a homicide out here a few years ago," said McGaven.

Katie thought about it but didn't remember. "I don't recall."

"Oh yeah, I keep forgetting that you weren't here then."

"What happened? Did they solve it?" she asked.

McGaven slowed the sedan as they drove over several sets of train tracks, rattling the car. The vast, wide-open area was deserted and there were no trains in sight as they zoomed farther down the road.

"I was on patrol and was the second deputy to arrive at the tracks about a quarter mile up," he said, gesturing to the westward area. "It wasn't my first dead body, but it's the one that I'll always remember. That call changed the way I conduct police work. I pay more attention to everything now—no matter how small the detail."

"That's what makes you a great detective." Katie turned to study her partner as he told the story. She could feel his uneasiness by the way he was talking. His voice was low and he seemed to be choosing his words carefully. Katie kept quiet and listened.

"I rolled up and Deputy Salinger was already there. He was walking back to his cruiser as I arrived. I could see his grimacing face, eyes looking down. He almost seemed to stagger to his car door as he called it in." McGaven took the next turn as instructed by the GPS. "Anyway, I got out and asked him if he was okay. He nodded and then pointed toward the tracks—so I walked over to take a look."

Katie watched him. She had never seen McGaven quite like this before—even with everything they had been through. She didn't know exactly why he was retelling this story, but she had a hunch it was something that haunted him. She could relate. It made her feel that much closer to her partner.

"I could see pink fabric billowing in the breeze. I didn't know if it was clothing or some type of a blanket. As I approached, I saw the body of a girl lying on her back. I saw her face, pale. She wore pink lipstick and had pink chipped fingernail polish. She looked like a little doll—because of her posed position, as if she were lying down and gazing at the sky. But h-h-her throat had been cut and you could still see the blood all around. She was seventeen. I'll never forget her name—Lily Bennet." He became silent.

"What happened?" she said, giving his arm a gentle squeeze. "Was her killer arrested?"

"Yes and no."

"What do you mean?"

"A man named Dean Hollis was arrested and convicted of her murder. The investigators put him in the vicinity of her last known whereabouts. He had a propensity for violence and liked young girls like Lily, but..."

"And..."

"There was a lot of circumstantial evidence, and he seemed to be the killer, but something has always bothered me about that case. I kept thinking that there would be more killings with the same MO—more girls murdered in this county and possibly the neighboring ones, but it never happened."

"I'm guessing something else bothered you about the case."

"It's probably my own personal feelings rather than me being objective. It seemed more personal. The way her body was left, innocent and posed, and in a place that would be easy to find. It was almost as if someone was taunting the police. If Hollis was the killer it would suggest that he hunted this type of victim, but if it was a revenge or payback type of murder—that would mean a completely different type of killer."

"Do you think we need to somehow get the case opened for another look?" said Katie, feeling his concerns. She made a mental note. There was something about McGaven and the retelling of the story that made her curious. She couldn't shake the feeling that somehow it would play into their case today that they had to pay attention to every small clue.

"No, at least for now. It's just that it reminds me that we need to be extra careful and mindful with our current investigation."

Katie nodded. "I'm beginning to see that this case is going to take everything we have."

They pulled up in front of a large beige building with navy awnings and a large sign that said "Randall Construction." It was a newer building compared to the automotive garage across the street, which had metal doors and was smaller. Blooming groundcover plants and small shrubs were neatly maintained in the long flowerbed across the front.

Katie and McGaven got out and briefly looked around.

There was a large, oversized black Ford truck parked next to the entrance. Behind the building in a heavily fenced area were various pieces of machinery, including two backhoes, an excavator, a bulldozer, trailers, chippers, and a bobcat. There was a large metal building in the corner, which most likely had lumber and various parts for construction.

"Let's see if Mr. Randall is around," said Katie. She realized that she was dressed in her casual clothes, so she adjusted her badge and holster. She would appear professional enough to conduct a police investigation interview.

Katie pushed the glass door open. A pleasant chime rang to alert whoever was inside. It was already nearly 6 p.m., so the reception and office areas were deserted.

"Hello?" said Katie as they moved farther inside. Both detectives took a careful look around.

There were two architects' tables with overhead lamps set up. A small couch and two chairs were placed in the corner with two six-foot potted palms. It was a nice area for clients to come in and feel comfortable as they talked about their dream home. Several colored house renderings were framed on the wall—some were modest and others were like that of Travis Stone's home.

"Anyone here?" she said again. "Hello?"

A dark-haired man appeared. "Hello. What can I help you with? Do you have an appointment?" he asked, moving around and putting paperwork in filing cabinets.

Katie flashed her badge. "I'm Detective Scott and this is my partner, Detective McGaven."

"Yes, Detectives, what can I do for you?" He took immediate notice of the badges and glanced at their holsters.

"Are you Seth Randall?"

"David."

"David?"

"David Randall. Seth is my brother," he said. "Is Seth okay?"

"I'm sure Seth is fine," she said. "We wanted to speak with him about a remodel job for Travis Stone. The house on Maple."

"Which one?"

"717 Maple."

"We're getting ready for a renovation—just fine-tuning the budget and timings. You know, the usual for an aging rental house." He moved closer to the detectives. "What's going on?"

"It burned down this morning."

"Oh no. Was anyone hurt?"

"No."

"Then why do you need to talk to Seth?"

"This hasn't been released to the press yet. It's confidential," said McGaven.

David studied McGaven for a moment. "Of course. Whatever you need."

"There were bodies found buried in the basement and backyard."

"Bodies?" he repeated. "What... how..." He stammered and seemed genuinely surprised. "I can't imagine..."

"It's now an ongoing investigation," said Katie. She glanced at the paperwork David had been moving around since they arrived. They were invoices and official-looking letters. "When was the last time you or your brother were at the house?"

David frowned as he tried to remember. "Wait," he said, and walked over to a large whiteboard with a list of projects and progress dates written up on it. "Let's see. We met with Mr. Stone two weeks ago."

"At the house?"

"Yep. He had decided that he wanted to just update the kitchen and leave the heating as is. He wanted it fixed, not replaced."

Katie thought about it. It seemed strange that he wouldn't want to just replace the old heating system so there wouldn't be any more problems. "Would you happen to have blueprints to the house? The electrical and plumbing?"

"Oh sure. Let me make a copy for you," he said and headed to another room.

Katie could hear the rustling of papers and then the sound of a copy machine. She turned to McGaven who was studying the area. "What do you think?" she said quietly.

"Interesting," he said.

Katie knew that was code for they needed to pay closer attention. She knew her partner well and understood that he was already making mental notes on the background checks he would perform once back at the office.

"I'm not sure how this can help you, since the house is now gone."

Katie took the rolled-up blueprints David Randall was holding out to her. "Thank you, Mr. Randall. It's appreciated. Everything helps."

"Anything for our finest." David forced a smile.

"Oh, and we would still like to talk to your brother. Here's my card," she said.

Taking the business card, he said, "Sure thing."

"One more thing," she said. "Did you ever notice anything unusual about the house? Something out of place, or anything that might be a problem for remodeling?"

David took a pause as if he was wracking his brain, but said, "Nothing that I can think of. It's typical of the houses in the area."

"You mean the Snyder Subdivision?"

"Yes. It wasn't supposed to be developed. Beautiful land though—can't say I blame them." He smiled.

"Thank you for your time, Mr. Randall," she said.

Katie and McGaven exited the building and walked back to

their car. Before they got in, an oversized black truck raced in and through the electric gates that had opened into the back storage area.

Katie looked at her partner as she opened the car door. She tossed the building plans in the back seat. "What do you think?"

"Seth?"

"Let's go and find out," she said.

They walked back across the parking lot and through the open gates cautiously.

A heavyset man dressed in dark jeans, long-sleeved shirt, and black cowboy boots stepped down from the high four-wheel-drive truck. He looked rushed and clearly had something on his mind, but he saw the detectives and stopped. "This is a private yard. What can I do for you?"

Katie stepped forward showing her badge. "I'm Detective Scott and this is my partner, Detective McGaven."

"Detectives?"

"We'd like to ask you a few questions," she said.

He walked closer to face Katie. "About?"

"The house at 717 Maple Road."

"One of Travis Stone's properties? What do you need to know?" He eyed McGaven curiously.

"It burned down this morning."

"Didn't hear about it."

Katie didn't believe him. He kept fidgeting with his wedding band on his ring finger—spinning it with his thumb. "Did you work on the house?"

"Wait a minute. Are you trying to blame *me* for the fire?"

Katie took a step toward him. "Do we need to?"

"Of course not. We haven't started working on it yet. Stone keeps changing his mind—first he wanted to do an entire remodel, then a partial, just enough to make it look good for prospective renters."

"Which involves?"

"He wanted us to open up the kitchen to make it look more spacious, replace the basic appliances, and the heater. That's it."

"Have you worked for Travis long?"

"Yeah, about ten years now. Mostly lower-end stuff, but work is work."

"How would you describe Mr. Stone? Easy to work with? Difficult?"

"Sometimes. He definitely knows what he wants, but it's the strict timelines he wants that can be a pain in the— a challenge."

"I saw the amazing renderings in your reception area," she said. She realized that she had probably started off a bit harshly, and didn't want to put him on the defensive. She lightened her tone and changed tack. "I realize that you guys probably prefer the larger projects."

"Of course. But clients like Stone help during the slower months over winter." He leaned back against the truck, crossing his arms. "So I'm getting the vibe here that there's more to the house burning down."

"Mr. Randall, it's an ongoing investigation, but as I told your brother there were bodies found buried in the basement. That's why we're investigating."

"Bodies? Jeez, that's horrible." He looked away.

"You wouldn't know anything about that?" said McGaven as he casually moved around, quickly assessing the property.

"Why would I know anything about bodies buried in the basement?"

"I left my card with your brother. If you think of anything that might be helpful about the property or hear anything, please don't hesitate to let us know."

"Of course, I'll do that." He turned and walked away from them, heading into the storage barn.

Once again, Katie and McGaven went back to their police

sedan and got in. McGaven got behind the wheel, made a quick U-turn and headed away from the construction company.

"I think he knows more than he's saying," he said as soon as they were driving away.

"I got that impression too."

Katie's cell phone chimed with a text from John. She quickly read it:

Bodies are uncovered. Ready for viewing before going to the lab.

"Was that John?" he said.

Katie nodded and McGaven pressed harder on the accelerator, heading back to the crime scene at Maple Road.

SEVEN

Wednesday 1855 hours

A few dark clouds moved quickly across the sky, threatening rain, but not delivering. The overcast evening was dull and depressing, matching the detectives' moods.

Katie remained quiet as they sped back to Maple Road. Her mind was assessing the demeanor of the Randall brothers as they answered the questions put to them. Something felt rehearsed, as if they had been waiting for the detectives to show up. She guessed they would know more when background checks were completed.

"I agree," said McGaven.

Katie turned to her partner as he stared straight ahead. "What?"

"I know you're thinking about the brothers back there." He smiled.

"We have to scrutinize everything. I know we're going to have a ton of evidence and even more interviews to conduct."

"Your gut?"

"I think Seth Randall is hiding something..."

"About the fire?"

"Maybe, maybe not, but he's hiding something that he's not wanting us to find."

"It could be that he's been in trouble with the cops, or that his business is dirty ... It could be anything."

"Yes. But still, there was some odd behavior from him. Didn't you notice the fidgeting?"

"I did," replied McGaven. They lapsed into silence and their own thoughts as the car sped on to Maple Road.

Minutes from the crime scene, McGaven glanced across at his partner. He seemed to hesitate before he asked, "Everything okay? I know you're dealing with a lot. How does it feel to have Chad as the lead arson investigator?"

Katie knew that she couldn't hide much from her partner in regard to what was going on personally. She sighed. "It's a bit weird for me."

"And?"

"You're not going to let it go, are you?"

"Nope."

"I'm having second thoughts about selling the farmhouse." Katie's words hung awkwardly in the air. The moment she said it, she wished she hadn't. "There, the cat's out of the bag."

"I know that hurt, but I also know that you will make the right decision for you."

Katie smiled. She felt a bit of relief saying it out loud to someone who wouldn't judge and was her true friend.

They drove down Maple Road, noticing that there were now fewer vehicles parked around the site of 717. The security team had finished setting up the chain-link fencing around the whole enclosure. There were two men watching the area dressed in plainclothes and combat boots. They were armed and had serious expressions on their faces.

"That was fast," said Katie.

"That's the sheriff—he definitely gets things done."

McGaven quickly parked and they jumped out of the car and headed over to the crime scene.

Katie flashed her badge at the security detail as one of the officers opened the gate and let them inside—locking it behind them. The entire property was sealed off, similar to a construction project in progress.

"Thank you," said Katie over her shoulder as she rushed to the backyard area.

She hurried around the burned structure, noticing that special tape and plywood had been secured to the house as precaution. There were signs already up saying "Keep Out" and "Caution." She thought it might have been a bit soon to attach anything to the remains of the building. She could still smell the aftermath of smoke.

McGaven must've thought the same thing as he paused to look at the handiwork more closely.

To Katie's surprise, the backyard area had been turned into a forensic examination area.

"Wow," said McGaven, echoing what Katie thought.

Heavy plastic and PVC piping had been transformed into a ten-foot-by-fifteen-foot room. It resembled a garden shed, but with a high-tech quality to it, fitted with lights and examining tables. Two figures were inside: the professor of forensic anthropology from the university, and John; they seemed to be in deep conversation as their voices were low and slightly muffled.

Katie walked where heavy plastic was draped over the structure to form a makeshift doorway. "Hello?" she said, grabbing a couple of pairs of gloves and handing one set to her partner.

"Detectives Scott and McGaven," said John.

"What do we have?" she asked, pulling the gloves on.

Two long folding tables housed the remains of four skeletons. Two were obviously adult size while the others were that of two children.

"Come see for yourself before they are transported back to the lab and the medical examiner's office," he said.

Katie stepped inside the plastic cocoon, her eyes fixed on the first table. McGaven was close on her heels. She was surprised that there was a little tissue and hair left on the bodies. The first appeared to be a woman—the body that had been on top and first to be discovered. The remains of a long-sleeved, dark denim shirt and dark jeans were one of the only things to aid with identity—no shoes were visible. Spotty patches of dark hair remained around the hairline. The obvious blunt force trauma was on the left side of the skull. Whatever the object used, it had made a shattered crater in three pieces. The teeth, almost all well preserved, would hopefully help match up with an official identity when searching dental records.

"You're quiet," John said. "I think that's a first. You usually bombard me with questions."

"There's a lot to take in," she said.

"Well, there's definitely a story here," said Dr. Rimini. He stood patiently in the background waiting for the professionals to get a firsthand look.

"Please..." said John as he took a step back.

Katie watched the young scientist.

"Well, here," he referred to the first body, "is a female between the age of thirty and thirty-five. Good general health. Her bones are exactly what they should be for that age and her teeth are in good condition. She had at some point in her life broken her left ulna and her right fibula."

"Her arm and lower leg," said Katie.

"Correct. You can see where it had healed," he said and gently pointed to the areas. "She also had given birth. That is usually where we can tell the age and sex, by the pelvic area."

"What about the other adult?" said Katie.

"This one's a bit more difficult. Male. Approximately the

same age as the woman. But his demise appears to be a gunshot to the chest," said the professor.

"We've recovered the evidence and we're in the process of removing the clothes and bagging them for further testing," said John. "Everything has been documented and you'll have it soon."

"How do you know it's a gunshot to the chest?" asked McGaven.

"We've detected a bullet to the chest, a nine millimeter. It had wedged itself into the area just to the right of the sternum. It will be removed once we get back to the lab." John pointed to the area. It was obvious the bullet must have caused mortal injuries.

Katie studied the male skeleton. There was more tissue on this body, making it easier to identify the skeleton as a man. He appeared to have been wearing a dark sweatshirt and jeans. Again, he didn't appear to have any shoes. *Were the shoes taken? Or, were they not wearing any at the time of death? Something that had happened so quickly that they hadn't had time to put their shoes on?*

"What's bothering you?" said John. He watched Katie closely.

"Just wondering where their shoes are."

He nodded. "Good question."

"Was there anything found that indicated restraints were used?"

"Not that we found."

"What happened here?" She indicated the other side of the chest. It looked almost melted and odd-shaped.

"It's from being buried next to the other skeleton. As the body goes through the decomposition process, within the first month or so before skeletonization it goes through the active process of rigor mortis, then putrefaction, and active decay. These steps make the gases microorganisms and bacteria leech into the dirt. It can cause two skeletons to almost adhere together," said Dr. Rimini.

"More than I wanted to know today," said McGaven. "So how long have the bodies been in the ground?"

"It's difficult to say with pinpoint accuracy. But based on the weather, temperature in the ground, and if the bodies were buried right away, it's anywhere from one to four months."

Katie was already adding up the timing of when the last tenants, the Cross family, had left. It seemed possible, but tests would have to be run to confirm her theory. She turned to McGaven who was already making notes for backgrounds and anyone who knew them including the neighbors. She also wondered why no one had reported them missing.

"Here are the two girls," said John.

His words stung Katie. She could never get used to children being murdered. The thought of the horrors that the girls must have gone through made her stomach churn. Her mind flashed back to her childhood best friend, Jenny, who had been murdered. No matter how hard she had tried to push those events behind her, the memories would occasionally crash uninvited into her mind.

Katie and McGaven turned to the other table, where two small bodies lay. It was difficult for Katie to see. Glancing to her partner, she knew it was challenging for him too. His jaw was clenched and his lips were pressed tightly together as if to keep from letting out what he felt.

Everyone was quiet and the atmosphere became hauntingly grim. There were remnants of clothing left on the girl's skeletal remains that hadn't completely disintegrated, leaving behind what appeared to be shorts and T-shirts. Katie imagined the girls had been simply enjoying the beginning of summer, until it had come to a terrible end.

"So," said the professor. His clear voice startled Katie, who had been lost in thought. "Some of these bones are much older."

"Older?" said Katie. "How much older?" She couldn't understand why one of the bodies was buried previously. *Who would do that? Why?* It immediately changed the dynamics of the crime scene.

"Ten or twenty years. Could be more. Let me rephrase, one of the bodies is older and the other is about the same timeframe as the adults."

"What?" she managed to say. The first thought she had was that it could possibly be a serial killer who had made this property his personal burial ground. *The same killer? Or two different killers that just happened to bury the bodies in the same place? The latter was highly unlikely.*

"Can you pinpoint anything more conclusive?" said McGaven.

Dr. Rimini smiled. "It's not that easy. For one, there appears to be some weathering on the bones, which could be from the ground freezing and thawing. There are other factors such as minerals from groundwater, heat, humidity, along with wetting and drying of the area."

"So only one set of bones is definitely older than the adults?" said Katie. She wanted to make sure that she put everything in order with the correct evidence to back it up.

"Absolutely, based on what I described. It's just that I can't say definitely that it's five years, ten years, or even twenty."

Katie sighed. At least it was a clue to the case, knowing that they weren't buried at the same time—at least not all of them. It just wasn't what she wanted to hear. They would have to dig through years of information from missing persons and everyone who lived at the house. First, they would have to contact the tenants who'd lived there before the Cross family.

"Detective Scott, I know it's not what you want to hear but dating how long bones have been in the ground isn't an exact science. We take several things into consideration."

"I'll have Dr. Rimini write up an official report for your investigation," said John.

Katie nodded, holding back her disappointment. She didn't know how much it was going to help in finding out who murdered and buried these two girls.

"Katie?" said McGaven. He had been studying the remains of the girls. "Take a look at this."

Immediately at his side, she saw what he was referring to. "Is that a bracelet?"

"Yeah, I think so." He used a pencil to gently move what appeared to be a braided bracelet around one of the girl's wrists —the older set of bones.

John moved in closer and examined it. "I missed this. Good eye, Gav." He immediately took several photos.

"I think it's like a friendship bracelet. But what I don't understand is why it's not disintegrated by now," said Katie.

"Let me see," said the professor as he adjusted his glasses. "I don't think it's thread, but more like wire, which wouldn't."

Katie thought about it and realized that the material used was like jewelry wire, which could be found in any craft store. It was easily braided into a pattern and generally came in colors. She thought that the find was significant into not only the identity of the victim but also a timeline.

"It's like craft wire," said John.

Katie continued to study the small bones. "What would be the approximate age of the two girls?"

"Judging by the pelvic area, I would say one is either seven or eight years old. And the other is preteen, maybe twelve."

Katie searched the bodies for indications of foul play or injuries. The skulls were intact—no blunt force trauma or bullet injuries. "How did they die?"

"It's inconclusive, but there are several broken bones that hadn't had time to heal before their deaths."

"We wouldn't be able to tell if they have been shot or stabbed?" she said.

John stated, "Not unless we find something that would corroborate that, like shell casings, bullets, or even the murder weapon."

"Thanks, John," she said, standing up and getting ready to leave. "Nice to meet you, Dr. Rimini."

"Pleasure is mine," the professor said.

Katie had already itemized everything in her mind, but knew that she and McGaven would receive all the reports from the scene in due course. After looking at the friendship bracelet one more time, she stepped through the temporary plastic door into the yard. The painstaking skill that it had taken forensic technician Jimmy to complete the job of removing the children's skeletal remains had been daunting. She watched the young tech catalog and begin to clean up the area. As the sun dwindled in the early fall day, three outdoor lights had been set up on tripods, lighting up the yard.

"Jimmy," said Kate.

The lanky tech turned and smiled. "Detective?"

"Is that all the dirt from the graves?" She indicated to a pile in the corner.

"Yes."

"Is there a way to sift through it to find anything that would be from the bodies or anything related to them?"

"Sure. That's next on my list. We have two-by-two-foot sifters made with a wood frame pressed with screening between them. That can be done fairly fast."

"Let me know what you find."

"Will do, Detective."

Katie turned back to the improvised crime scene lab just as McGaven came out. "What do you think?"

"I think we're done here today. Now, we have to wait for

further examination, test results, and a fresh list of witnesses to talk to."

"Like?"

"Once we get back the results of the neighborhood canvass and any possible security videos, we'll be back to question the neighbors themselves." Katie sighed, her hands on her hips as she looked around the property. "We won't be releasing this crime scene until sometime tomorrow."

"Call it a day?" he asked.

Katie nodded. "Since there are no exigent circumstances—because it's basically like a cold *cold* case—we get to get some sleep tonight."

The detectives walked back to the locked entrance, where one of the guards, now a different one on a new twelve-hour shift, opened the gate for them.

"You've been really quiet. More than usual at the beginning of a case," McGaven said.

Katie sighed. "We have a *ton* of paperwork and reports to get through tomorrow."

"That doesn't scare me. Nor you, usually. What's really bothering you?"

"We have two sets of bodies that had been buried at different times—years, maybe even a decade apart."

"Again, this doesn't scare me. We'll get to the end of it and find the killer."

"It may be two killers, from two different timeframes. We almost need a time machine."

"It could have been an accomplice of the first murders, using the same burial grounds. Or, the killer of the couple who, until we know otherwise, might have had a long career."

Kate stood next to the car. "Either way, whether there's the same killer or an accomplice, we're still dealing with a potential serial killer, no matter how you look at it."

"I'll check out other police jurisdictions to see if there are any outstanding cases with the same types of MOs."

Katie nodded, thinking about everything they had learned today.

"C'mon," he said, opening the car door. "I'll buy you a beer."

EIGHT

Wednesday 2015 hours

Katie found Cisco happily waiting for her when she got home. He zoomed around the living room and kitchen areas a dozen times with pure glee, wagging his tail furiously. A few whines were added to the mix.

"Oh, Cisco, I'm sorry it's been such a long day for you," she said, going straight over to the kitchen area.

A handwritten note was on the counter:

We watched football and had dinner. Hope you don't mind that I ate the rest of the baked chicken in the fridge. I owe you a lunch. Love, Uncle Wayne.

"So, you watched football and I'm sure he gave you some chicken too." She petted the dog furiously and scratched behind his ears, much to his delight. "Missed you so much, buddy. We'll get some training in soon—I promise."

Katie turned and looked at the house. The plastic tarps and freshly painted walls were still the way she had left them just that morning. It was a work in progress. She sighed and went to her bedroom to change into more comfortable clothes. Peeling away some of the plastic and tarps, she found her bed. It suddenly seemed very inviting.

Her cell phone rang. "Scott," she said.

"Hey, babe," said Chad. She could hear the background sounds at the firehouse.

"I've been thinking about you."

"About me or about the case?" he laughed.

"Do I need to choose?"

"I suppose I wouldn't want to know the answer to that. You doing okay?"

"Yeah, it turns out that we not only have one set of victims, but two, from different times of death and burial."

"Wow. So I guess I won't be seeing you anytime soon."

"I'll always make time for you." Looking around at the house, she said, "I've been painting today. Well, at least I was, until Gav came and got me for the crime scene."

"That's great. Save some painting for me. I'm happy to help."

"I don't think we would get any work done."

"You're probably right," he said, laughing again.

Katie closed her eyes and began to relax.

Cisco jumped up on the bed, wanting more attention.

"Hey, I've got to go, okay? Love you," he said.

"Love you too," she said.

"Love you more. See you soon. Goodnight."

"Night," she said and the phone connection ended.

Katie lay back on the bed. She knew that Chad was feeling a bit awkward working on the same case but for different reasons. They didn't talk about their work and that was fine with her. They seemed to be on the same track of keeping work and personal separated. The day slowly faded as she realized how tired she was once she quit moving.

Cisco snuggled up against her and within minutes Katie fell into a deep sleep.

In the darkness Katie's cell phone suddenly rang and vibrated, waking her immediately. "Scott," she said sleepily.

"Katie, sorry to wake you at this hour," said John. His voice sounded strange—he strained as he talked.

"John?" She looked at the clock on the nightstand. It read 1:30 a.m. "What's wrong?" She sat up at once, now fully awake.

"There's been a murder... one of our own."

Katie struggled to breathe. She could barely ask, "Who?"

"It's... It's Jimmy Turner," he said, in a voice almost too hard to hear.

"Jimmy?" she said in shock, remembering his smiling face only earlier that evening when she had asked him to sift the earth at the crime scene for any clues.

"He's dead."

"When? Where?"

"Um, I'm at his apartment. I don't think I can be objective right now. Can you come?" His voice was shaky and Katie had never heard him like this.

"Of course. I'll be right there. Text me the address."

NINE

Katie drove as fast as she dared to get to the Skyline Apartments, which were located fifteen miles north out of Pine Valley. They were rustic residences, but the reward was the amazing forests that lay around them and the stunning views of the area. She marveled at how deserted the roads were at that hour and tried to shake off the feeling that she was driving into the unknown. She couldn't get over what John had told her.

Jimmy was dead...

She kept flashing back to Jimmy working the crime scene. She hadn't known him well, but she'd always liked him nonetheless. He was so diligent and thorough with his work. He could've been a deputy, but halfway through the academy he had decided that he wanted to work in forensics instead. That said quite a bit about his character and professional calling.

Katie took the main road up to the apartments, rehashing as she drove the brief conversation she'd had with John on the phone. He'd been through so much personally, and had always gone the extra mile to help Katie, ever since she was hired and appointed cold-case detective. To hear his voice and his grief had shocked her and only added to the uncertainty and the heartache that laid ahead in the investigation.

She took several deep breaths to calm her nerves, loosening her grip on the steering wheel as she drove into the parking lot. Looking for apartment 17, she spotted John leaning against his black pickup truck.

Jimmy was dead...

Katie parked next to his truck and jumped out to meet him.

"John," she said. "Where is everyone?" Katie had been expecting to see fire, rescue, police, and the CSI van. Instead, it was quiet and most residences were dark.

He finally looked up at Katie and met her gaze. His eyes were red, shoulders slumped forward. The man standing there wasn't the John she knew. "Thank you."

"For what? I'm here, but..."

"I just... couldn't..."

Katie could see that John was struggling to make sense of everything. "Okay, start from the beginning. Why are you here?"

Taking in a breath, he began, "I got a call from Jimmy around midnight. He sounded scared. It wasn't like him. He's sound. A strong guy." He broke off.

Katie waited patiently to let John tell the story in his own way.

John glanced up at the apartment that Katie assumed was Jimmy's. "He said that he thought someone was following him."

"Following him?"

"After he left the crime scene with the chain of custody for the evidence, he went straight to the forensic division. Then he left for home... He said something about someone following him from the house to the department, and then again coming home."

"What made him think that?"

"The same vehicle was in several places where he was..."

Katie's mind immediately went to the bodies and evidence she'd asked Jimmy to look for at the burned house. What had he found? She kept her demeanor calm and gently pushed John. "Then what happened?"

"I told him if he thought there was trouble to call the police. But something really spooked him."

Katie glanced around the area. Everything was quiet and still around them. She didn't see anyone sitting in a car waiting or watching.

"I thought more about it and then I tried to call him back... no answer. I started to get worried. I don't know anyone who lives in this complex, so I drove up here. And I found him..."

"Why didn't you call the police right away?"

"Katie, after what I saw... Jimmy... the fight that must've happened... and his body. Once I knew he was dead, I backed out of the apartment immediately. I didn't want deputies coming here and possibly messing with the crime scene. I just thought... who was going to process this scene... The only person I could trust with the evidence... I thought of you."

"John," she said softly. "We have to call the police."

"I didn't think I could explain this to the first responding officers without falling apart."

"Okay, I'm going to call this in and I'll take lead. But you're going to have to tell them what you told me, okay?"

"But—"

"I'll call the sheriff and he can coordinate what needs to be done."

"Okay."

"John, are you going to be okay?"

"Yeah."

"Stay right here and I'm going to call this in, okay?" She squeezed his hand for support.

He nodded as he stared at the windows to Jimmy's apartment.

Katie ran back to her Jeep and grabbed her cell phone. Her hands shook and she had to wait until she had gathered her thoughts and calmed her voice before making the call to her uncle. He would direct what she needed to do next.

Three deputy sheriff cruisers and one plain detective's sedan pulled into the parking lot at the Skyline Apartments without lights or sirens. Within five minutes of their arrival, the sheriff arrived followed by McGaven's truck.

In the time they were waiting, John had pulled himself together and his usual strong character surfaced. He spoke with the deputies, Detective Hamilton, and the sheriff as Katie waited with McGaven.

A few neighbors peeked out windows and more came out in their robes and pajamas. They were hustled back inside their apartments and told that officers would be speaking to them shortly.

"Do you know what happened?" McGaven asked Katie.

"Just that John found Jimmy dead in his apartment. He had called John saying he thought someone was following him."

"I can't believe this..." McGaven looked around at the buildings.

"What?" she said.

"I'm trying to see if there are any cameras, but I don't see any. Or if there are, they're not easily visible." He walked toward a section of apartments. "Wait. There's one there and I think another one of the other side."

"We'll need to get that footage."

"I'm sure that Hamilton will be working this case," he said.

They waited another fifteen minutes and Sheriff Scott met with them.

"Detective Hamilton will be handling this case."

Katie wasn't surprised. "Of course."

"But," he said, "under the circumstances we need you and McGaven to search, document, and process the crime scene."

"Absolutely," she said.

"Whatever we can do," McGaven added.

"John has anything you might need in his truck." The sheriff left Katie and McGaven to get to work.

Katie watched her uncle return to the officers. She could see that he was deeply saddened, but as usual he had to keep his personal feelings reined in to stay in charge.

Detective Hamilton approached Katie. "I'm glad that you both are documenting the scene. Before the evidence is collected, I would like to walk through."

"Of course," she said.

Hamilton nodded and walked back to the patrol officers.

"You ready?" said McGaven.

"Let's go get what we need."

Katie grabbed gloves, evidence containers and bags, numbered markers, measuring devices, fingerprint powder and application cards, tweezers, various other items in a metal case, and the digital camera.

Katie and McGaven, gear in tow, walked up the stairs to apartment 17. There were a couple of tenants peeking out their doors as the detectives passed by. Jimmy's apartment was located at the end of a section, near an exit stairwell that led around back—meaning two ways the killer could've entered or exited.

Katie stood at the slightly opened door with a gold 17 on the front identifying Jimmy's residence. She glanced to her partner. "Okay, you ready?"

"No, but I'm right behind you."

TEN

Katie hesitated before she pushed the door open—so many memories and thoughts tore through her mind about the crime scenes she had worked. But nothing could have prepared her for this. As she stood at the threshold of the apartment, she could immediately see that there had been a struggle. Furniture was overturned, couch cushions torn, pictures smashed and lying on the floor, items that had been on surfaces now scattered everywhere across the carpet. A cell phone was on the kitchen tile and it was smashed as if someone had crushed it under the heel of their shoe.

As they entered the living room, adjacent to the open kitchen area, they found the battered lifeless body of Jimmy Turner on the floor. His face was severely beaten, his body crumpled and shoved partway into a tight hallway. Bloody handprints and crimson smears were on the lower parts of the walls indicating that he had fought hard and tried to escape his killer to one of the other rooms, but hadn't made it.

A rope was twisted around Jimmy's neck. His eyes were

now fixed open, as if he would watch his own crime scene being processed and documented.

Katie stopped, her arms shaking. Her breath caught in her throat. She wasn't sure if she could work this crime scene of someone she knew and had worked with on so many occasions.

"I'm right behind you, partner," said McGaven, as if he felt her hesitation.

"Okay," she said softly. "Why don't you photograph the area and then take the close-ups while I document evidence?"

McGaven started taking the series of photos of the apartment. He methodically recorded everything; it was like telling a story to someone who hadn't heard it before.

Katie started at the entrance and kitchen areas. She documented the evidence even if she thought it didn't seem important. There was no chance at getting back to this part of the investigation if they cruised over potential evidence. She placed numbered markers around the area, from fingerprints to probable clues. She kept her focus and tried not to think about the life of the helpful and capable young man who had excavated the bones of four people earlier today.

Katie and McGaven worked together in efficient silence. No matter how traumatic the situation, they could be comfortable performing their duties side by side, knowing as they did one another's moves and mindsets.

It wasn't until Katie stood over Jimmy's body that she felt the sensation of falling apart. Jimmy stared back up at her. She had to force herself to imagine for her own benefit that if he could speak he would tell her it was okay. And that for his sake, she needed to examine every bit of evidence on and around his body.

Jimmy was dead...

The endless loop played over in her mind. Was there something that could've prevented this tragedy? If he had only called the police when he first thought someone was following him. If he had stayed at the police department and not driven home. *If only...* plagued Katie's thoughts and she found it incomprehensible that she was bagging Jimmy's hands and feet to preserve potential evidence. There could be viable evidence that could help identify the killer. Blood. Saliva. Something that transferred from the killer to the victim—anything at all.

Katie realized that there was what looked like possible skin under his nails, giving some hope to finding the killer. She also noticed that there was some type of dust or fine pieces of an unknown substance in his hair.

"Gav," she said. "Take a look at this."

McGaven leaned down to check it out. "I see it."

"What do you think it is?"

"It could be something from the fight in here, or food. Get as much as you can and bag it."

Katie retrieved a small round metal box. Unscrewing the lid, she carefully used tweezers to pick the larger pieces from his hair, tapping it into the box. She used adhesive tape to get the rest.

Her thoughts went to who would be receiving the evidence for investigation. The only person would be John and she didn't know if he was going to be able to face it. He needed some time to set things straight in his mind. But she hoped he could do it. He was a former Navy Seal and he knew how to move through extremely difficult situations and what it was like to lose friends along the way.

Katie carefully examined Jimmy's face and noted the wounds. McGaven took numerous photographs of the body as she did so.

They heard heated voices outside the door along the walkway. It sounded like there were neighbors expressing their concern about what had happened and officers trying to calm them.

Katie and McGaven turned and faced the door expecting

someone to burst into the scene causing problems. But no one did. The boisterous voices soon quieted and then there was the deadening silence falling over the apartment once again.

"How should we protect the rope? There could be trace evidence on it as well," she said. Her voice sounded hollow to her.

"Protect it like his hands and feet."

The scene was so shocking that Katie hadn't really taken an objective examination of the rope. It was older, made of a natural material like jute or sisal, and about two inches wide. It was worn and discolored with some debris stuck in the twists. "Gav," she said.

"What's up?"

"Does that look like dirt to you?"

Leaning in closer, he said, "Yeah, it does."

"I'm taking some examples before I cover the rope for transport."

McGaven nodded. He was quiet and Katie could almost feel his stress. The atmosphere was a heavy static one that made her skin prickle. She felt a deep sense of tragedy, and yet also as though this were all a bad dream or some cruel joke. Either way, she wanted to leave as soon as possible. At the same time, she felt a deep responsibility to Jimmy not to overlook anything that might help identify the killer.

Katie knew that Detective Hamilton was in charge of this investigation, but she couldn't help but let her mind wander as she carefully retrieved evidence and bagged everything appropriately so that it couldn't get lost during transport.

Who killed Jimmy?

Was it someone he knew?

Someone who had a problem or disagreement with him from his past—or present? Or was it connected to one of the cases he worked?

Time ticked by as McGaven documented everything. He

even took photos outside the apartment, carefully capturing images of the front door, walkway landing, the video cameras, and the stairwells, in order to give Detective Hamilton everything he needed to conduct the investigation.

Katie discovered and tagged all the potential evidence she could find. There were twenty-seven markers. She stood in the middle of the apartment and did one last three hundred-sixty-degree turn, cataloging everything in her mind and making sure she didn't miss anything.

Katie and McGaven handed everything over to Detective Hamilton and gave him time to walk the crime scene himself, making his own notes and assessments. The detective seemed as quiet as they were as he carefully walked through the apartment making quick sketches and notes on his small notepad. Katie watched him out of curiosity as his tall slim frame bent over to look at something more closely, taking his time before moving on to the next clue. He looked older than he was due to his receding hairline. She remembered the first time she had worked with him at Whispering Pines at the crime scene of a murdered young woman—he definitely hadn't been happy that the sheriff had ordered that she should be there. Now as she watched him, she realized that he must've finally made peace with her working at the department. Or maybe it was just the fact that this time, it was one of their own who had been beaten and strangled to death. It hit too close to home for there to be jealousy or resentment.

McGaven was now filling out the sheets for the evidence and the chain of custody. He looked up. "Who is taking the evidence back to the forensic division?"

"Probably Hamilton or the sheriff," she said. "The body will be released to the medical examiner when he gets here and gives the order."

Hamilton finished up and left the scene without saying

much to the detectives, other than that he appreciated their great work.

Katie and McGaven bagged and identified each piece of evidence, which took them more than an hour. In the meantime, one of the medical examiners serving under Dr. Dean came to the apartment and officially signed the death certificate, which in turn allowed the release of the body.

The crime scene was officially completed.

They walked back to their cars. There was still one patrol car there, along with Hamilton and the morgue van.

Katie looked around for John, but didn't see him or his truck. She assumed he had given Hamilton his statement and then gone home. She was worried about him—this must have really shaken him up. She imagined that it would have brought back horrifying memories of losing friends and comrades in Navy Seal combat.

Glancing at his watch, McGaven said, "Wow, it's almost getting close to sunrise."

Katie moaned. She was exhausted. Her arms and legs felt extra heavy. Her mind was now fuzzy and her body was in desperate need of sleep. It seemed a lifetime ago when she was painting the interior of her house.

"What's that you say?" he joked.

"I'm so looking forward to bed—we have a big day today. I can't even think about it right now."

"You? I find that hard to believe."

"My brain has officially stopped."

"What time do you want to meet at the office?" he said.

"How about ten or ten thirty?"

McGaven walked to his truck. "See you tomorrow. Stay safe. Keep watchful and if you think anything seems wrong, call the police."

Katie got into her Jeep and sat a moment trying to make

sense of everything that happened today. She watched McGaven drive out of the Skyline Apartment's parking lot.

She turned over the Jeep's engine and it roared into life. All she could see was the bodies of the day—the skeleton remains and Jimmy.

How were they going to sort through everything?

Driving out of the parking lot, she followed the lights of McGaven's truck in front of her. It gave some comfort to her to be behind him, until he turned off to go toward his neighborhood and she had to continue on alone.

She got home just as the sky was getting lighter. Soon the sun would be up on another day.

Jimmy was dead...

ELEVEN

TWENTY-FIVE YEARS AGO

Snyder Fields, Pine Valley
Summer

Sara Simms was excited that morning as she hurriedly made her bed, tidied up her clothes, and picked out the perfect summer outfit in mostly pale blues. She couldn't believe that she had been invited to the party of the summer. It was usually something that was only for the sixth graders. She brushed her blonde shoulder-length curls and applied pink lip gloss. She had received a special note left in the mailbox—it was written on yellow paper folded twice and addressed in her name.

It was difficult for Sara to not whistle or sing while she was getting ready. It was going to be a happy day.

The clock read 12:35 p.m. She made sure that she had her favorite bracelet as she affixed it to her wrist. Grabbing her backpack, she left her bedroom.

"Bye," she said as she approached the front door.

"Bye, honey, have fun," said her mother from the kitchen.

"Where do you think you're going?" said Kent, her older brother, appearing out of nowhere.

"*Me to know and you to find out...*" She tried to pull open the front door, but it slammed closed again.

"*What are you doing?*" she said. He always tried to ruin anything fun in her life by belittling or bullying her.

"*You really think that you're so special?*"

"*The difference between me and you—people actually like me.*" Sara tried to open the front door again.

"*Yeah?*" he said, pushing his face close to hers.

"*Uh-huh.*" She tried to stand up to him, but he was stocky and tough. She was no match for him.

He pushed her.

"*Better not. I'll tell Mom.*"

"*Fine,*" he said and opened the front door. "*Go, but I guarantee that no one really likes you.*"

Sara took her opportunity and rushed out the front door just as it slammed behind her. It startled her, but once she caught her breath, she vowed that she wouldn't let her brother ruin her fantastic day.

She carefully unfolded her note and reread the instructions, which directed her to the Snyder Fields. Replacing it into her backpack, she gave a couple of skips and walked down the driveway heading toward the grounds.

TWELVE

Katie drove to the Pine Valley Sheriff's Department sipping on her fourth cup of coffee from a stainless thermos. No fancy latte drinks today—only pure bursts of caffeine would sustain her. She had made sure that she ate a complete breakfast, because she knew that it was going to be another busy, long day. Sadness still engulfed her as her mind swam between the previous day's arson scene and Jimmy's apartment.

She had managed to get a couple hours of sleep, but when she closed her eyes she saw Jimmy's face—watching almost as if he were overseeing her search. This was going to hit the department hard. Usually, if someone was killed in the line of duty it was an officer—not a forensic technician.

She tried to push away the memory of his face with its fixed expression, but its place was only taken by other images of the evidence, the rope, and the ghostly atmosphere when she had arrived at the apartment. Something bothered her about the scene—an inkling, a gut feeling that something was out of place. She wasn't completely sure yet what it was. Maybe it was just the fact that it was someone so close to home, someone who was part of her working family. It was making it difficult to concentrate.

Driving into the employee parking lot, Katie noticed that John's truck wasn't there. She frowned, worrying about his state of mind. It had obviously hit him hard because it was someone from his team. She surmised that he probably partly blamed himself because he didn't get there in time.

Katie parked and grabbed her briefcase along with the extensive files they'd received from Travis Stone. It was going to be a heavy load of reading and sifting through information.

Entering the building and heading down the hallway, she stopped at the usual door, which had a camera aimed down at whoever was standing there. She inserted her keycard. A soft buzzing emitted, which allowed her access into the forensic division.

It all worked like clockwork, and felt like an almost comforting reprieve from the outside world. The scrubbed air that was piped into the offices and laboratories made her wrinkle her nose. The hum of the ventilation system kept a constant background sound similar to white noise. The cold-case section consisted of two unused offices that between them acted as the working office and the storage room for anything related to Katie and McGaven's investigations. It was partly due to the lack of space for another division upstairs, but she thought it was more likely it kept her away from the whispers and gossip that she was the sheriff's niece. Either way, it had worked out well for them.

Her boots clipped down the long hallway, echoing slightly. Katie glanced into the large forensic examination room, full of many tables and computers. That was where she usually witnessed John bent over a scanning electron microscope. But today, the forensic division was vacant. Quiet.

Hurrying, she reached the end of the hall and opened the

door on the right. She walked inside and spotted McGaven already at work in the cramped space. He sat at his desk, pecking at the keyboard, searching for clues and follow-up information to assist them and start pointing the investigation in the right direction.

"Hey, morning," she said, trying not to sound as tired as she felt.

Without looking at her, he said, "Been lonely here for the past half hour."

"I noticed that John wasn't here." She ignored her partner's remark about the time she had arrived.

"He might be taking a personal day."

"Maybe." She didn't think so. It was more likely he was trying to make sense of everything, following his intuition and trying to get some answers.

She dropped her files and briefcase on her own desk. Noticing that McGaven had already posted the blueprints of the home on Maple Road up on their investigation wall, she saw a few notations indicating where the bodies were located.

"I think we might need another space to spread out everything," she said.

McGaven looked up. "Like where?"

"I don't know, but maybe we can move some of the storage files across the hall to free up a wall."

He nodded. "That might work."

"I was thinking that everything pertaining to the property should be across the hall and everything about evidence, suspects, and profiles should be in here." She studied the house plans and where the electrical and plumbing had been located. "We need the remodel plans and permits here too. I'm assuming these might be from before Stone owned the property."

"Maybe."

Katie scrutinized where the bodies were buried and made

some notations of her own. "I think we also need an overall plan of the street. I want to know if there are any anomalies. Maybe the entire neighborhood had some updated plumbing, which would point to when—giving us a possible timeline when the bodies were buried." She stepped back, still staring at the blueprints.

McGaven looked up at his partner from his desk. "Denise is gathering that information now and should have something before the end of the day." He looked back at his email. "Looks like something from Detective Hamilton."

"Oh good," she said and squeezed in next to her partner, reading the names of the files. "There's a list of the neighbors. Let's start there."

McGaven hit a key for two copies. The printer churned out pages of what information had already been gathered from the initial crime scene and canvass of the neighborhood.

Katie skimmed through the write-ups of the brief interviews held with the neighbors, but nothing seemed of interest and no one seemed to have anything useful to add to the investigation, but... "Hmm," she said.

"Anything?" McGaven asked.

"Not really, except..."

McGaven turned his attention to her. "Except what?"

"Read the neighbor's account of that morning, a Cara Lewis, forty-seven-year-old writer who works at home and lives alone."

McGaven shuffled the pages and stopped to read the woman's account. "What's caught your interest?"

"Here she says that she let her dogs out around 7:30 a.m. and they barked and sniffed the fence that is at the other side of the yard. She didn't think much of it—it could've been anything, like a squirrel or someone walking by."

"It could give us an idea of the timing of what went down on the property, but we need to get back the report from Chad to find out the details as well. The accelerant or whatever ignited the fire could've been set on a timer."

"True. No one else seemed to hear or know anything," she said. She opened her laptop and began to bring up aerial maps of the area and then zoomed in on Maple Road. She zeroed in on the house and the immediate neighbors around it.

McGaven sorted through other neighbors' statements.

Katie printed out the map so she would have a better visual of all the close neighbors. She snatched up the printer copy. "Okay," she said. Looking at the layout of the burned-out home, she scribbled notes and approximate locations of how the surrounding houses faced the property.

McGaven studied the map. "I see how Ms. Lewis would be the closest to the house. In fact, she would have the best view."

Katie flipped through some notes. "Do we have the contact information and addresses for the Crosses' employers before they gave notice?"

"Yep. William Cross worked at Thomas and Young, Architects, which is over on Pine Street—his manager is Stan Bates. And Mrs. Cross, Heather, worked for Serenity Spa, which is next to the Royalty Hotel. Her manager is Tiffany Moore-Benedict."

"That's what was filled out on their rental applications."

"At least it's a start."

Katie thought about organizing paperwork. She also wanted time to get started on the preliminary profile. "It's going to be a busy day. Let's drop in on the neighbor Cara Lewis first and then make our way to the architect and spa."

"We might need the spa after all that," he chuckled.

Katie grabbed her notes and keys. "We need more caffeine."

"I can't survive on caffeine alone."

THIRTEEN

Thursday 1245 hours

Katie drove to the Snyder Subdivision and on to Maple Road. She remained quiet and lost in thought, constantly revisiting the arson crime scene in her mind. McGaven was also quiet beside her, using his laptop to find out more information about Ms. Lewis.

As they neared what had been 717, Katie slowed her speed, scrutinizing each of the homes in turn before stopping at the residence of Cara Lewis. It was one of the smaller homes on the street, but the landscaping was far more complex and beautiful than that of her neighbors. It was miraculous that the flames hadn't jumped the fence and tree line to ruin the flowers and plants that had been so carefully tended. Katie parked and cut the engine. She sat waiting a moment.

"Cara Lewis," read McGaven beside her. "She's been a mystery writer for the past fifteen years. And she's successful. She's divorced. No children. Her blog talks mostly about writing, but she also shares her joy and enthusiasm for her dogs. She shows them on occasion, but it seems that she keeps a low profile and enjoys her quiet life." He shut his laptop.

"She sounds nice," she said. "Since her life is so quiet, she might be one of those neighbors who is aware of what's going on around the street. Who comes and goes, for instance."

"She has no criminal record."

"Okay, let go see what Ms. Lewis has to say."

The detectives got out of the sedan and walked up the path of carefully placed stepping stones with deep green moss growing in between.

Katie spotted a hard rubber dog toy on a rope on the front porch, which made her think of Cisco. Two tall vases with small manicured bonsai trees were located on each side of the porch, and there were two hanging pots and several other small pots with annuals planted in an array of bright colors, along with two ceramic dog statues. In contrast, the door mat was plain rubber.

Both detectives glanced around at their surroundings. Each scrutinized the area and what the vantage point would be to the rental house, then stepped up to the porch.

Katie knocked. Instantly dogs barked. She recognized the distinct sound of German shepherds.

"Quiet," said a female voice from inside.

Slowly the door opened. A blonde woman with hair twisted up and pinned in a large silver barrette, who looked to be in her forties, poked her head out. "Yes?" she said to the detectives.

"Ms. Cara Lewis?" said Katie.

"Yes. What can I do for you?" She eyed Katie curiously and then looked up at McGaven.

"I'm Detective Scott and my partner, Detective McGaven," Katie said, showing her badge.

"You must be investigating the fire next door."

"That's right. May we have a few moments with you?"

The woman hesitated, glancing back inside, but then finally opened the door wider. "Please come in."

Katie stepped inside. McGaven followed and shut the front door behind him.

Three large German shepherds surrounded the detectives, making a greeting circle to sniff every inch of them.

"They are friendly, just a bit pushy," said Cara.

"They're beautiful," said Katie. She noticed that one was older than the other two with a grayish face. He seemed to be the most interested in them.

"Please, come in and sit down." The woman gestured to the living room, where there was a large beige sectional couch.

The three dogs stayed with Ms. Lewis and followed closely behind her. Their temperaments were calm as each took their place, two on the floor and one on the couch next to her.

The large living room was heavily decorated with many knickknacks, framed photographs, and a writing desk in the corner that faced the backyard. Katie made a mental note of the location.

"I don't know what else I can tell you about the fire—I've already spoken with the patrol officer who came to my door."

"Yes." Katie took a seat while McGaven stood looking at photos hanging on the wall.

"It is so terrible. We, actually the neighborhood, were so worried that the fire would spread. It nearly caught my back fence." Her eyes were dark and expressive. Katie believed the woman was being truthful.

"Did you know the previous tenants—Mr. and Mrs. Cross?" said Katie.

"Yes."

"And their daughter?"

"Of course. Raven. Sweet girl."

"If you don't mind me asking... How well did you know them?"

"Well now, let me see. They lived here a little over two years. We were friendly, neighborly friendly. Raven would come over to play with the dogs and I would take their mail inside when they were gone." She thought a moment. "We had a couple of barbecues... that kind of thing."

"Have you spoken with them since they moved out?"

McGaven turned to watch Ms. Lewis's response.

"I had sent Heather an email, but I haven't heard back. I just figured that they were getting settled and were too busy with everything to respond yet."

Katie watched the dogs lying close to the woman. "Do you know how to get in touch with them, besides email? A forwarding address? New place of employment?"

"No. Just their email. They disconnected their cell phones, which seemed odd. I know they have my address—I just figured that they'd get in touch when they had time."

"Do you know where they moved?"

"Arizona."

"Do you know where they would be working?"

"I know that Heather didn't have a job, but Bill was going to be moving somewhere for his work. I don't know if it was a city job or in the private sector."

"I see," said Katie.

Cara's face clouded as she frowned. "Detective? What's wrong?"

"We're just trying to locate them."

"Do you think something happened to them?"

"We don't know. We're just trying to locate them, that's all."

"I may not be law enforcement, but it doesn't take a cop to realize that the type of security guarding the burned-down house is more than the usual. Something more is going on." She petted the dog sitting next to her.

Katie wanted to tell her about the bodies, but there was no reason to share that information with her. "We're following up on anything we can. Would you happen to remember the moving company or rental truck they used?"

"I think they hired one of those storage moving companies—Alpine Storage Company. You know, where you pack up everything and a big truck comes by and picks it up and stores it until you're ready to move it to another location."

Katie made a mental note—at least they had a name to find out more. "When was the last time you talked to them or saw them?"

"Let's see," the woman said, looking at the calendar on her desk where she had many small handwritten notes. "It's been two months and six days." She looked back at the detectives, concerned.

McGaven joined Katie on the couch. "We just wanted to talk with them just to get some insight on the house."

"The house..." she said, trailing off. "Well, you should be talking to their so-called landlord, a Mr. Stone, I believe that's his name."

"Why do you say that?" said Katie.

"Heather used to tell me that he would harass them."

"Harass them how?"

"He would actually come to the house two days before the rent was due and demand the money—in cash. He would offer a small discount if they gave him the money right away. He would even bring some other man with him."

"Anything else?" Katie tried to be calm and respectful, but she really wanted to know all about Mr. Stone's behavior.

"He felt that he could enter the house anytime he wanted—and did. He wanted to make sure they weren't ruining the home. He said something about the basement..."

"Basement?" That ratcheted up Katie's attention.

"From what Heather had said, he wanted to make sure they weren't doing anything around the basement area. He wanted the house to stay intact and in its original condition. I think he was planning on remodeling it and didn't want to pay for anything they might ruin."

"Anything else?"

"He was really pushy and it made Heather uptight because she never knew when he was going to show up. I think she was frightened."

"I see."

"Have you spoken to the landlord?" She watched the detectives closely.

"Yes. We had a preliminary interview about the house."

"Well... he should know more than I do. But something's not right about that man."

Katie stood up and looked out through the sliding doors to the backyard. She moved toward it and calculated how close she was to the other house. All three dogs got up and followed her. "Did you call in the fire?"

"I did call, but they said there were already two calls and that a fire truck had been dispatched."

"Did you notice anything unusual that morning? A car? Noise from the backyard? Anything?"

"I'm sorry, Detective. When I let the dogs out at around 7:30 a.m. they were pacing and barked a few times along the fence. But I just figured it was a neighbor's cat or a squirrel.

I didn't notice anything else unusual."

"Ms. Lewis, you work at home?" said Katie. She had noticed her laptop, paperwork, and a thick pile of printout that resembled a manuscript.

"Yes, I'm a writer," she said. There was no further explanation and she didn't offer details about what she wrote.

"Thank you, Ms. Lewis. If you think of anything, or if the Crosses contact you, please give us a call." Katie left her business card on the coffee table.

Ms. Lewis walked the detectives to the door with her three German shepherds in tow. "I'm sorry I wasn't much help. I hope you find what you need."

Katie nodded. "Thank you."

As soon as Katie and McGaven were back inside their car, Katie said, "That was interesting."

"You think she knows more?"

"Yes, I do. And for all the time she spends at the desk writing novels, she could see and hear more than anyone else. She knows more than she's saying." Katie started the car. "Check with dispatch and see if she did call 911 about the smoke."

"So the neighbor's cat and squirrel assumption was just a ruse..." said McGaven.

"More like deception."

"What about Travis Stone?"

"We need to dig a bit more about him so that we're prepared for the next visit—we will definitely be paying him another visit —this time unannounced."

FOURTEEN

Thursday 1350 hours

The two-story office complex seemed to be mostly occupied by small businesses such as accountants, attorneys, and investment-planning firms. Every door had its business name stenciled in black lettering. The detectives quickly found the upstairs office of Thomas and Young, Architects.

Katie pushed open the glass door followed closely by McGaven.

They were greeted by a small reception area barely big enough for two chairs, where a middle-aged woman sat behind a desk. She looked up over her glasses. "Yes? May I help you?"

"Hi. We're Detectives Scott and McGaven," said Katie flashing her badge. "We're here from the Pine Valley Sheriff's Department."

The woman's eyes grew bigger. "Is there someone you need to speak to?"

"Yes, Stan Bates," Katie said. "Is he here?"

"One moment." The woman left her desk and disappeared around the corner.

Katie loved to speak with people unannounced. It generally caught them off guard and they seem to answer questions more truthfully—better than hauling them down to the interview room at the police department.

The detectives looked around, but there wasn't anything memorable on the walls or anywhere else in the reception area. Katie thought it odd that an architects' office wouldn't have some of their work hanging on the walls for clients to see—she remembered at the construction office there were many carefully framed photographs and artist's renderings of their projects.

Within five minutes, the receptionist returned with a nervous-looking man in his forties. His sparse hair had been gelled and combed carefully to one side. "Thank you, Misty," he said to the receptionist. He turned to Katie and McGaven, resting his gaze on Katie. "I'm Stan Bates. What can I do for you?"

"I'm Detective Scott and this is my partner Detective McGaven. Can we talk somewhere private?" she said.

"Of course. Follow me to the conference room." He turned back into a long hallway off which Katie could see six cubicles. Drafting boards were set up in them, and employees were diligently bent over drawings.

The conference room had double glass doors and one big rectangular table that would accommodate about twelve people. There were several inspirational framed photos on the wall with quotes about motivation, ambition, and life dreams.

"Have a seat," he said, nervously adjusting and readjusting his glasses.

"Thank you," said Katie, sitting down. "We won't take up much of your time. We're basically conducting a background check."

The manager looked a bit confused but patiently waited.

"You had a William Cross in your employ?" she said.

"Yes. He worked here for about two years. Just recently resigned about two and half months ago and said that he and his family were moving to Arizona for another job."

"What was his position?"

"He was a level-two draftsperson."

"Was he a good employee? Showed up on time? Turned in work on time?"

"Always. Bill was a great employee and a nice guy."

"Have you heard from him since he left?"

The manager shook his head. "No, I haven't heard from him. I did email him his letter of recommendation, but didn't hear back. That was a couple of months ago. We've been swamped and I haven't thought much more about it." He seemed to study the detectives carefully. "Did something happen to him?"

"I'm sorry but we're not authorized to comment about our investigation," she said. "But we are trying to locate him." Katie stood up. "If you hear from Mr. Cross, please call us." She dropped a card on the table. "Thank you for your time."

Katie and McGaven moved toward the door.

"Oh," said McGaven. "Did Mr. Cross have any problems or seem upset about anything? Anything you might notice?"

"No, not at all."

"Thank you," he said.

Katie and McGaven retraced their path and exited the building.

Walking to their car, Katie said, "It's clear that they don't know anything—we've just given them some angst."

"I agree."

Just as Katie was about to open the car door, the receptionist came running toward them, her hands waving. "Detectives..." She looked behind her as if someone might be following.

Katie caught McGaven's eye as if to say "interesting."

"I'm so glad that you haven't left yet," the woman said.

"Is there something you want us to know?" said Katie.

Still winded, the slightly heavyset woman that Stan Bates had called Misty said, "Yes. I couldn't help but overhear what you were asking about Bill Cross. I'm sorry but it's no secret at the firm that you can hear people talking in the conference room."

"Go on," said McGaven. "Do you know something about Mr. Cross?"

She took a deep breath. "I saw Mr. Cross in the parking lot one day..."

"How long ago?" said Katie.

"About a month before he resigned. Anyway, he had just come back from lunch and I was going to say hi, but I saw he was talking to a man. They were arguing and Mr. Cross was angry. I've never seen him like that before. He was waving his arms and I think he even poked the man in the chest..."

"Who was he arguing with?"

"I don't know, never seen him before or since."

"Can you describe this man?" asked McGaven.

"Well, I guess he was sort of handsome, if you like that kind of look. He had blondish hair that was long, maybe shoulder length, but he had it pulled back in a ponytail. Muscular. And I think there was some older, thin man standing near a very nice black car."

"Anything else you can remember?" said Katie.

"No, but it wasn't like Bill. I never saw him ever raise his voice to anyone before that."

Katie gave her a card. "If you think of anything else, please feel free to call us."

"Okay," she said taking the business card.

"Thank you," said McGaven.

The detectives got in the sedan.

"Looks like Mr. Travis Stone has some explaining to do," said Katie.

"So now a neighbor and a receptionist from Mr. Cross's work, neither with a connection to one another, have talked about the Crosses having confrontations with Stone."

"Wait," she said. "Looks like Stan Bates had to leave in a hurry." She watched the awkward man leave the office.

The detectives observed the supervisor hurry to his car, looking all around him, before getting in and driving away.

"Maybe the supervisor does know something?" said McGaven.

"More follow-up. We still can't connect the Cross family to the skeletal remains until they are officially ID'd. We need to run down every lead we have and see where it takes us." She drove out of the parking lot.

"Where there's smoke there's usually fire," said McGaven.

"I can't believe you just said that."

FIFTEEN

Thursday 1545 hours

Katie drove to the Serenity Spa, which was situated next to the pricey Royalty Hotel, located at the outskirts of Pine Valley on one of the most picturesque drives in the area. The tall, magnificent pine trees lined the road as though they were directing you to the most wonderful secret place.

Katie rubbed her neck and grimaced. Her muscles were achy from the lack of sleep and the results of painting the interior of her house.

"I haven't been here in a while," said McGaven, watching the scenery pass by his window.

"You've been to the hotel?"

"Yes. Well, no. I had a call-out here once."

"Robbery or disorderly?"

"Disorderly. Domestic issue. Nothing big. Just loud. Drinking involved."

Katie pulled up into the visitors' and delivery parking areas. "I was here once for a surprise birthday party."

"Wow, nice surprise," said McGaven.

"It is really nice, but all the grounds are laid out in a way that's meant to keep most of the natural elements intact."

"Which is code for 'we have to walk a ways.'"

"Exactly," she said. "At least I'm not in heels this time."

The detectives got out and looked for the best path through the landscaping. They headed up to the main entrance of the hotel, walking across the grand threshold into a massive reception area. Signs instructed visitors where to go. Main Desk. Lobby. Restaurant. Spa.

Katie followed the signs toward the spa area. She was trying to keep her focus, but it was starting to prove difficult to keep the momentum going. A few minutes after entering the luxurious hotel, walking on the plush burgundy carpeting and hearing the faint, soothing classical music, she was overcome with fatigue and exhaustion. But they had to keep moving until they'd heard from the medical examiner's office and forensics as to the identification of the remains.

Finally the detectives reached the entrance to the spa. Katie slowed her pace, straightened her jacket, and made sure that her badge was visible. She actually would have loved to spend an hour at a spa, but there never seemed to be a convenient time.

The serene music and the aroma, a lovely mixture of lavender and geranium with hints of rose, was comforting and relaxing. Katie walked to the front desk, where a young woman was dressed in a pale pink uniform similar to scrubs in a hospital. She smiled at the detectives. "Good afternoon. May I help you?" she said.

"Yes, would it possible to speak with Tiffany?" said Katie.

The woman opened a large appointment book and checked times. "She's just finishing up a facial and will be out shortly. I can let her know you're here. And you are...?"

"Detective Scott and Detective McGaven," she said.

"I see," the woman said. She gave an extra smile at McGaven before she left the desk.

Katie turned to her partner. "I think she likes you," she whispered.

"I feel uncomfortable here," he said. "It's weird for me. I feel too conspicuous."

Katie giggled. "Why? Haven't you ever been curious about manicures and facials before?"

"Uh, in a word, no."

"You might not be able to escape this spa without a massage first."

McGaven stared at Katie and it was first time that she had seen her partner panicky.

"Don't worry. I'll protect you."

"Good to know."

They waited almost ten minutes before a tall brunette woman who obviously had had some surgery done on her face came out to meet them. It was clear that she was well over forty, but her perfectly toned and wrinkle-free face resembled a preserved doll-like image of a much younger woman. She was dressed in the same pink uniform as the receptionist.

"Detectives," she said happily. It was a first that they were treated this way upon meeting any witness or suspect.

"Tiffany?" said Katie.

"Yes, I'm Tiffany Moore-Benedict. I'm the manager here at Serenity Spa. What brings you two in here?"

"We're doing a background investigation on one of your previous employees, Heather Cross."

"Yes, Heather. What an absolutely lovely girl. She was one of my best estheticians. We really miss her." Tiffany stepped to the side of the entrance. "Did something happen to her?" she whispered as concern washed across her face.

"Is there somewhere we can speak in private?" said Katie.

"Of course, please, this way."

Katie and McGaven followed her to an office, which smelled as lovely as the rest of the spa. There were large framed photographs of beautiful beaches and waterfalls on the walls. Tiffany took her seat behind the desk, leaving two overstuffed chairs for the detectives.

"Please, Detectives, tell me what this about. I'm getting the feeling that this isn't just a routine background check."

"We can't divulge why we need this information, but we wanted to check to make sure that Ms. Cross had worked here and see if there's anything you might like to tell us," said Katie.

"Like?" She glanced back and forth between the detectives.

"Like, did she always show up on time? Or, if she had any problems you know about," said McGaven.

"I..." she said and hesitated. "I don't know."

"Please, if you know something."

"I haven't heard from her since her last day more than two months ago. Her cell phone has been disconnected and I haven't received a reply from her email."

"Did she tell you anything about any trouble she was having?" said Katie.

Tiffany sighed and leaned back in the chair. "She mentioned that her family was being harassed by the landlord."

"Harassed how?"

"He would show up at odd hours. He wanted the rent earlier and earlier before it was due. I think he even showed up at her husband's work. She was really scared of him."

"Did she say that—about being *scared*?"

"She didn't have to, I could tell by the way she talked about him. The trouble was they had to wait until their two-year lease was up before they could move."

"Do you know where they were moving to?"

"I think it was Arizona."

Katie felt disappointed that they weren't finding anything new. But Tiffany did corroborate the statements from the neighbor and supervisor at the architects' office. "Thank you for seeing us, Tiffany. You've been helpful." She put a business card on the desk. "Please call if you hear from Ms. Cross, or if you have anything else you can remember that might help us."

"Of course. Oh, and, Detective?" She looked at Katie. "If you ever want a facial and a mani-pedi, it's on the house."

Katie smiled. "Thank you. I might take you up on that, but I'm more than happy to pay for the services."

"And," she said, gesturing to McGaven, "if you ever need a massage after a long day of detecting, we would be more than happy to accommodate you."

McGaven smiled awkwardly and followed Katie out of the office.

After the detectives finally reached their car, McGaven was the first to speak. "If we ever have to question someone at a spa again, leave me back at the office."

Katie laughed. "And leave your fan club without your presence?"

"That was uncomfortable."

Looking at her cell phone, she had missed two text messages.

First text was from Denise in the record's division:

Found records and permits for 717 Maple Road and video came in from two of the nearby neighbors.

The second text was from John in forensics:

I'm back in the office and will have some preliminary information for you soon.

"What's up?" asked McGaven.

"Things are starting to come in. We have records and permits for the arson house and John just let me know that he's back in the office."

"Sounds good. More to go through until we hear from the medical examiner."

"I'm afraid we're going to have to go back and talk to Travis Stone."

"Yeah, that goes without saying. He's quite a piece of... work."

Katie stayed quiet.

"What do you think? Is it possible he could have killed the Crosses and buried them in the basement?"

"I've learned that you can't eliminate anyone when it comes to murder, but Travis Stone obviously has some issues and I want to know what skeletons are in his closet."

"Did you really say that?" he said.

"Payback."

"I see."

"I don't mean any disrespect to the victims, but this case is becoming convoluted." She turned the key and the V8 engine immediately roared to life. "Let's see what we can find out back at the office before we pay a visit to Mr. Stone again."

SIXTEEN

After Katie and McGaven returned to the office back at the sheriff's department, they found several bundles of paperwork and security DVDs. There was also a sticky note with a scribbled message from John to come to his examination room.

Katie began looking at the paperwork.

"Hey, I'll sort everything out and get it organized. Why don't you see what John has to say?" said McGaven.

"Okay." She headed to the door.

"Hurry back," he called after her.

Katie closed the door behind her. She stared down the long hallway and for the first time she was hesitant to see John. Remembering his distress and extreme sadness, she wouldn't be able to not think about Jimmy every time she entered forensics.

She walked to the door, it was slightly ajar. Softly knocking, she heard John say, "Come in."

Katie pushed the door open and saw John working as usual. Everything seemed just like it was—but it wasn't and they would all have to grieve and support each other to move on.

"Hey," he said, looking up from one of the microscopes.

"Hi," said Katie.

"Okay, let's get everything out in the open so there's no weirdness between us."

Katie nodded.

"I apologize for calling you in the early morning, but I couldn't think of anyone else who I could trust—or run a crime scene the way it needed to be done." He paused as if searching for the right words. "If I had to do it all over again—I would make the same decision. And I'm grateful—thank you, Katie."

"It's okay, John. We're like family—you know that. Right?"

"Yeah, I do. I've never really had any family, so this place and people like you and McGaven are the closest thing."

Katie moved forward and hugged him—he hugged her tight for a moment. Stepping back, she said, "We'll all get through this. We've been through a lot together."

John nodded.

"Now, what did you need for us to see?" she said. "Gav is sorting out all the arson house paperwork and security DVDs."

"Don't most people upload their security to the internet or wherever?"

"I thought so too, but these are dated security camera systems. We have to take what we can get. So what's up?" Katie avoided looking at John. She felt slightly awkward now after the emotional hug they'd shared—it was no secret to her that there were some slight sparks between the two of them. But it was just familiarity. That was what she kept telling herself.

"Oh, of course," he said. "Come with me."

John went out a different door from the main examination area, turned the corner, and opened a door. The room was about the size of a small bedroom. There was an eight-foot folding table with two fold-out chairs—two more were leaning up against the wall.

"Okay. I don't understand. What is this room?" she said.

"Well this room was used for storage and we recently cleaned it out. We're not using it right now, so I thought the cold-case unit could use it on this case. I can only imagine how much evidence and information you must have—and keep accumulating."

Katie was surprised. "Really?" She had to admit it would make things easier. There was so much evidence, not to mention two investigations going on at the same time—the homicide and the arson.

"Yes. I know there's a lot of stuff from the arson house. You can use all these walls to lay out your investigation. I know that Chad will be bringing more stuff to you about the arson—and I can update your forensic evidence when it becomes available. I'll make sure you get keys."

"I don't know what to say. This is great." Relief filled Katie as she looked about the room and imagined how much evidence they could lay out in it. The four bodies were actually two cases —this would help separate both investigations in order to see them clearly.

"Good. Bring what you need and set it up as your command center."

"Thank you, John. I'll let Gav know right away."

She stood to face him. Paused. She gently squeezed his hand in support before she returned to her office.

Katie and McGaven grabbed the architectural plans and everything pertaining to the construction and remodeling of the arson house on Maple Road, including aerial maps and street views.

"This is great," said McGaven. He tacked up the maps, blown-up photographs, and aerial views of the house."

Katie stood back to where she could look at the whole wall and follow the chain of events. She could see what the home looked like before and after the fire, and where the bodies were found. According to the planning department, there had been only one major remodel besides the current permits that had been pulled by Randall Construction. Interestingly, there wasn't a name for the construction company on the previous permit, which was to build a fence two years after the home was built.

"What do you think?" said McGaven admiring his handiwork.

"It's looking like a real command center. We're going to need to know everything about this neighborhood and property." She took a step closer to the maps. Her hands rested on her hips as she lightly bit her lower lip—it was how she concentrated as she worked through the recent events, scrutinizing everything.

"I think this is good for now," he said.

"Let's take a look at the security footage from around the time the fire started."

Katie and McGaven slipped the first DVD into a laptop back at their smaller office and watched the footage an hour before and after the 911 call. The video was from two neighbors who had had the cameras for many years and had never bothered to perform any maintenance or upgrades.

"Wow, I feel like I'm watching footage from another era," he said.

"It's better than nothing."

"But you can't identify anything with certainty—except maybe when the fire trucks rolled up. Everything is black and white, and extra grainy. I don't think there's infrared."

Katie agreed, but she had hoped that there was something that would help with the timeline pointing them in the right direction.

Before the fire ignited, there were only a couple neighborhood cars leaving for work. Both vehicles were four-door sedans.

No one stopped or slowed down. Nothing suspicious. A large truck was seen slowing and then leaving. From the camera angles, it was impossible to see the entire truck and if it was indeed stopping and looking at the property.

"Rewind that again," said Katie. As she watched the truck, she knew there wasn't enough detail. It might be important—it might not. "Not enough time for someone to set up the incendiary device. Maybe someone was dropped off?" She leaned in. "Can't even see the entire truck and wouldn't be able to tell what make and model it is."

"Maybe we can rule out what makes it isn't," McGaven said.

"It's not one of the smaller makes like Toyota, Honda, or maybe Nissan if they even make them. I don't claim to know much about big or small trucks." She sighed. "I don't think it's going to help us."

"We're still investigating without knowing who the bodies are yet," he said.

"True. I know that Dr. Dean will get in touch soon." She yawned. "We need a timeline for the Cross family, the week before they moved out. Their movements. Anyone who visited the house."

"May not be easy, but we have the name of the moving company—Alpine Storage Company."

She yawned again.

"I think someone needs their beauty sleep."

"And a hot bath."

"Let's get out of here and begin updating everything again... and maybe we'll hear soon about the IDs."

"You know what?" she said, pushing her chair back. "I'm not going to do anyone any good if I'm falling asleep."

The detectives left their office and forensic division for the day. They walked into the parking lot together.

Katie thought about Jimmy and wondered if Detective

Hamilton was making headway on the case. Her cell phone rang. She answered, "Scott."

"Detective, it's Travis," he whispered. "Something is wrong, very wrong. I need your help. I wasn't completely truthful... There are some issues..." His speech was hurried and slightly slurred.

She waved to McGaven. "Slow down, Mr. Stone. What is wrong?" She tapped her cell phone's speaker option so that McGaven could hear.

"I can't talk on the phone. Please, Detective, *please* come over."

"Why are you whispering?"

"Someone might hear me..."

"Mr. Stone, I'm going home right now. If you have an emergency, hang up from me and dial 911."

"Please come over... I... I have some things to tell you... Please... I won't waste your time..."

Katie looked at McGaven. He nodded to agree that he would go with her to Travis Stone's house. "Okay, we'll be there in about ten minutes."

The phone connection went dead.

SEVENTEEN

Thursday 1925 hours

Katie drove her Jeep to Travis Stone's house, followed by McGaven in his truck. They parked on the street. The house was dark. No outside lights. Nothing illuminated from the inside except for a dim light in the upstairs corner of the house.

Katie stepped out of her Jeep, assessing the area. She switched on her flashlight.

McGaven joined her. "I don't like this. It's like we're stepping into an ambush situation."

"Something's off." Redialing Travis Stone's number, she listened to it ringing and ringing with no voicemail. "No answer." She returned her cell to her pocket.

"How do you want to play this? Call for backup?"

"Not yet. You met Stone. Eccentric. High minded. These super-rich types operate by a different set of rules... usually with some type of drama. He did say that he had information for us."

"Still," wavered McGaven. "Not really liking this."

"Let's check it out. It's probably nothing. If anything's off, we'll call for backup." She headed for the door, sweeping the flashlight's beam across the front yard, alert and keeping her attention on the surroundings. Nothing appeared unusual or out of place.

McGaven jogged behind her, clearly not wanting to be at the house again.

Katie decided to knock on the front door. No answer. She rang the beautiful chiming doorbell. They waited. Still nothing.

Instinctively, Katie put her hand on the door handle. She pressed the lever and the door opened. Looking at McGaven as he towered over her like a protective big brother, she said, "Do we go in?"

McGaven didn't immediately answer.

Katie slowly pushed the large door inward, but after a foot it stopped. Something was jammed behind it, not allowing her to push any farther. She pulled her weapon. "Mr. Stone? You home?"

"Go," said McGaven as he readied his weapon.

Katie tried to push the door open wider, but it would hardly budge. She squeezed through the opening and saw the lifeless body of Simon sprawled out on the tile floor, blocking the entrance. His torso was bloodied and a sticky crimson pool lay around him. His eyes were in a permanent stare on his ghostly face, his hands were curled into fists, dipped in blood. It was obvious that he was dead.

Bending down, she pressed her fingers gently against his neck and couldn't find a pulse. His skin temperature was already cool to the touch. "Call for backup." She pulled the body slightly, just enough to allow the door to be opened farther, while trying not to contaminate the scene.

"Travis! Travis!" she yelled.

"I'll clear this side of the first floor—you take the left." He turned on his flashlight. "Wait for me before going upstairs. Okay, Katie?" said McGaven.

She nodded. There were long blood streaks from the butler's body, indicating that someone had dragged him to block the front door.

Who killed him? Was it Travis? A burglar? Maybe a contract killer?

Looking to the left, she remembered when they were here in these rooms barely twenty-four hours ago. She stealthily moved through the faux office, taking a moment to comb the darkened corners with the flashlight sweep. Everything looked to be in place.

Katie kept moving slow and steady with her gun trained and flashlight leading her advance. The door to the solarium was open and she felt the humidity wafting through, hitting her face with the wet heat. The lights were off, giving a strange vertigo feeling as she stepped onto the patio area. Her mind was playing tricks, making it seem like every footstep was spongy and unbalanced.

She stood her ground, straining her senses to the surroundings. "Travis?" she said. "Travis?"

With her flashlight, she slowly panned the beam from left to right and back again, ensuring that she could see any possible shadow behind the large palm plants.

A click and motor sound came from the pool. The automatic skimmer had turned on, making its rounds cleaning the pool's surface.

She crept up to the side of the pool expecting the worst, kneeling down; she peered into the deep end directing her flashlight into the depths—nothing. No sign of Mr. Stone. No body. No clues.

Katie walked around the pool area, searching for any sign of foul play or evidence of any kind. The table and chair that she had sat in were now empty—no paperwork or other items on top. It was clear. The solarium was vacant.

Katie hurried back through the faux office and into the

grand foyer as McGaven returned from the other side of the estate.

"Anything?" she said.

"No, clear."

"Same." She made her way to the staircase. "I don't want to wait for backup if Mr. Stone is in need."

"Go, I'll cover."

There was a smashing sound upstairs.

"Go, go, go," said McGaven.

Katie didn't need any urging as she ran up the massive slightly winding staircase, followed closely by McGaven. When she got to the top, she wasn't sure what direction the sound had originated from. She looked over the wrought-iron banister to where the front door was located to gain her bearings, but she was moving on faith instead of knowledge.

She took the long hallway, where there were numerous rooms—all with closed doors. They both scaled close to the left side, skirting around the decorative tables and various pieces of huge bronze artwork. Their flashlight beams cast exaggerated shadows from the figurines so that there appeared to be giants and monsters dancing across the walls and ceiling.

Katie slowed her pace. She fixated on the room at the end of the hall, which had two large doors. There was a silver tray with a plate and a wineglass sitting on the floor. It had to be Travis Stone's master bedroom. She was caught in a dilemma between clearing each room down the long hallway and barging into the master bedroom.

With her back against the wall, Katie turned to her partner who was keeping the areas behind them clear. McGaven would make sure that they weren't going to be ambushed.

She moved her head toward the master bedroom, indicating that she was going to enter. He nodded okay.

That familiar prickly feeling ran down her arms and legs, her breathing became shallow, and everything told her that the answers they desperately needed were behind that door. Katie was on the verge of an adrenalin rush.

McGaven put his hand on her shoulder to let her know he had her back and it steadied her nerves.

Katie tried one of the golden doorknobs. It turned easily under her hand. She held it for a moment and then slowly nudged the extravagant door open. Pushing her Glock out in front of her, guiding the way, she could see that the dim light seen from outside was a small lamp with a stained-glass shade. The lighting cast a soft peach radiance around the bedroom.

"Travis," said Katie. Her voice sounded hollow and an octave higher than normal.

McGaven swooped to the right, clearing the immediate area. It was the sitting room portion of a grand bedroom suite, with two couches and an oversized chair in front of a fireplace. The décor was consistent with the rest of the house.

A door was open across the room, leading to a bathroom. The curtains and French doors were also slightly open, leading out on to what seemed to be a balcony or terrace.

Katie crept forward. She eyed the four-poster bed. It looked like the dark red bedding was rumpled and twisted. Still moving forward as if drawn by a magnet, she heard a low moan. There was no mistaking the sound.

"Gav," she said.

Katie heard his footsteps hurry up behind her. The top of the bed pulsed—at least that was what Katie saw. It reminded her of a nightmare she had when she was a child after seeing a sci-fi movie about an entity that consumed you when you slept.

Katie was hypnotized by the bed. She stood on the left side and slowly took a corner of the burgundy blanket; it felt wet in her fingertips, and strangely warm. She flipped the corner back and it revealed an arm.

She gasped. "*No*," was all she could say in a strangled whisper. She ripped back the blankets, revealing the body of Travis

Stone dressed in a silk robe. The front was wide open, exposing his chest with a number of slices and a severe stab wound. Blood had seeped quickly into the bedcovers.

"Travis," she said.

The bloodied man moaned. "*Help me...*" he managed to say. His blond hair was soaked in blood. His eyes were wide. Face eerily pale with a waxy complexion.

Katie turned and grabbed a towel that had been draped over a chair. It was still damp. She guessed that he had taken a shower and had been attacked, ending up at the bed. "Call for an ambulance."

McGaven put in the call and demanded backup to respond immediately—saying some choice words as to why deputies weren't already there by now.

Katie holstered her weapon and climbed onto the bed to apply pressure to the wound with the towel until help arrived. "Travis, who did this to you? C'mon, stay with us. You're going to be okay."

"Someone grabbed... me... from behind and..."

"Who?"

"I don't know," he wheezed.

"Help is coming," she said. "Who would want to hurt you?"

"So many..."

Sirens sounded and rolled up fast in the driveway.

"Did you see the person?" She couldn't hear him, so she leaned in close. The towel had turned completely red beneath her hands.

"Had mask... man... thin..." He managed to get the words out. "Familiar... don't know..." He tried to move. Then with a burst of strength, he grabbed Katie's hand. "Si... mon?"

"He's downstairs. Just relax until the paramedics are here." She didn't want to compound the seriousness of the situation by telling him his butler was dead at the front door.

They heard the sound of several people entering the house,

boots hitting the European tile, and voices yelling to ask where they were.

McGaven yelled back, "Up here at the end of the hallway. Hurry!" He grabbed a couple of tissues and turned on all the lights he could as the paramedics arrived. Not wanting to contaminate anything more than they had to, he kept his position at the door.

"Find him..." Travis wheezed, choking on blood as it came out of his mouth. "Be careful..." He continued to grip her hand and then released it as the last big pocket of air released from his lungs. His body went limp.

"No, Travis. Hang in there."

Katie climbed off the bed to give the emergency personnel room to work. She stood next to McGaven watching everything unfold. Dozens of scenarios fluttered in her mind.

The two paramedics quickly assessed the extent of the wounds and realized that the man wasn't breathing so they began trying to resuscitate him.

Several deputies came down the hallway opening doors, making sure the areas were clear.

Katie looked around the bedroom, but it wasn't the shocking scene of the paramedics trying to get Travis Stone's heart to beat again, it was the condition of the room—blood had spilled everywhere. It wasn't easy to see at first. There had been insurmountable violence. Blood was not only soaked into the dark rug, but also spattered on the surfaces and walls.

"Let's get this house locked down as a crime scene now," said Katie to the deputies, trying to erase the image from her mind of Travis Stone's last breath.

EIGHTEEN

Thursday 2 1 o o hours

Katie and McGaven stood out on the front lawn, watching everything unfold and waiting to talk with Detective Hamilton. After someone from the medical examiner's office declared Travis Stone and Simon officially dead, the morgue technicians stood ready to wheel out two body bags.

John had arrived to document and process the scene. After changing into protective gear and grabbing two metal cases, he nodded casually to the detectives as he made his way inside the estate.

Katie felt bad for thinking that Travis was a high-minded jerk. No one deserved to die like that inside their own home. She felt that he was trying to tell her something with his last words, but she couldn't read between the lines. Did he know who attacked him? He was in shock and his statement could be something made up in his mind that he thought was real. His words, which seemed not helpful, continued to resonate in her mind. His face. His intenseness.

Someone grabbed... me... from behind and...

Had mask... man... thin...
So many...
Be careful...

Detective Hamilton appeared at the front door ordering a couple of deputies to work the area and canvass the neighborhood. After taking a cell phone call, he headed out to talk to the detectives.

"So," he began, "you received a call from Mr. Stone when you were leaving work?"

"Yes. He said something was wrong and needed our help," said Katie.

"You specifically? Not the police?"

"I told him if there was an emergency to call 911."

"Did he say anything else?"

"He wanted us to hurry, and said that he had to whisper because someone might hear him."

"Was there someone already in the house?"

"He didn't say, but now I'm assuming there was."

Detective Hamilton asked some more questions and made his notes. Katie and McGaven told him everything they had experienced and heard.

"Well," said Hamilton. "I think this is enough for now. I'll keep you both in the loop due to the fact that Mr. Stone is part of your investigation on Maple Road." He kept a poker face and it was difficult to ascertain if he was annoyed by Katie and McGaven or just trying to make sure he was crossing all the T's and dotting all the I's.

"Thank you," said Katie. She thought that their investigation was getting complicated and murkier by the hour. "We'll have our reports copied and sent to you as well."

Hamilton nodded as he flipped his notebook closed and walked back toward the house.

"Well, that was fun," said McGaven as he rubbed his forehead. He looked at his partner. "You need to go home and burn those clothes." He referred to the blood that was all over her shirt and dried on her hands.

Katie looked down and was horrified by her appearance. Partially dried blood stained her shirt. Her hands looked as if they had been dipped in blood. "It's been too long of a day." She sighed, wanting a hot shower and a nice long sleep, but her mind wouldn't let her forget all the details of the day.

Katie left Travis Stone's crime scene and hurried home. She had received a text during all the commotion from her uncle saying that he was staying with Cisco until she got home—and not to worry. What would she ever do without him? The only blood family she had and he was the sheriff—but he still made sure that Katie was taken care of, and that included Cisco.

Katie eased her Jeep into her driveway, parking next to her uncle's large white SUV. Slouched in the driver's seat, she waited a moment before stepping out. The weight of the world pressed down hard on her shoulders. Too many crime scenes, too many unnecessary deaths that led back to the burned-down house on Maple Road. She knew in her gut that there would be one thing, event, or person that would tumble everything so that they could solve these cases. The cases seemed to overlap. She knew that she was missing something—but had to get a good night's sleep to even begin to contemplate what it was she wasn't seeing clearly.

After securing her car, she walked up to her front door. It was always a welcoming feeling whenever she came home. Home, she thought. This was her home. This was where she felt safe and relaxed. How could she sell it?

She heard Cisco's signature bark before she opened the front door. "Hey, big guy," she said to the ecstatic German shepherd.

"There she is and..." Her uncle stopped talking. "I know

you were at a crime scene of Travis Stone, but now it looks like you took on an army by yourself."

"Yeah, I know," she said, dropping her briefcase on the counter. She noticed that there was an empty plate on the coffee table—and she knew well that Cisco had got some tasty treats as well.

"Go take a shower and I'll warm up something for you to eat."

"Oh no, Uncle Wayne. You've done enough."

"Nonsense. It's an order."

Katie smiled. She knew that she wasn't going to win this conversation. Besides, she was too exhausted to even attempt to do so. "Okay."

"By the way, I like the new paint," he said.

"Really?"

"Yeah, it looks fresh. This old farmhouse could use it."

Katie went to her bedroom and peeled off her clothes, dropping them in the corner of the bathroom. The waterfall from the hot shower soothed her bones, her muscles, and her mind. The earlier events of the day seemed so far away now—because she couldn't get the last breath of Travis Stone pushed out of her memory.

As she dried herself, she saw her reflection in the mirror. There was a haunted look about her eyes—common among police officers and soldiers after a traumatic incident. She stared at her mirror image and it stared back.

A wet nose interrupted her contemplation of her life. Cisco had pushed the bathroom door open and poked his nose at her hand as if he knew how hard the past two days had been and wanted to console her. "Hey, you're not mad at me for being away so much?" She petted his big head and scratched behind his ears in the way she knew he loved. He gave an appreciative snuffle and nuzzled against her.

Katie quickly pulled on sweats and a T-shirt before rejoining her uncle.

Walking into the kitchen, she said, "Wow, what smells so good?"

Her uncle was heating up some chicken noodle casserole she'd had in the freezer. He smiled as he stirred the mixture in a skillet. "Much better," he said, looking at her.

Katie hugged him tight. There had been so many times she needed a hug at work, but had to save them up for in private. "I feel better. I think I'm going to burn those other clothes."

"I'm sorry you had to go through that." He spooned the casserole onto a plate.

Katie took a seat at the counter. "It's okay. It's just part of the work."

"Well, I think you've had your fair share of gruesome crime scenes."

She hated to admit it, but he was right. "I don't have to go it alone—I have Gav."

"That is truly a blessing. He's a good man," he said and put the plate in front of her.

She nodded in agreement.

"Katie, I probably shouldn't be telling you this…"

"What?"

"It's been requested that McGaven be officially transferred to robbery-homicide."

Katie sat for a moment and stared at her plate. She had figured as much about Gav. And why not? He was a detective now and great at what he did.

The sheriff sat down next to Katie. He was dressed casually in jeans. She hardly ever saw him that way these days. "I know you don't want to hear it, but I thought you should know."

"And what do you think?" She kept her uncle's gaze, wanting to know his thoughts about the partnership in the cold-case unit.

He sighed and appeared to take a moment to gather his thoughts. "I have to do what's best for the department and this community. And right now, there's no doubt in my mind that you and McGaven are a fantastic team. The community is that much better for it."

"I don't know what I would do without him. Working these cases is... sometimes I don't think I can do it but he always helps me through."

"Well, for one thing, you both complement each other, and if I didn't trust his abilities, he wouldn't be your partner." He went to the refrigerator and took a bottle of wine out. Pouring two glasses, he gave one to Katie.

She began to eat. She hadn't realized how hungry she was.

"Raise your glass," he said.

Cisco barked.

Katie laughed. "Good boy." She raised her glass and gently touched it to his. "To more case closures and to enjoying life."

"To the best detective and most wonderful niece I could ever ask for."

NINETEEN

Katie stood at the doorway in the medical examiner's office waiting for Dr. Dean to show up. She had received an early morning text that he had important information for her and wanted to meet in person. But she found her nerves were always twitchy in this place, had caught herself once or twice breathing very shallowly.

As she looked around the division, she realized it seemed busier than usual. That's when the reality hit home of all the bodies she had witnessed over the past few days. Was it the time of year? The moon? There had to be something going on that she couldn't see that was contributing to the body count. Her sadness for all the unnecessary deaths caused her soul to ache.

She watched now as bodies lying on stainless steel surfaces were wheeled to different areas. Some had a sheet covering them while others were naked. She tried to avert her eyes, as if they would be embarrassed by her seeing them. But there was nothing anyone could do for them now—except find justice. The burden of the heavy load she felt weighed her down so much that she thought for a moment she might fall to the floor. It took a great effort to push her focus back to professionalism, but she stood firm, held her head high, and took a cleansing breath.

She couldn't help but notice a particular person as he was rolled by her. She had spotted the blond slightly wavy hair combed back from the dead man's face—no doubt it was the body of Travis Stone. He was cleaned up and there was no indication that he had been bloodied just the night before. Just the bluish-red wounds on his chest remained now like a waxy remnant. He was Detective Hamilton's case, but she still felt a tug at her investigative senses and wanted to know more. She wanted to see the report. So many questions plagued her.

A hand touched Katie's shoulder, making her slightly jump.

"Hey," said McGaven. "Didn't mean to startle you, but in this place, I don't blame you if you're on edge." He stood next to her wearing his usual brown slacks and white dress shirt. Today he also had on a navy tie. "Hope you slept well."

"As a matter of fact I did."

"Really?"

"Yep. I guess there are other forces making sure that I get my sleep."

"And that could mean we've got an extreme schedule ahead of us."

"What's the occasion?" she said.

"What?"

"Your tie. It looks great by the way."

"I don't know. Just thought that I needed to look more official as a detective, instead of just the really tall guy." He forced a smile.

It was true. Katie also had picked out one of her best pantsuits today. It was strange that they were on the same page: making sure they stood out, showing their professional expertise.

"Detectives," said Dr. Dean as he rushed into the room. He always made for a dramatic entrance in his Hawaiian shirt, loose khaki pants, and sandals, toes showing. Today he wasn't wearing his usual white lab coat over his vacation attire. "I can see you've both been quite productive." It was his way to begin with some dry humor—breaking the ice in such a depressing place. Fact be told, he had respect for the detectives and enjoyed their conversations.

"Dr. Dean," said Katie.

The medical examiner picked up a file, flipped it open, and quickly re-familiarized himself with the information. "We have good news and we have *really* great news."

Katie glanced at McGaven quickly. She steadied her nerves. "What does that mean? How could good news be even better?"

"Ah, Detective. It's not often that we can identify bones, but it's an entirely another thing to identify bones from twenty-five years ago."

There was a momentary silence while the doctor's comment sank in.

Katie realized that all four skeletons had been identified. Her heart skipped a beat and she could barely breathe. It was fantastic news. "Really?" was the only thing she could say because she was absolutely elated by the news. They were on the right track.

"Really," the doctor said. "Computers can be an amazing tool. We were able to identify William and Heather Cross from their dental records. Their teeth were in good condition and it was easy to compare—especially when we had their names to begin with as the potential victims."

"That's fantastic news. We've been investigating on the understanding it was probably them. And the little girl?" She watched Dr. Dean closely.

"Yes, one of the child skeletons was identified as Raven Cross, the daughter of William and Heather Cross. She was eight years old and has very distinct baby teeth. It was easy to confirm."

Katie felt a wave of conflicting emotion crash over her. She was thrilled that they'd made a breakthrough in identification. On the other hand, after meeting the Crosses' employers and neighbors, all of whom had spoken so highly of them, it was tragic to have to confirm their fate. They had been so excited to get out of their rental lease to move to Arizona to begin a new life, only to have it brutally derailed.

It saddened Katie to think that such a family could be so easily murdered and buried under the house they had rented and no one would know, until... someone set the house on fire. Was it a coincidence? The little investigative voice in her head said: there are no coincidences in homicides.

Dr. Dean leaned back against a table. He was relaxed and didn't seem to mind that he was taking some time out of his extremely busy schedule to explain everything to the two detectives. "First, I've sent you everything on the identification of the Cross family and my findings of the cause and manner of deaths." He watched the detectives. "But, I wanted to talk to you in person in case you have any questions—I know time isn't your friend with homicides. Besides, you're my favorite detectives—just don't tell the others."

"We appreciate that," said Katie. She was anxious about the findings of the older remains.

"Follow me," the doctor said as he led the detectives down the hallway to his office.

Katie thought it was unusual that Dr. Dean decided to have a meeting away from the usual area in the examination room standing over a body.

Katie and McGaven took a seat in the molded plastic chairs across from Dr. Dean's cluttered desk.

"Okay. As I said, I've sent you the reports of my findings but..." He leaned back and his chair made a shrill squeak. "Let's begin with Mr. William Cross, thirty-nine years old. Health appeared to be in good condition based on overall analysis of bones and previous medical history. Cause of death was a bullet through the chest, namely the sternum area. The bullet was recovered, a nine millimeter. Manner of death is homicide."

"I see," said Katie. She wasn't surprised by his analysis.

"Now, Mrs. Heather Cross, thirty-four years old and in fair to good health. When we examined her bones and their density, she was showing signs of early onset osteoporosis, which could account for her recent fractures. Cause of death was an intracranial hemorrhage, which was caused by blunt-force trauma to the left side of the skull—she wasn't struck just once, but two, maybe three times. It's unclear if she died right away, but with an injury of this magnitude, it would cause immediate bleeding between the brain tissue and skull or within the brain tissue itself. She would have died within minutes to maybe a half hour if she didn't get immediate medical treatment." Dr. Dean watched the detectives and politely waited for questions.

"So it's a homicide too?" said Katie.

"In my opinion, it would be highly unlikely to be categorized as anything else, such as accident or suicide based on the position. My professional opinion is that, yes, it is a homicide."

That's what Katie needed to hear. "What would cause such an injury? Some type of tool or a baseball bat?"

"From the position of the injury and the damage, the murder weapon would have to be something with some weight, easy to wield. My guess, and I've seen many blunt-force traumas to the skull in my career, it would be more like a tool, such as a hammer, wrench, or crowbar." He glanced at the photos again. "It would be difficult to tell any more than that because we're not dealing with a body with all the tissue still intact."

Katie took some notes. "What about their daughter?"

"It was easy to ID her from recent dental records, but at first, my ruling was undetermined."

"Undetermined?" said McGaven. "Isn't that determination rare? Wouldn't it be pending?"

"At first, we couldn't ascertain if it was accidental or not. But, one of my technicians caught that the hyoid bone was crushed, indicating strangulation." He slid a couple of photos toward Katie and McGaven to view.

Katie studied them and could see that the small horseshoe-shaped bone was broken.

"It's located in the anterior midline of the neck between the chin and the thyroid cartilage," the doctor explained.

She tried not to imagine the horror that the Cross family had endured. Mr. Cross shot at point-blank range, Mrs. Cross bludgeoned, and their daughter strangled. Katie's first question: was this the work of one person? Was it planned? Was one of them the actual target and the other two victims collateral damage to cover up the crime?

"It's a small bone and sometimes it's difficult to identify, especially after decomposition. It lies between the base of the mandible and the third cervical vertebra," continued Dr. Dean. He patiently waited for the detectives to study the photos.

"Was the Cross family all buried around the same time? Can you tell by the bones?" asked McGaven.

"We can't pinpoint with absolute accuracy in this condition, but I'd be willing to testify that they were all buried within the same time frame—approximately a few hours to a full day."

"Is there any way to tell who had been killed first?" said Katie.

Dr. Dean leaned back and held up his hands in apology. "I'm sorry, not with any certainty with what we have to work with. But I imagine that you will find out in your investigation."

"You have more confidence than I do," said Katie.

"Nonsense. Your track records are inspiring, to say the least."

Katie looked up at the doctor. "What about the other bones?"

"I was waiting for you to ask," he said. He rose and retrieved a thicker folder from the top of one of the filing cabinets. The folder was brown and well-worn, resembling the cold-case files she had back at the office.

"Is that a cold-case file?" said Katie. She wondered how he was able to get the file without going through her or McGaven.

"Yes. I'll explain," he said. "I spoke with the commander of the detective division when I couldn't get in touch with either of you. The commander had John in forensics pull the file. I put it in the email that you both will receive."

Katie wasn't happy that the file went through this process without her being aware.

"I apologize for any misunderstanding or stepping on toes, but I remember this case when the girl went missing. I was young and working at Memorial Hospital at the time."

Katie tried to remember the case and the girl that went missing—but couldn't recollect it. She would have been too young.

"When the bones were brought in and it was obvious they were much older than the others, I had a feeling it might be her," Dr. Dean said.

"Who is it?" said Katie.

"Sara Simms."

"That name seems familiar," said McGaven.

"Yes, she left her home one day during the summer to see some friends, but never showed up. And that was..." he skimmed the information in the file, "twenty-five years ago."

"Sara Simms," said Katie. "Was there any information or gossip around her disappearance?"

"There was some, but I'll hand this file back to you and you can read it yourself. I included my report and photos," said the doctor.

"Thank you."

"I heard how you had the crime-scene technician search the yard. You should be very proud. She may have never been found."

"Yes, it's an all-around sad set of circumstances," she said quietly.

"Could you tell how she had died?" asked McGaven.

"It's very inconclusive," he said. "There were broken bones, but it could've happened when the body was buried. There were indications that she could've been moved. I have this case officially 'pending.'"

"Humor us," she said.

"Well, I don't like making guesses. But, if I'm forced to, not for court of course, I would say that she was beaten or that she possibly fell from a high place."

Sara Simms…

Did someone push you?

Where? Why?

"I see," she said.

"Everything is in the file, but if you have any questions don't hesitate to ask. The family has been notified."

Katie stood up, taking the cold-case file with her. "Thank you, Dr. Dean, for your time and expertise. It's always enlightening."

"Thank you, Doctor," said McGaven.

"Always my pleasure, Detectives."

Katie and McGaven left the medical examiner's office.

"We have some checking to do," she said, squeezing the file.

"I'm on it. We'll see what family is still around and retrace the case." McGaven took the file and flipped it open.

"Looks like we have a recent case and a twenty-five-year-old case—and they all ended up in the same grave of a torched house."

"You know who the original officer was on the callout for a missing person?"

"No, I didn't read that far."

"You're going to love this." He grinned.

"Who?"

"Deputy Wayne Scott."

Katie wasn't really shocked. She knew that her uncle had worked many cases in the day. "This investigation is sure taking us for a ride."

"What are you thinking?" he said.

"I'm thinking there are no coincidences in homicide."

TWENTY

Katie and McGaven returned to their regular office and began poring over tons of paperwork for Sara Simms. The story was tragic. School had just finished for the year and summer had begun. Sara had apparently been excited about all the fun activities she was going to do in her time off. But she never got the opportunity to do them. She left her house one day to go meet some friends, but never showed up. No one ever saw her again. The last person to see her alive was her brother Kent.

The case had been thoroughly investigated at the time, with family, friends, teachers, and townspeople interviewed. It appeared that the persons of interest were her brother and a next-door neighbor who had since moved away. But nothing ever came to light.

Katie pinned up the school photo of Sara Simms. She had a lively beautiful face with shoulder length curly blonde hair and crystal blue eyes; she looked as bright as the future that should have been ahead of her. Next to the headshot of the young girl, Katie also pinned up photos of her skeletal remains, the yard on

Maple Road, the route and distance to the school she attended, and her home.

Katie stepped back and scrutinized all the locations.

"Looks like Sara Simms's parents and brother moved away about two years after she was reported missing," said McGaven. "I'll see if I can get in touch and if they have anything to add— especially after all this time."

"She would have been about thirty-seven today, older than me."

"What are you thinking?"

"Well, I know from when I was a kid growing up here, we had places where we liked to hang out, especially in the summertime. Tree forts, rope swings over the creeks."

"I see where you're going. Maybe we need to talk to your uncle about the case and what was going on at that time? Maybe he was aware of kid hangouts."

"I was thinking the same thing."

Katie's cell phone rang. She quickly picked it up. "Scott."

"Is this Detective Katie Scott?" said a woman's voice.

"Yes. Who am I speaking to?"

"This is Cara Lewis. We spoke the other day."

"Yes, Ms. Lewis. What can I do for you?"

McGaven looked up from the computer.

"Well, I was wondering if you might have some time to stop by today."

"Well..."

McGaven nodded.

"Of course," said Katie. "We can come by in a little while. Will you be home?"

"Yes, I'm here all day. Thank you, Detective." She disconnected the call.

Katie made a sour expression. "I guess the conversation is over. What's this all about, I wonder?" She watched her partner, who was smiling broadly. "What?"

"We get to go see the three-dog lady."

Katie and McGaven arrived on Maple Road less than an hour after Ms. Lewis had called. Katie observed that the arson crime scene was still enclosed with chain-link fencing and locked up tight. The security detail had been relieved, but she noticed some cameras had been installed until the scene was officially released.

"What do you think she wants to talk to you about?" said McGaven, breaking the silence.

"I don't know—she didn't say."

"Maybe it's something that she didn't want to tell us but now..."

"But now she doesn't want to get caught lying."

The detectives exited the sedan and walked up her driveway. They spotted Cara Lewis in her front yard weeding some flowerbeds next to the house—a small spade and a rake lay nearby.

"Hello, Detectives," said Ms. Lewis smiling. Her attitude and greeting seemed friendly—more so than the last meeting.

"Ms. Lewis," said Katie. "What would you like to talk about?" She gently pushed the older woman, wanting to get to the point. She was suspicious. What could this neighbor have that would need the investigating detectives to come back?

The woman stood up, dusting off dirt from her jeans. "Please come inside. I made some lemonade—from my own lemons."

"Where is your entourage?" said McGaven.

"Oh, they are outside in the backyard."

Once inside, Ms. Lewis went to the kitchen and poured two glasses of lemonade.

Katie went to the sliding door and peered out to see the German shepherds running and chasing each other. It made her smile, remembering all the times of play she enjoyed with Cisco in between work.

Katie took the lemonade she was offered. "Thank you. What would you like to tell us?" she asked again.

Ms. Lewis's smile faded and she became serious. "It's not what I want to tell you—it's something else."

That comment piqued Katie's interest. "What do you mean?"

"Here, let me show you," she said.

Ms. Lewis opened the sliding door and gave several German dog obedience commands to the three shepherds. They obeyed and all sat down in the grass in a shady area, patiently waiting as everyone stepped into the yard.

Katie was impressed by Ms. Lewis's training techniques. It was clear the dogs paid attention to her. Stepping into the yard, she felt the thick grass compress under her feet, reminding her of her youth. Nothing was better than thick grass to play on. It made her think about where Sara Simms was twenty-five years ago, when she had thought she was safe but in fact been the target for murder.

"Detectives?" said Ms. Lewis. "It's over here." She gestured to the fence area.

Katie and McGaven followed the woman across the garden. Katie took a quick scan of the area, comparing it to the crime-scene yard. It was approximately the same amount of space, but was in the shape of a square instead of a rectangle. The grass was the anchoring center, with carefully built-up flowerbeds edged with light, neutral-colored bricks. There were perennials popping up from the bulbs and plants that Ms. Lewis had culti-vated—beautiful asters, dahlias, and various other colorful flowers.

"This is what I wanted to show you." She pointed down at the flowerbed she had been clearing and adding soil to, which ran along the fenced boundary of the arson house. "I was working here yesterday. I had been meaning to clear and ready the soil for ages, but when I began to dig... I saw..." She couldn't finish her sentence as she lifted a box and uncovered the object of interest.

Katie glanced at McGaven before she moved forward to see what was in the dirt. Focusing, Katie realized that it was bones. More specifically, bones from a finger. It was clear that's what it was—it had been separated from the wrist with a clean cut, and it clearly had the metacarpal bone, middle and distal phalanges for a complete intact finger. "A finger?"

"That's what I thought after I looked at it. My spade scooped it up and then I've left it just as I found it." She shuddered a bit. "I wanted to let you know as soon as possible. It's gruesome."

Katie said to McGaven, "Let's have John come out and document."

He nodded, took out his cell phone, and dialed John.

"Thank you for showing us, and for making sure it's been kept as it is to ensure the integrity of the bones." Katie turned to join McGaven.

"Wait," the woman said. "I know that you found remains over there," she said and nodded her head in the direction of next door. "A few of us neighbors were talking about it. Was it... the Cross family?" Her expression was concerned and deeply saddened.

"I'm sorry, but this is an open and working investigation and we can't disclose anything right now. But, we do appreciate your input and telling us what you found. A forensic technician will be coming over to document and retrieve it," said Katie.

"Oh, okay. Well, I guess we still must hope it isn't them. But thank you for coming out, Detectives," Ms. Lewis replied. She said a command that Katie didn't immediately catch, which released the dogs from their stay positions. They romped and played once more. Once they discovered McGaven, they nudged his hand for attention.

"They like you," the woman said smiling. The three dogs circled around her again, keeping close.

The detectives left the house with one more piece of evidence to add to their case board.

TWENTY-ONE

TWENTY-FIVE YEARS AGO

Snyder Fields, Pine Valley
Summer

It didn't take long for Sara to shake off her brother's rude behavior. It was typical. He thought the world revolved around him. But once out in the sunshine, feeling the warmth on her face, she became happy again. She was anticipating how fun the party was going to be and summer was just beginning.

She began to make her way to the Snyder Fields. First she walked down her street, then she took a cut-through that ultimately led to one of the local trails. She stopped for a moment in the shade and put her backpack on the ground. She quickly unzipped a small pocket and retrieved the folded paper. There was a small map drawn indicating where she needed to go. Excited about being included, she memorized the instructions.

Once she had slung her backpack on again and secured it, she headed on down the trail. She had never walked it before. The only thing she thought would have made this journey even better was if her best friends Tessa and Clare could have been with her, but she assumed they would already be at the party.

The path began to narrow as the small branches and bushes scraped her bare skin. It was darker without the sun and seemed scarier too. She kept walking, hoping to see someone familiar. The damp ground that never saw sunlight made her shiver. She held tightly to the shoulder straps, steadying her balance, and hurried.

TWENTY-TWO

Friday 1255 hours

"I don't see why you wanted to come back here right now," said McGaven.

"Why not?" said Katie. "We were already here anyway." She walked with purpose from Ms. Lewis's house, bypassing the car.

"Well, we have more people to talk to and everything has already been documented and retrieved at the arson site."

"It's still officially a crime scene and it hasn't been released yet. So... we can take another look around without worrying about someone or something contaminating it." She was still bothered. This case seemed to develop more clues and evidence every day.

Katie tried the gate but there was a padlock still attached to the door. "Damn." She waved cheerfully at the cameras in case she needed to explain their reason for being there.

"Oh well, we'll have to come back—maybe," he said.

Katie looked around and followed the chain-link fence line. They were put together in sections that were seven foot high by twelve foot long, each piece held together with rail clamps and screws. She walked around the fencing until she found what she was looking for—a section that wasn't as secured as the others. "Here. We can gain access here," she said.

McGaven sighed loudly. "Fine."

"Cheer up, Gav," she said and squeezed through the gap with relative ease. "We're waiting for tests, callbacks, and reports. I think we can take a look at the place where everything began..."

McGaven followed suit, with a little more difficulty.

"You know we could've requested the keys," he said.

"Now, that's taking up time. We're here. Why are you grumpy?"

"I didn't get to play with the dogs next door."

She laughed. "Come over tonight and play with Cisco."

"Great idea." He watched his partner re-enter the house by squeezing underneath the caution tape.

Katie made her way down to the basement. This time, she stalled on what was left of the landing, staring down.

Who would want the Cross family dead?

Was it something they had found out?

Were they forced down there—one at a time to their deaths?

She closed her eyes, half expecting McGaven to make a comment—but he didn't. Instead he was waiting patiently for her. Her methods might have seemed silly to onlookers. But they helped not only to clear her mind, but also to imagine what it had been like living here. The only sound she heard was the heavy plastic rippling in the breeze. The pungent smell of basement moisture became stronger than it had been, while the smoky remnants were almost completely gone.

Opening her eyes, she took each step one by one. It still seemed peculiar to her that they didn't squeak or groan under her weight as wooden stairs to the basement should. Once reaching the bottom, the packed earth felt solid underneath her boots.

Katie walked around the side of the staircase and inspected the stairs.

"What are you looking for?" said McGaven. He had to scrunch his body so as to not hit the upper floor with his head.

"I'm not sure."

He came to her assistance and snapped on a small flashlight. The beam bounced around the stairs making it easy to see the distributor's identification marking on the wood in white paint.

"Seems fairly new?" she said.

"Looks like. I'm not a contractor but these stairs haven't been in place much longer than a year."

"Maybe less?" She ran her hand along underneath the stairs but they were clean. "Did Randall Construction say they had worked on this house within the past year?"

"No, they said they were working out a deal to do some remodeling before the next tenant."

Katie frowned. "Someone was here within the last year. More likely within months."

"Replacing stairs wouldn't necessarily need a contractor—only if they were replacing everything."

She turned to face her partner. "What if..."

McGaven listened with curiosity.

"Based on Mrs. Cross's injuries. What if she was standing at the top of the stairs, was struck by an object and fell, causing a broken bone or two?"

"It's plausible."

"Then the daughter comes home and she was strangled."

"Okay."

"And then Mr. Cross comes home and it was easier to shoot him at point-blank range. Then the hard part ensues—how to get rid of the bodies."

"Plausible. But that would mean someone was inside this

house and that they knew the person and knew the house layout," he said.

Katie moved toward the wall with the scratches. "Like Travis Stone?"

"Possibly. It could've been someone from either one of their workplaces."

"But what if..." She thought about it more. "What if someone was working on the stairs?"

"And you think that whoever replaced the stairs killed the Cross family?"

"Pretty thin theory, I know, but something seems out of place here. I think everything happened within this area and it ended up being the Cross family's final resting place."

"Then who burned down the building?" he said.

"Who would benefit? Travis Stone."

"So if Travis Stone burned down the house, or had it torched by someone else, he would have to know that the bodies would more than likely be found."

Katie ran her fingers along the wall. Her hand retraced the area where the deep scratches were. "Do you think these could be caused by someone trying to claw their way out?" The thought was horrifying, but it was the first thing that had crossed her mind when she saw them.

"I don't know. John should have some theories on that."

An unexpected chill ran down Katie's spine. She shook it off and walked past the burial area for Mr. and Mrs. Cross and pushed open the door leading to the backyard. A barrage of information and possibilities confronted Katie. The area was left the way they had last seen it. The makeshift room made out of heavy plastic and PVC poles was still intact, but it was empty and the tables that had held the skeletal remains were gone too.

"I thought everything would have been cleared by now and the trench filled in," he said.

"I guess not." Katie walked to the corner where there had

been a pile of dirt that Jimmy was going to sift. "I wonder if Jimmy sifted everything." She looked further. There was now a pile of dirt on the other side of the yard. "It appears he did and that is the examined dirt."

"He must've finished," said McGaven. "That was the kind of guy he was."

Katie continued to look around. They had not one investigation but three, the connection with the house and property being the common factor.

Why?

"I know you're on to something. I know that look," he said.

"It's nothing that we don't already know, but... standing here, I realize how important the house is. Like maybe we're not looking objectively enough at it."

"Meaning?"

"We have a residential arson, a murdered family buried on the property, the skeletal remains of a murdered girl from twenty-five years ago, more bones at the boundary, the owner of the property murdered, and... our forensic technician murdered at his apartment."

"Wait a minute. I see where you're going with this..."

"Just think about it. No coincidences—especially in homicide. Right?"

"Right," he said slowly.

"Jimmy told John that he thought someone was following him—on more than one occasion *after* he left this property?"

McGaven didn't look convinced.

"Think about it. What if the killer has been watching the whole time and is now eliminating everyone to do with this property so they can't discover the clues that would lead us directly to him..."

"That would answer a lot of questions. But, Katie, do you really think that the killer is going to go to those extremes?"

"Wouldn't be the first time."

"But by your theory, that would mean we're all in danger."

Katie realized that seemed like quite a reach—but her gut instincts were fired up.

"What about the little girl from twenty-five years ago?" he said.

"That's the key—to where all this began and where it's going until we stop it."

TWENTY-THREE

Friday 1355 hours

Katie and McGaven returned to their office to dive back into the massive amount of paperwork waiting for them. They were still reeling from the possible connections of the arson house. But the cases had to rely on fact, not coincidence. It was a complicated puzzle that needed the precise pieces to solve the full investigative picture.

McGaven worked on the list of previous tenants and applicants for 717 Maple Road. There were six previous tenants and fifty-six applicants in total that he had to sift through before running background checks for anything relating to the investigation.

A while later he ended his second call. "Well, I just spoke with the previous tenants to the Cross family. A Thomas Rhodes and Sadie Myers. They were roommates and lived at the house for three years while going to school and working nights at a restaurant—the Sunshine Diner."

"Did they have anything to say?"

"They each referred to Stone as a pain and said he was intense about receiving the rent. Otherwise nothing noteworthy, but..."

"But what?"

"They said that for the last six months, before they gave their notice, Stone locked the doors to the basement. Both the one from the kitchen area and the one that led outside."

"Interesting. Did they say why?"

"Nope. They came home from work one night and there were heavy locks. They had about six boxes they were storing down there that had been moved and were sitting in the kitchen."

Katie made a face wrinkling her nose. "Doesn't necessarily mean anything. It just shows that Stone was paranoid for whatever reason—nothing criminal. He would have said that he let them know twenty-four hours before he entered—most likely saying something about their safety."

"It does show that Stone was fixated on that house in particular. I spoke with his other tenants on the other two houses he owned on Maple Road and they said they never saw him, only had a phone call or two."

"He was murdered, which could show that he knew something he shouldn't have, something to do with that basement."

They returned to their work. Katie read through the applications that Travis Stone had filed with the building and planning department—more specifically the ones for the houses on Maple Road. There were no permits or anything official that mentioned the stairs in the basement. Her frustration showed. "I can't find any connection through the building and planning department."

"I'm not getting very far on this either," he said in a distracted tone.

"Gav, I've never heard you like this before. You never give up."

"Sorry. I need something that will bring my attention to what I'm supposed to find."

"I contacted my uncle," she said. "We can talk to him at the end of the workday about the Sara Simms case."

Shuffling paperwork, McGaven looked up. "The day is improving already."

A soft knock at the door interrupted the detectives' gripes.

"Come in," said Katie as she looked at McGaven, shrugging her shoulders.

The door opened and Detective Hamilton stood there awkwardly, holding files in his hands. "Is this a good time?" he said, looking around at the investigation affixed to the walls.

"Uh, sure. What can we do for you?" she said, surprised to see him. She watched the detective hover—he seemed to have something weighing heavy on his mind. "Sorry, we don't have enough room in here for another chair, I'm afraid."

"It's okay," he replied, absently scratching his head as he stood in the doorway. "In working the Travis Stone homicide, we found some interesting paperwork that I thought would be helpful to you."

"Great. What is it?" She eyed the folders.

"I made copies of the insurance policy of the house, which he had made changes to about two months ago."

"Around the same time as the tenants gave notice," said McGaven.

That grabbed Katie's interest.

Hamilton gave Katie the paperwork. "And, we've been able to possibly connect a man called Stewart Fitzgerald to his murder. Does his name mean anything to you?"

"No. Should it?" she said.

"Nope. That name hasn't crossed my desk," said McGaven shuffling through paperwork.

"He's a known killer for hire and he also supplemented his resumé with arson for hire."

"What do you have on him?" she said.

"Circumstantial stuff. We could probably make an arson case quite easily, but not murder. He goes by the street name of Flash. He's in custody."

"We'll make a note of that."

"I actually came here to ask a favor," said Hamilton.

"A favor?" said McGaven. He tried not to smile too big as he glanced across at his partner. It seemed a little ironic, considering the history between Hamilton and Katie.

"We've interviewed Flash and we've found out that he went to Mr. Stone's residence, but it was just to talk about the arson job. But the murder scene and what we believe was the escape route for the killer was the master bedroom."

Katie thought about that for a second. She felt mad at herself for not pursuing the obvious exit for the killer. "Did you find a murder weapon?"

"Nope. And that's where the favor comes in. We've searched the suspect's apartment and Stone's property, but there was no sign of the weapon—a knife."

Katie understood where he was coming from. "So you need me and Cisco to do a sweep of Stone's property and any nearby areas to find the knife?"

"Yes." He averted his gaze.

"Did you clear it with the sheriff?" she said.

"Yes. He said under the circumstances it would be prudent."

"What about one of the department's K9s?"

"They are training at the moment, and anyway, they aren't as experienced in tracking and trailing as Cisco—they are mostly drug and apprehension."

Katie glanced at her watch. "We can do it this afternoon before our end-of-day appointment."

"Great," he said and smiled. "I'll text you everything and meet you there." He looked from

McGaven to Katie. "Thank you."

"I can't guarantee anything. We don't know for sure if he even tossed the knife or took it with him and dumped it somewhere else."

"Of course, Detective. Thank you."

It took Katie more than an hour to go home and change into more appropriate clothes for the search and get Cisco ready. He was ecstatic to have a job. His high-pitched whines and other happy noises continued all the way to Travis Stone's house.

Katie had left McGaven in the office to continue sorting through paperwork and make calls. She thought there was some irony in what she was going to do, working with Hamilton on the homicide, but right now she would do anything to help solve these cases. After all, they were all on the same side.

She sat in her Jeep parked on the street, waiting as Cisco spun several times in the back seat, knowing that he was going to do something fun. "Take it easy, Cisco," she said. "I need you to do what you do... find that weapon."

A detective's dark-brown sedan pulled up and parked behind her. She recognized Detective Hamilton as he exited the car wearing a police windbreaker and accompanied by another officer he must have pulled off patrol.

Katie stepped out and greeted the detectives. "I'm not familiar with the outside of the property," she said.

"It's about half an acre, with dense landscape. Beyond that back gate is about another acre that leads to a neighbor's property line. It's not landscaped professionally, but there are quite a few obstacles."

"Okay," she said. "Since this isn't an exigent or security situation, I don't need a cover officer. It's just me and Cisco, understand? We don't need the scent of you or anyone else blowing downwind and taking him away from his track."

The detective nodded.

"Has anyone been on the property since the murder?" she said.

"No. And we locked the gate." He handed her the key.

Katie went to retrieve Cisco. While he was still in the Jeep she hooked up his long lead, so that she could allow him some leeway while still keeping him safe under her control.

After letting him out of the vehicle, she walked with him to the black iron gates on the left side of the estate. The memories of her first visit to Travis Stone's home and then the arrival at the scene of his murder weren't far from Katie's thoughts. The solarium. The grand entrance. And the magnificent master suite where she had found his bloodied body.

Katie unlocked the gate and dropped the key in her pocket. She examined the layout of the initial part of the estate and saw perfectly manicured bushes, trees, and flowering vines. It was beautiful, but also a wonderland of hiding places.

Once inside the yard with a very excited dog, she took a moment and looked up to where the master bedroom's balcony was located. She estimated that the killer had probably taken that exit—over the railing and across to a fairly easy climb down the lattice attached to the house on which creeping fragrant vines had intertwined. It wouldn't take long for him to escape the yard and disappear.

Calming Cisco down, she slowly petted him so that he would focus on the track. There was little wind, which made it easier to follow the scent. Katie decided that they should begin near the balcony and sweep the fenced area in a circle grid pattern.

"Okay, Cisco," she said, moving her free hand around the area so he would be alerted to catch a scent. "*Such.*" She used the German track command.

Cisco didn't waste any time. He sniffed a few things around

the lattice and balcony area. Keeping his nose down, tail down, but senses extremely keen, the dog moved his attention to a track, taking them to the farthest side of the property.

Katie let out some slack on the lead, giving Cisco a few extra feet ahead of her. She watched carefully for him to snap his head, change his body language, or hesitate on a scent. Once they reached the area closest to the street, she saw Hamilton and the officer waiting patiently near their vehicle.

She kept close attention to any area where a knife could have been stashed or tossed to be picked up at a later point. The killer would probably have wanted to get rid of the weapon as soon as possible so he wouldn't risk being caught with it.

Cisco led for about ten minutes before he slowed his pace. Katie stopped and waited. Something was activating the dog's senses. He backed up and rounded a large pot about the size of a small bathtub. Then he seemed to hesitate. It was clear he wanted to go around and behind the pot, but the space was too small, so he backed out, looking up at Katie and barking.

Katie pulled him back and broke off a small branch—one large enough that she could poke around behind the plant container. She leaned over, pushed her arm down and flicked the branch back and forth. When she struck something she stopped. She lit the flashlight on her cell phone, and shined it downward. Something shiny was reflected back at her. She'd remembered to bring a glove, so she pulled it out of her pocket now and slipped it on. Reaching over with every bit of range and strength she had, she felt around until her fingertips hit something solid. She carefully grasped the object and eased it out.

Katie held a seven-inch hunting knife with a bone handle, blood dried along the jagged blade. She gently laid it down on the ground, wanting Hamilton to document it and then retrieve it as evidence with the appropriate chain of custody.

She dialed Hamilton's cell. He answered quickly, almost breathless. "You got it?"

"We got it."

TWENTY-FOUR

Friday 1710 hours

Katie ran up the stairs to Sheriff Scott's office. His secretary had already gone home, so the outer area was deserted. The front desk was cleared and extremely tidy. Her uncle's door was ajar a couple of inches. She could hear voices inside.

Katie steadied herself. She had run all the way up from the parking lot and employee back entrance. She had barely had enough time to take Cisco over to the department's kennel and make it back. She smoothed her hair and tried to calm her nerves. She was still elated from finding the murder weapon in the Stone murder case.

Taking a breath, she knocked on the door.

"Come in," was the response.

She pushed the door open to find McGaven sitting across from the sheriff with the file folders open.

"You're eleven minutes late," announced the sheriff.

"Cisco and I found the murder weapon at the Stone estate," she said casually.

"Well, we can overlook the tardiness then." Her uncle smiled.

Katie took a seat. "Did I miss anything?"

"We were just going over the reports of when Sara Simms went missing," said McGaven.

"Did anything seem unusual or as though it didn't fit?" said Katie.

"Meaning... did I think someone wasn't telling the truth?" said the sheriff. "No. It was one of those missing persons' cases where the longer that time went on, the more I knew that we were looking for a body. And don't forget, I was still a rookie."

"What was the consensus?" she said.

"The detectives with the help of some of us deputies retraced her last steps many times, canvassed every inch, and we always came back with the same thing—she had to have been abducted."

"But her remains were found right here."

McGaven scanned through some of the statements. "I assume there was a search party."

Sheriff Scott leaned back in his chair and thought a moment. "That's where things got different."

"Meaning?" said Katie. She watched her uncle and she knew when he was troubled. He did everything by the book—no matter what. Now she could see that he had some doubts.

"It was one of the biggest searches that Pine Valley had ever assembled. Everyone wanted to help: friends, family, neighbors, business owners, kids from school... It was a huge undertaking."

"I've been trying to contact her family but I haven't heard back," said McGaven.

"I remember that the family moved away a couple of years after the disappearance." The sheriff looked at his detectives. "Why do I get the feeling that you have something on your minds?"

"You know Katie. She *always* has something on her mind—another angle, perspective, you name it," said McGaven.

"Tell me."

"Well," she began, "I understand that Detective Hamilton has the possible killer of Travis Stone—and now the murder weapon, along with various other pieces of evidence. During our investigation for the Cross family, Stone was a person of interest. He had harassed the family, showed up at their work, came over whenever he wanted—and yet... he ended up dead too."

"He had access to the house and to where the bodies ended up."

"And," she said, "he must have ordered the arson for the money. I guess he was tired of dealing with an older property and just wanted to start over."

"And your point about the Cross family?" said the sheriff.

"I now believe that it's likely Stone didn't kill the family. And this has left me thinking what if both cases—the Cross family and Sara Simms—were somehow connected?"

"That's a bit of a stretch. It's been twenty-five years. You mean you're saying the same killer killed all of them?" the sheriff said.

Katie held her ground and glanced at her partner. "It does make sense."

Sheriff Scott raised his brows and patiently listened to his niece.

"First, the arsonist was hired by Stone. Wouldn't you think that if Stone was the killer he would either move the bodies or figure out how to deal with the property another way?"

"In other words, why would he take the chance that those bodies would be found if he had his house burned down?" said McGaven.

"I see your logic and I agree to an extent," said the sheriff. "But the same killer twenty-five years apart... I don't know."

"How do we know there weren't other murders just because they weren't buried in the yard?" she said. "We could search for other similar murders with the same MO, but all of them were killed in different ways. It makes it difficult to profile the killer or even to search for case linkage."

"It makes me glad that I'm not in your shoes," said the sheriff.

"And," she said, ignoring her uncle's comment, "I don't think this case is cut and dried. I also believe that the murders of the Cross family, Jimmy, and Mr. Stone are related—or interconnected."

"What's your reasoning?" the sheriff said.

McGaven was staring down at the paperwork as if he wasn't completely on board with Katie's assessment.

"I know that we don't have the direct evidence to back this up—but I've been thinking about it. It's all I think about. We know that the killer didn't want anyone to find those bodies. But what about all the people who are helping in the investigation, or who have important information for us?"

"It would make the killer nervous—before long the police would be closing in." The sheriff thought a moment. "Interesting. But your theory would mean the killer wouldn't stop before trying to kill everyone who is investigating the case or helping with it."

"I know, Uncle Wayne, it sounds crazy."

"It's the sign of a good detective to look at *all* angles, but that can leave you vulnerable to tunnel vision. Too many cops have fallen down that rabbit hole."

The detectives stared at the sheriff. No one said a word. The unnatural quiet was uncomfortable but necessary.

Katie rationalized that she should have kept her theories to herself until there was something to report. She didn't want the investigation to stall or, worse, go cold again.

Down that rabbit hole...

Leaning forward, the sheriff closed the case files and pushed them toward Katie and McGaven. "I would suggest that you follow all leads. Recheck some of the things that the original detectives and myself investigated. Create a timeline."

Katie nodded. She knew her uncle was right. Taking the files she said, "Looks like we have our work cut out for us."

"Now that doesn't mean you can't explore your theories. After all, they have been known to pan out." He smiled broadly. "I have confidence in you both. I know you'll find the answers you need to solve these cases."

TWENTY-FIVE

Friday 1915 hours

Katie's head spun from everything they had learned as she drove home in her Jeep, but she still felt confident that once they solved one case, all the cases would be closed. She kept running the investigations backward and forward as she had on previous cases. It was important to keep a careful balance of what she knew and what she had a hunch on. Otherwise, the situation could, and would, drive someone insane. What she needed now was a real timeline—a tight account of the last week or so for the Cross family.

Katie decided to take one of the back roads to cut through to her neighborhood. It was a Friday evening and she wanted to skirt around the evening traffic.

Cisco was asleep in the back seat softly snoring.

The only thing on Katie's mind, besides the case, of course, was that she was ravenous. She hadn't been to the grocery store for a week and her uncle had cleaned out the last of the chicken casserole when he had stayed with Cisco. She thought she would call her favorite small Italian restaurant—Little Sicily's.

From her car dash, she pressed her cell phone icon and said, "Call Little Sicily's."

The phone rang three times before someone answered. There was background noise of voices and clanging dishes. It was obviously a busy night.

"Hi, this is Katie. I'd like an order to go."

"Ah, Katie, hi," said a man with a distinct accent who she recognized as Riccardo.

"Hi, Riccardo."

"What would you like, sweet Katie?"

"The usual chicken Caesar salad and your daily soup special, please."

"Minestrone?"

"Perfect."

"You got it. How about ten minutes?"

"Sounds good, thanks. See you then," she said and ended the call. "Did you hear that, Cisco? Dinner in ten minutes."

She slowed her speed as she knew there would shortly be a sharp turn in the road. Just as she reached the beginning of the curve, a car came round the turn with the headlights on high. The brightness was overwhelming. She took her foot off the gas pedal, and honked her horn.

"What a jerk," she said, waiting for her pulse rate to return to normal. She glanced in the back seat and saw Cisco was standing at full attention, looking from the windshield and then to the side windows. His hackles were up, which made him look fierce, and his low guttural grumble was menacing if you didn't know him.

Katie continued driving around the long bend just as rain sprinkles hit the windshield making an almost musical tone. The road became wet quickly. With her wipers on slow, she increased her speed slightly in order to get to the restaurant on time. The trees were dense and hugged the side of the road on this section, making her feel like she was in a sudden tunnel of forest.

Bright lights approached from behind at high speed. Katie looked in the rearview mirror to see nothing but the high beams from a sedan—it appeared to be the same car that had blinded her only moments ago.

Katie increased her speed.

The pursuing car also sped up, keeping barely a foot from her bumper.

The bright lights meant that she couldn't read the license plate on the front of the vehicle. She couldn't be certain of the make and model either.

Katie pressed the emergency button on her GPS screen.

"911, what's your emergency?" said the woman dispatcher. Slight static cut in and out.

"This is Detective Katie Scott of PV Sheriff's Department, badge number 3692. I'm on Cold Creek Road, going northbound about three miles before Chester Avenue. I have a dark gray sedan trying to run me off the road. Please send any available units to my location. Officer needs backup. Do you read me?"

"Copy that."

Just as Katie finished speaking the car behind her lurched erratically and made contact with her bumper, throwing her car forward. She managed to grip the steering wheel, keeping control of her Jeep.

"Cisco, down! Now!" she yelled. The dog knew that it meant to get down on the floor behind her seat. She hoped he would be safe and partly contained instead of possibly being catapulted forward. The dog immediately jumped down and stayed, but high-pitched whines ensued.

There were no cutoffs or driveways for more than a mile. No streetlights. No visible landmarks. She had to keep the Jeep on the road ahead of the car pursuing her. She hesitated, but then she began to weave side to side from her lane to the oncoming lane, keeping the vehicle behind her guessing where she would go next. The defensive driving she was taught back in the police academy came crashing back to her and she was glad she had participated and paid attention to the instructors.

With the increased speed, her tires squealed going around corners. She maintained handling of the vehicle even though the car was slightly hydroplaning and with every turn she ran the risk of losing control and crashing into a tree.

The sedan tried to keep up to her unpredictable driving but couldn't make contact again. The light flashed from low beam to high, trying to distract or scare her—even more than she was already.

Katie gritted her teeth and held firm to the wheel, biding her time until she could get off the one-lane country road.

The light sprinkles turned into a full downpour, pummeling the Jeep's windshield and roof. The sound became louder, pounding like drums above her. As the wipers pushed to top speed, they still weren't fast enough to keep Katie's view clear. The road looked strangely distorted, morphing into an abstract roadway.

The car still kept up to Katie, pushing its speed despite the rainstorm. It pitched, and this time it connected to the Jeep's rear left quarter panel, causing the latter to sharply turn to the right.

Katie didn't fight the steering wheel. She let it loosely turn underneath her hands in hopes of the Jeep righting itself. It was a technique that had been proven to work in this sort of situation.

Katie and Cisco spun several revolutions on the road. The dizzying rotations made her squeeze her eyes shut for a couple of seconds. She prayed that they wouldn't smash into one of the enormous tree trunks aligning the road. She wasn't sure if her prayer was silent or if she had said it out loud. It didn't matter, she still hung on, waiting for the ride to stop.

The Jeep finally skidded to a stop facing the opposite direction. The engine gave a few puttering sounds and stalled.

Katie had both feet on the brake now.

The pounding of the rain was the only sound battering in her ears.

She instinctively reached her right arm out, feeling the coarse coat of Cisco tucked behind her seat—he was okay.

Putting her hands to her face, Katie took a deep breath, trying to make sense of everything that had just happened. Her heart raced. Her arms and hands tingled. It wasn't like the typical adrenalin rush she experienced in her job or in the military; it was her body trying to protect itself from an overflow of stress.

Cisco whined and panted loudly.

The rain had subsided a little but still stippled across the windshield. The wipers went back and forth across the glass and it was the only sound competing with Cisco's pants.

Katie opened her eyes and stared out through the flickering headlights. The Jeep now faced its nemesis at an angle. Her driver's door was less than twelve inches from a large tree.

The dark sedan was in the middle of the road, straddling the solid white lines between lanes, engine idling, lights extinguished, with a darkened interior. There was no license plate. Her headlights didn't penetrate the cabin. It reminded Katie of a phantom car without a driver. It sat like a thirty-five-hundred-pound predator waiting for its prey. A metal killing machine that wasn't going to stop until its target was dead—or permanently out of commission.

She looked at her cell phone and saw there was no signal—typical for the region, in one of the deepest areas of the forest. Most people didn't drive this particular road, especially after eight in the evening. Her racing thoughts now began to settle down and she knew that there were only two options—stay in the car and hope for the best—or get out. She contemplated her choices carefully and gambled that police backup would arrive soon. There was only one thing that she could do and she would have to muster every ounce of strength to accomplish it.

Her first worried thought, even before her own safety, was to get Cisco away from the cars if things went sideways.

The sedan revved its engine and steam rose from the exhaust pipe. It was telling Katie that war was eminent. She had to act now.

"Cisco, *hier*," she called him to her.

The black dog immediately rose and climbed to the front seats.

Katie opened her door and said, "*Voraus*," which commanded him to go out. It meant that he needed to get away from the situation until she recalled him.

The dog did what he was ordered to do. He easily jumped over Katie and made his way out the door into the forest until she couldn't see him anymore.

Katie then squeezed out the door with her back against the tree. She slowly pulled her weapon and moved to the rear of the vehicle, watching the revving car.

Using the Jeep's back corner as partial cover with her Glock pointed at the car, she yelled, "Turn off your vehicle and step out!"

Katie waited.

Nothing.

"This is the Pine Valley Sheriff's Department—turn off your engine and step out now!" She braced next to the car to steady her hand.

It had been a two-minute standoff when suddenly the headlights of the sedan ignited, blinding Katie momentarily. She heard the other car's engine rev beyond its capacity. Tires squealed. The metal monster catapulted toward her.

Katie didn't have a choice; she fired her weapon twice and then a third time. The bullets pinged off the exterior as the sedan skirted close to her and then raced off down the road.

She could hear the gears grind as the vehicle disappeared. There were no license plates for her to identify it—most likely the car was stolen.

Just then sirens sounded south of her and coming up Cold Creek Road fast. She grabbed her flashlight and backed away from the roadway as far as she could. She felt a cold nose on her hand as Cisco reappeared and stayed close to her side. Extremely relieved, Katie fought back tears.

Two deputy cruisers closed the gap, lights and sirens blazing, followed closely by a large white SUV. A few seconds later a fire truck pulled up behind the police. Moments after the last emergency vehicle, a black truck parked next to the SUV as an ambulance was quickly approaching.

All lights spotlighted Katie and Cisco.

TWENTY-SIX

Friday 2045 hours

"That's all the information I have. I'm sorry I couldn't get anything else," said Katie explaining everything to one of the deputies who took notes. She now sat in an ambulance with Cisco at her side.

The faces of deputies, the sheriff, McGaven and Chad all looked in the ambulance at her, asking questions ranging from whether she was alright to what did the perp look like.

"I'm fine, really. Just a little shaken up."

Sheriff Scott had sent out an all-points bulletin for the car, but nothing had been reported back yet.

McGaven hung up his cell phone. He reported to the sheriff, "Looks like a car matching that description was found crashed north on Eagle Ridge Road. No occupant. Car was empty. Prints wiped clean."

Katie watched as everyone began to go about their duties. She could see that her uncle was extremely stressed—even more so than usual.

Chad climbed in and sat next to Katie. "Are you sure you're alright?"

"Yeah, I'm fine," she said, snuggling closer to him. "I'm so glad that you're here." She felt her pulse return to normal.

Cisco snuck a few well-placed licks on the side of her face.

"I'm on a twenty-four-hour shift," he said. "I'd rather be with you."

"It's okay. I'll be fine home alone."

"No, you're not staying home alone tonight," said Sheriff Scott. "We don't know what we're actually dealing with here. Someone tried to run you off the road—a Pine Valley detective. This isn't random or a road-rage incident." He looked at everyone. "It seems that our own are being systematically targeted."

"Wait a minute," she said. "With all due respect, we don't know that for sure. I don't want any of our resources wasting their time at my house." She knew that her uncle was going to have some type of security detail. "I have security and Cisco. I'm fine."

"Sir," said McGaven. "I can stay with her."

The sheriff contemplated it, but his scowl and intense energy didn't lessen. "Since you two work together and we need every available officer, fine. You'll stay with Scott until further orders."

"I feel better," said Chad as he readied to leave. "I'll call you later," he said to Katie, giving her a peck on the cheek. As he stepped from the ambulance, he said to McGaven, "I don't need to remind you..."

"Nope. You have my word that Katie will be safe," said McGaven.

The sheriff ordered the fire truck and all patrol cars to depart, ordering just one to stay to control any traffic until the scene was completely cleared.

"Looks like we're going to be roomies," said McGaven, trying to lighten up the situation.

"I feel guilty. What about Denise and Lizzie?"

"They'll be fine and they would want me to have your back."

"Detective," said the paramedic. "You're good to go. Your blood pressure was a little bit elevated, so take it easy the rest of the evening."

Standing up, she said, "Thank you."

Cisco kept close and trotted next to her.

Katie met up with McGaven, who had been examining her Jeep.

"What?" she said.

"This fender is bent against your tire."

"Crap."

"We'll have the tow truck come and pick it up. Where should they drop it?"

"Pine Valley Garage," she said.

"Got it." He made the arrangements.

Katie met up with her uncle and moved away from the others. "What's going on?"

"What do you mean?"

"C'mon, Uncle Wayne, I know you. Besides, I'm a cop and I can tell there's something wrong—more to this scene." She watched her uncle as he let down his guard a bit.

"This isn't an isolated incident."

"I didn't think so."

"But what you don't know is that Detective Hamilton was attacked leaving the Owl. But he's fine. Luckily there was a good Samaritan in the parking lot who stepped in."

"Who was it?"

"They didn't see. The guy had a mask. And..."

"What?"

"A call also came in that a couple of deputies have been attacked. Some kind of ambush set for them. They're okay, but still."

Katie was in shock. It appeared that all the law enforcement personnel and emergency responders were under attack.

"I've rounded up a preliminary task force just in case it's needed."

"But..."

"I know you want to help, but right now just go home and get some rest. We'll know more in the morning. Maybe it's just an overreaction, but I didn't want to take any chances."

Katie's thoughts returned to Jimmy's apartment and the garrote around his neck. Was this killer now targeting those people who were working the case? Or was it something different altogether? "I think there's more here and we're just scratching the surface."

"Detective Scott, please go home. Get some sleep so you can be back at the department early tomorrow. You have a job to do." The sheriff looked around until he found McGaven. "Detective, please take Katie home."

"Yes, sir. C'mon, Katie, let's go." He steered Katie and Cisco to his truck.

"Wait," she said. "I need some things from the Jeep." She ran to the car and grabbed her briefcase, some files, and her cell phone.

"Let's go, Scott," said McGaven yelling out his window.

Katie and Cisco jumped into McGaven's truck and they began to make their way out of the dark forest pass.

Sometime later, McGaven drove into Katie's driveway and parked.

"Oh no," said Katie. "I forgot. I put in an order at Little Sicily's. And I don't have much to eat in the house. I'm sorry."

"No worries," he said. "I'm two steps ahead of you."

"What do you mean?"

Katie and McGaven, with Cisco in tow, walked to the front

door where there were two grocery bags and an overnight bag. Hanging on the door handle was a clean suit.

Cisco sniffed the bags thoroughly.

"You see, I thought that might be a problem, so I had Denise drop off some food while I was coordinating other things."

"Gav, you're the best," she said, relieved. "Denise is amazing, not to mention speedy."

Opening the door, they were met with the fresh-paint smell.

McGaven grabbed the bags and headed to the kitchen. "I'm starved." He began pulling Tupperware containers filled with various foods out of one bag and grocery items like eggs, bacon, and bread from the other.

"Me too. I'll be right back."

Katie hurried to her room and quickly changed her clothes into something more comfortable. She sat on her bed a moment to catch her breath. She could hear McGaven talking to Cisco in the kitchen along with the sounds of dishes and pans.

It finally hit her—the full impact of what had happened that evening. Her heart began racing again and she fought the urge to cry. Something awful could have happened to both Cisco and her if things had gone differently and if she hadn't been able to call for backup in time.

Katie knew with her cop's gut instinct that tonight's event hadn't been opportunistic. It was strategic, deliberate, and it had everything to do with the Cross family and Sara Simms. She couldn't see the whole picture yet. There had to be an overlapping of evidence. She had to find it before someone else from the department was hurt—or worse.

She pulled herself together, washed her face, and combed out her hair.

"Hey, Scott, I don't know how long I can wait," McGaven hollered from the kitchen.

Katie laughed. "You better leave me something."

TWENTY-SEVEN

Saturday o815 hours

Katie and McGaven stood at the front gates of the Alpine Storage Company, waiting for them to open. She kept glancing at her watch. The company was supposed to open up for the two detectives at exactly o8:oo and she was getting impatient.

"Take a breath," said McGaven.

"What?"

"Your tenseness is making me nervous."

"I'm sorry, but we're trying to retrace the last days of the Cross family here. I don't want to waste any time. We don't even know if their storage container is still here."

McGaven had tracked down the container, but since no one had paid for it in two months it was about to be transferred to a different holding facility—and if they still didn't receive payment it would be set up to auction all contents.

The slow mechanical gates began to open.

"It's about time," she said.

The detectives got back in the police sedan and drove into the facility.

It wasn't set up like personal storage units where someone rented a space, used their own lock, and then put their stuff inside. This was more like an industrial storage company, the kind where they brought customers a box to be filled, then took it away to store until requested again. The space Katie and McGaven were in now was the facility used to store those individual boxes. It wasn't single story, but rather had storage boxes stacked in several levels in a holding area.

"Wow," said Katie. "I've never seen so many storage containers."

"Welcome to the new technology."

Katie scanned the area, craning her neck to watch the large loaders move the containers around. The complex was massive.

They spotted a sign that read "Office Check In."

"Looks like this is the place," said McGaven as he pulled up to the two-story building.

The detectives got out of the car, still looking at the working area unfolding in front of them.

McGaven walked up to the office and entered, followed by Katie.

There was no waiting area or place to sit. The front desk consisted of a person behind glass who spoke through a small section that looked like a breathing hole.

"May I help you?" said the man behind the glass. He didn't have a smile or offer any other comment. Looking intently at them from behind the clear window, he waited for an answer.

"I'm Detective McGaven and this is my partner, Detective Scott. I spoke with a Terry West earlier about a container belonging to a customer by the name of Cross."

The man keyed up the information that McGaven had given him. It was unclear if he found it or not. "First name?"

"William or Heather Cross," said McGaven.

"Address?"

"717 Maple Road, Pine Valley."

As Katie waited for the preliminaries to ensue, she slowly scrutinized the area. There were high-tech cameras everywhere. They were small, but they were still visible if you knew where to look. She wouldn't have been surprised if cameras were in the restrooms. There were two mirrors on each side of the office entry. They weren't just ordinary mirrors, but two-way ones. A prickly feeling rose up and down her arms, one that usually meant she knew someone was watching and she couldn't see them.

"Thank you," said McGaven.

"What now?" she said as they exited the office. "Is the container here?"

"Yep."

"And where is it?"

"We wait for someone to take us to it. Right now, they are recovering it and dropping it at a *discovery* location—as they called it. And, they are emailing the information that Mr. Cross filled out."

"Wow, I feel like we need the CIA's approval to be here."

McGaven shrugged. "That's the way the company does business and it seems they're doing well."

"I think we—we meaning the average person—all have too much stuff."

"It's not just extra storage. It's another way of moving, taking out the moving companies themselves."

Several big rigs slowly drove in and were navigated by a man directing them to other areas to pick up containers.

Within another ten minutes, a woman driving an electric golf cart drove up. She had curly dark hair piled up on her head and held in place with several shiny barrettes. Dressed in overalls with a pink T-shirt peeking out, she stopped and said, "Detectives?" with a slight southern drawl.

"Detectives McGaven and Scott."

"Hop on."

Katie rode shotgun and let McGaven sit in the back seat, which faced the other direction. Barely seated, the electric cart took off. The woman drove without saying another word. After taking a couple of sharp turns and weaving in and around different mobile containers, the woman suddenly stopped the cart.

"Here you go," she said.

Katie and McGaven got out of the cart, but before they could say anything the woman zoomed away.

"Well," said Katie. "I guess this is our stop."

There were several containers, but only one, blue and white, that appeared to be a residential size. It was approximately ten by fifteen feet and about ten feet high. Fixed on the side was paperwork that listed the destination as "AZ" and a routing number identifying it in the computerized system.

Katie moved to the roll-up door and noticed that it didn't have a lock. She bent down and pulled it up. Inside, it was packed from floor to ceiling, with boxes up front and furniture toward the back. It seemed to have shifted to one side, most likely during the moving from one location to the next.

"Okay," said McGaven but he didn't move.

"Where do we start? We only have so much time." She began reading lists of contents handwritten on the sides of boxes. "Let's... start with anything personal."

"You got it," he said, retrieving a small knife from his pocket ready to cut through packaging tape.

Katie looked around. She noticed that they had some space beside them, and if they used it, they wouldn't be interrupted by the bustling of the rest of the storage area. "I think we can stack boxes here," she said, gesturing to the left of the container next to them. "Then it will be easier to return them."

"Ten-four."

The heat from the early morning sun reflecting off the dark blacktop made it hotter than it really was. Katie felt tired after removing only five boxes. She shed her suit jacket and rolled up her blouse sleeves. She noticed that McGaven had done the same thing.

"Is there any shade?" she said.

McGaven looked around and spotted an area on the west side of a large storage container that had a strip of shadow. "Over there." He pointed.

"Okay, it'll have to do." Katie carried the boxes over to that area and began searching through them.

McGaven followed her example.

After forty-five more minutes Katie and McGaven were exhausted from searching, but had found some items that might prove useful in their investigation.

Whenever Katie had to go through someone's belongings it made her uncomfortable. When the person had packed these things, they had likely never thought that anyone, let alone police, might be going through them later.

Katie walked over to McGaven, who had perspiration running down his face. "What do you have?"

"Some personal items, photo albums, household invoices, and banking information from about a month before they supposedly moved. And their paperwork for the rental."

"I have a calendar that Mrs. Cross wrote family things and appointments on, which might help build a better timeline of their last days. And a small bag with flash drives dated the same year, some miscellaneous paperwork including mail, and more family photos."

"Sounds good. Put everything we're taking into that empty box over there. I have to list everything that we're taking for the investigation." He leaned against the side of the container. "I feel like I've been running a marathon in the middle of summer in Phoenix, Arizona."

"Katie laughed. "I didn't know you hated the heat so much."

"It's not fun unless you're in the water on vacation."

"You mean like a water park?"

"That sounds good too—especially right now."

Katie looked at the storage container. "Is it worth more time to keep searching?"

"I think we have what we need. Everything else is kitchen stuff, clothes, books, and the usual stuff besides furniture."

"Did you find anything from Raven? Like personal stuff? Journal? Yearbook? Letters?" she said.

"No, I didn't."

Katie frowned and thought for a minute. "Let's take ten more minutes before we pack this up."

He nodded.

The detectives didn't find any boxes with Raven's name on it, so they decided to repack the unit, make a complete listing of the items they were taking, and head back to the office.

Katie and McGaven finished up some sandwiches and sodas in their office back at the sheriff's department as they went through their storage-container findings.

"Looks like Mrs. Cross wrote everything down," said Katie.

"Except their killer," said McGaven quietly.

"Now who is the pessimist?"

"C'mon, don't you think this case has become convoluted?"

"Every case seems that way once we start digging in," she said.

Sipping his ice-cold soda with extra ice, he commented, "You may have a point there."

"Now we're beginning to fill in the days before the murders."

Katie opened a small, black velvet bag with a drawstring similar to a jewelry pouch. Inside were two flash drives with recent dates written on a small piece of masking tape. "Let's see what we have." She inserted one of them into her laptop.

Several files came up: *Going Away Party, Mom and Dad*, and *Celebration*. Looking back at the dates, she realized that the writing was more like that of a child.

"What's up?" said McGaven. He rolled his chair next to his partner.

"Look at this," she said and clicked on the first file.

Instantly the video opened up showing Mrs. Cross in the backyard. The picture shook and moved at funny angles until the videographer steadied their cell phone. "Stop videoing me, Raven," she said with a smiling face but a stern warning. Her dark shoulder-length hair shined in the sun. She was wearing a light blue loose sweatshirt that was off one shoulder and a cropped pair of jeans. She wasn't wearing shoes.

"Why?" said a little girl's voice behind the camera. She giggled.

"What are you doing?"

"I'm documenting our going-away party."

"What do you mean?"

"Well... we get to move and go to Arizona. It's like a going-away party and a new adventure."

Mrs. Cross kept walking. The grass was greener and seemed to have been mowed recently.

"C'mon, Mom, don't you have anything to say?"

Mrs. Cross stopped and faced the camera. "I'm very happy that we're finally moving from this house."

"Me too. Now you won't be scared anymore..."

Then the video stopped.

Katie and McGaven didn't speak. The room remained quiet.

Katie was taken aback and had a lump in her throat. It was bad seeing bodies at crime scenes, but seeing the victims on video made it more personal—more real—more exigent. The only other photos they had had until now were from the Crosses' driver's license photos. She had been able to keep it all impersonal—at arm's length—but seeing Mrs. Cross's face and hearing her talk upped the intensity of the case.

Katie clicked the second video. *Mom and Dad.* She took a breath and waited for the picture to become clearer.

The video was inside the home, where there were packed boxes everywhere. Mr. and Mrs. Cross were sealing up boxes and stacking them.

"What's the best thing about packing?" said Raven.

"That we can move and decorate a new place," said Mr. Cross. He was handsome with light brown hair, wearing shorts and a T-shirt with a baseball team name on it.

"And," said Mrs. Cross as she stood up, "we won't have to have a weird landlord."

The camera movement became muddled and jerked from side to side until the lens changed where you could see all three of them—the Cross family.

"Say yay, we're moving," said the beautiful little girl who resembled her mother.

All three in unison smiling at the phone camera said, "Yay, we're moving!"

Then the picture went dark.

Katie let out a breath and blinked a couple of times. The juxtaposition was sharp in her mind—the smiling, happy family, excited about moving—and the skeletal remains in the basement and yard.

"Makes it seem surreal, doesn't it?" said McGaven.

"To say the least."

"They remind me of someone who we might be friends with, or neighbors, or go to the same coffee house."

Katie clicked the screen and froze the image of the smiling family. They stared back at her. The longer she looked at them the more it seemed that they were criticizing her for not working fast enough to find their killer.

"We now know that the Alpine Storage Company dropped

off their empty storage box only three days after this was taken," she said, pulling the invoice from the company copies they were given. "And two days after that the company picked it up to store—until notified of what address to ship it to."

"The window's closing in on when the killer had access to the family."

"After the storage container was picked up," she said. "It could have been minutes or a couple of days when they were murdered."

TWENTY-EIGHT

Saturday 1415 hours

Katie had buried herself for the past hour in paperwork, reading through everything she could and extracting anything that would be pertinent to their investigation. She knew that Detective Hamilton was overburdened with the homicides of Travis Stone and Jimmy Turner, but Katie had to keep her concentration and efforts on their cold cases of the Cross family and Sara Simms.

McGaven had been on the phone trying to get hold of anyone in Sara Simms's family.

Katie organized several piles of rental applicants—categorizing them for further background checks to see if any of them had any connection to anyone they had spoken with so far. She then went through the file that Travis Stone had given them at their first meeting, cross-referencing them with the Crosses' rental paperwork.

"Wow," she said under her breath.

"What? You have something?"

"Not yet. Mr. Stone certainly kept impeccable paperwork. I've never seen anything quite like this."

"Did you not see that guy?"

Katie turned to her partner. "What do you mean?"

"C'mon, Katie, that guy spent more time in front of the mirror than he did working. That tells you quite a bit. If his notes were that detailed it meant he didn't have a life."

"Funny. He made some interesting memo notes." Pulling one of the rental application forms, she said, "Listen to this, and I quote: 'Mr. H. doesn't have the skills to keep his current job. Doubt he will be able to pay rent after six months'."

"Harsh. Did he have a crystal ball to see the future?"

"But don't you see? He went the extra mile on everyone. It's like he profiled every applicant. He was careful, methodical, and a bit unnerving."

"Now that sounds like a serial killer."

"He was a serial *something*, that's for sure."

"What made the Cross family the winner?"

"I don't know. His notes were just initials. BGC."

"BGC? Maybe background check?"

"Could be. I think he had his own way of taking notes—like shorthand. We probably won't know for sure because he had his own way of coding and interpreting things." Katie kept reading. "It seems that Stone spoke to both bosses—Stan Bates and Tiffany."

"Seems reasonable."

"Do you think he might've known either one of them?" she said.

"It's possible. But they didn't say anything except that Stone was harassing the Crosses. You still don't think that Stone killed the family, do you?"

"No. But he's connected somehow, part of the picture, not just the fact that he owned the house and paid to have it burned down." She flipped through her notes. "Remind me when

Stewart Fitzgerald was arrested? Can you see if he's in the system?"

McGaven typed in the parameters into the police database: *Fitzgerald, Stewart, moniker, Flash.* He waited. "Got a hit. Yep, he's been taken into custody for arson and looks like he sees a judge next week for his bail hearing."

"How long has he been there?"

"Since... yesterday, like Hamilton said."

"Hmm," she said. She leaned back and stared at the investigation board, which was now mostly empty since most items had been transferred to the forensic room. "My gut says the killer's not Flash—he was just an arsonist for hire. The timeline doesn't add up. The killer has to be connected to the victims, to a twenty-five-year-old murder, and the house on Maple Road. There must be a connection. But... such conflicting behaviors at the crime scenes... bludgeoned, shot, strangled..."

McGaven's phone rang and he picked up. "Detective McGaven." He listened. "Yes, hello, Mr. Simms. Thank you for calling back."

Katie sat up, hoping that the brother might be able to shed some light on the investigation. She continued to go through her rental paperwork and Stone's other properties while McGaven talked, checking off names of applicants and sellers and then entering some in the police database, hoping to get lucky.

What was she missing?

McGaven hung up.

"Well? Anything?"

McGaven shook his head no. "There's nothing new to add to the family's statements, but he did suggest checking with the school Sara attended and talking with her teacher, Mrs. Betty Anderson."

"Good idea. Let's get some of their old yearbooks too."

"On it. I'll set up an appointment with Mrs. Anderson. And I'm going to send sweet Denise a text to see if she can get some background on what was going on twenty-five years ago and if she can get anything from the school."

"Great." Katie's cell phone rang. She answered, "Scott."

"Katie, it's John." His voice was stressed.

"What's wrong?" She didn't like the strain in his voice, immediately fearing the worst.

"It may be nothing, but can you and Gav check on Dr. Rimini?"

Oh no, she thought. The professor worked on the case too.

"I just didn't want to call patrol to check on him, because of everything else going on. It may be nothing."

"No problem. Of course we'll check on him."

"He called me earlier and sounded cryptic. That's not like him. He's at the lab at the university."

"Did you call one of the security guards?" she asked, thinking about how large the campus was. It was Saturday, so it might be a little trickier finding their way to the professor's lab and office.

"I left a message with the security office and haven't heard back."

"What's the make and model of his car?"

"I think he drives a white Mercedes—four door."

Katie glanced at her watch. "We'll head up there shortly, okay? Can you let Sheriff Scott know? A heads-up just in case."

John sighed. "Will do. Thank you, Katie."

"No problem. I'm sure it's nothing," she said, trying to sound casual.

"I hope so. Bye."

The call ended.

The more Katie thought about it, the more worried she became. What if the killer was continuing to try and kill anyone who had anything to do with the investigations—even Dr. Rimini from the college?

"Katie, what's wrong?" said McGaven. "I know that look. Was that John on the phone?"

"Yeah."

"Did they find something out?"

"No, it's not about the crime scene at Jimmy's house." Many thoughts paraded through her mind—each one worse than the last.

"Then what?" He rolled his office chair closer to his partner.

"It's Dr. Rimini," she said.

"The bone professor?"

"John can't get hold of him."

TWENTY-NINE

Saturday 1745 hours

Katie drove the police sedan while McGaven searched for more information about the campus. He keyed in the location for the science building parking area, and where inside the building Dr. Rimini would be found.

Katie entered the main entrance of the Pine Valley University. She drove slowly, looking at everything she passed and wondering if the killer was nearby—or if it was just her anxiety working overtime. The familiar sensations of lightheadedness, strange tingly limbs, and difficulty breathing in a normal relaxed manner tried to take hold of her. Pushing her concentration was crucial because so much was at stake—the investigation and lives. She tried not to compound her stress with physical symptoms, but it was becoming increasingly difficult.

But with everything that had happened since Wednesday, she wasn't going to take any chances on finding the professor. There was no room now for mistakes.

As McGaven looked at the campus map on his phone, he

said, "Okay, you make a right here and keep going up, passing two parking lots."

Katie kept her speed slow, still surveying everything around them as they drove up the hill. Maybe a car or truck would give pause. There were still students moving about, and some parking lots were half full and others empty with only a couple of cars.

"See anything unusual?" she said.

"I'm not sure what I'm supposed to be looking for, but unusual generally finds us." He glanced at his phone map. "Okay. Make a right and there should be a faculty parking area."

Katie turned into the parking lot listed "Faculty." "Not a lot of cars here," she said. "Wouldn't there be classes today? Or maybe he was working in the lab?"

"I don't know." He looked out his window as he saw a white car. "Wait."

Katie stopped the sedan. "Is that a Mercedes?"

"Yep, and it's a four-door sedan."

"Okay, let's run the plates." Katie took a moment and ran the license plate number on the police computer in the car. They waited, still watching the area. "Here it is. The car is registered to Salvatore Antonio Rimini."

"That's quite the name," he said.

"So he's supposed to be here." Katie pulled in next to the professor's car. She quickly got out and touched the hood—it was cold and had been parked for a while. She looked inside and it was clean except for a gym duffel bag in the back seat.

McGaven stepped out of the car and scanned the area. "Anything?" he said.

"Nothing except for a gym bag." She looked around. "Let's go find his lab."

They went into one of the main science buildings. Forensic

anthropology was listed as one of the disciplines and Dr. Rimini as the lead professor.

The detectives walked past several labs for other studies. A male student wearing shorts and T-shirt and with a backpack hoisted over his right shoulder came out of a door.

"Excuse me," said Katie.

The student stared at her. "Yeah..."

"Where's Dr. Rimini's lab?"

"Oh," he said, noticing her badge and gun. "It's in the next building behind here, building C, but you can get to it by going out the back way. It's faster."

"Thank you," she said.

"No prob." He left through the way they had come in.

Katie hurried to the back exit and opened the door. It wasn't a parking area, but more of a garden area with tables—she assumed a place to eat lunch and study. It was vacant. No students sat at the small cement tables.

"Where now?"

"Over there," she pointed. "It's a nice nature path."

They hurried down the path to building C.

Katie eyed everything around them. The bushes moved from the slight breeze and the boughs in the trees floated back and forth as if under water. She was glad when they saw an entrance door, which seemed to be more of a maintenance entrance.

As they neared the door only identified as C-M, McGaven put his hand on Katie's arm, slowing their pace. Neither spoke.

The door was slightly ajar. At first it looked as if someone had put a dark rock at the bottom to hold it open, but upon closer inspection the obstacle holding the door was the bottom of a black work boot. A low buzzing noise emitted every fifteen to twenty seconds. It was inaudible but sounded like a walkie-talkie or police radio.

Katie and McGaven both retrieved their guns and

proceeded with caution. They did a sweep in a three-hundred-sixty-degree turn, back to back, making sure they weren't going to be ambushed. The area was clear, but the wind was picking up faster than the slight breeze earlier. Dry leaves rose up in a funnel and swirled against the side of the building before dropping to the ground.

Katie took the left side of the door as McGaven covered the right. They made eye contact and Katie nodded. She gripped the door handle and pulled.

McGaven went in first. "Clear," he said.

Katie followed.

On the ground was a security guard who must have been a part of campus police, dressed in a dark blue uniform with a utility belt. He lay on his side with his leg bent behind him. Blood oozed from his scalp, trickling down the side of his face. His eyes were closed. He looked middle-aged and appeared to be fit.

Katie knelt down slowly next to the man and felt for a pulse in his neck. She nodded and whispered, "He's alive and his pulse is strong. He's been knocked out."

On the ground were his cell phone, work radio, and a large round silver ring with numerous keys dangling from it.

The security guard murmured something and then opened his eyes. He stared at the detectives and tried to get up.

"Take it easy there," said McGaven helping the man to his feet.

"I'm Detective Scott and this is my partner Detective McGaven. We're from the Pine Valley Sheriff's Department," said Katie.

"What happened?" asked McGaven.

"I... I don't know. I was doing my rounds after five and someone hit me from behind."

"Do you remember anything about the person who hit you?" she said.

"I didn't pass out right away, so when I was on the floor I saw boots and the bottom of jeans." He winced at the pain on his head. "I couldn't tell you if it were a man or woman."

"Is Dr. Rimini here today?" said McGaven.

"Yeah, he's always here on Saturdays. Usually stays late."

"Okay. I'm going to ask you to sit down and stay right here, okay?" said Katie.

"Can you call this in?" said McGaven.

He nodded. "Yeah."

"We're going to borrow these keys, okay?" Katie snatched up the keys from the floor.

He nodded again.

The detectives took off, running down the hallway in the direction of Dr. Rimini's lab. Both pulled their weapon. This section of the building was eerily quiet and there were no students around on a late Saturday afternoon.

Katie slowed her pace. She noticed there were security cameras secured high at each corner, but that the rooms and lecture halls were all dark—a perfect place to hide or set up an ambush. She thought maybe they shouldn't have been so hasty and should start moving more carefully.

"What?" whispered McGaven.

"Too many dark classrooms and lecture halls."

He nodded, knowing exactly what she meant, slowing as they approached the lab at the end of the long hallway with more cautiousness.

Katie's approach was inaudible. Her boots made almost no noise. She tried not to think about something happening to the professor, but at this point, considering the attack on the security guard, anything was possible.

The small windows above the doors behind which anyone could be hiding made them an easy target. The detectives crouched down and moved forward carefully around each door entrance. They didn't have time to search every room, every closet, and every office at this point. The only concern was Dr. Rimini's whereabouts and his safety.

Katie was the first to reach the large double doors leading into the lab. They were locked. It was a good sign. The intruder might not have been able to enter the lab. She retrieved the large key ring and began by a process of elimination to find the right key for the lock.

McGaven kept watch behind them as Katie kept trying different keys. He pulled out his cell phone on which he still had the map of the school and the sciences building.

"There's another entrance down the maintenance hallway," he said. Looking to the right, there was a door labeled "Keep Out: Maintenance Only." "There are two exit doors from the lab."

Katie was beginning to get frustrated. Finally one of the keys fit the lock. She looked at her partner. "Try the maintenance door."

McGaven pulled the door open.

"Go around and I'll meet you inside. We can cover more area and contain the intruder," she said.

McGaven hesitated. "I don't—"

"It's the only way we can trap the intruder," she interrupted her partner. "I don't like it either, but we can't take the chance of letting this guy escape." She retrieved her cell phone, inserted her Bluetooth earpiece, and pressed McGaven's number. "Keep your phone on and the line open." She slipped her phone back in her pocket.

"Okay," he said. He inserted his earpiece so he could hear her.

"Watch your back."

He nodded. "See you inside."

Katie watched her partner disappear and the maintenance door shut quietly behind him. Taking a long look behind her to scan the hallway they'd just come through, she inhaled a breath and opened the lab door, stepping quickly inside.

She had never been to a science lab before, especially one for forensic anthropology. Dim lights were the only illumination. She noticed that the floor was covered with a low-grade carpet similar to those found at entrances. It also had a slight downhill slope from the student seats to the teaching podium.

She moved slowly as she didn't want to announce her presence just yet. She saw the large lecture room with a podium and an oversized computer screen adorning the wall. The audience chairs were all empty, making the atmosphere strangely lonely.

"I'm making my way," whispered McGaven in her earpiece.

"Me too. I'm heading to the exam lab area," said Katie.

There was a sound behind her. She spun around to face nothing. She thought she heard another sound. A squeak. A slight bump. She swung her weapon in the direction of the noise, but there was nothing there. Was her mind playing tricks? The last few days had been painful and horrifying, leaving her nerves on edge.

Could her fear be playing right into the enemy's hands?

Katie retraced her steps and then continued moving toward the lab. There was only one light on in the corner. It was hanging over an examination table similar to the ones found in the sheriff's department's forensic lab. There were carefully laid out bones in several groups with index cards with writing on them. She couldn't ascertain from her position if the bones were modern or from another time.

Moving on toward the lab, Katie kept watch all around her. It made for slow progress. She expected to see McGaven soon, but still inching forward herself. The door leading into the exam room was a large sliding one and was open a few inches. She put her hand on the frame of the door and slowly moved it wide enough for her to slip her body through.

The urge to call out to Dr. Rimini was overwhelming, but

Katie's law enforcement instincts overruled that impulse. She still needed to keep the sound of her presence at a minimum.

There were shelves in front of her filled with plastic containers, buckets, and pieces of heavy butcher paper. It appeared that all types and sizes of bones were catalogued and stored here. More bones were in heavy plastic bags. An area with signs that read "Animal Species" and "Prehistoric" had yet more bones. Along the other wall were numerous computers, microscopes, large format monitors, and all types of printers including 3D ones.

Katie looked underneath tables and into the corners, but there was no sign of anyone in the room or its adjoining sections. And luckily no sign of any struggle. She moved toward the area where she could see an office desk with three filing cabinets. A desk lamp was on and there were several files opened along with a teacher's grade book. A gold pen and a mechanical pencil were neatly positioned next to the files. It was as if Dr. Rimini had just been seated there but something had brought his attention away from his work.

Katie continued to move.

"You here yet?" she said into the headset microphone.

"Got turned around, but I should be there in T-minus five minutes."

Katie smiled. Even at times like this, her partner knew how to lighten a tough situation.

Katie swept around and through the administrative and records areas.

Nothing.

She continued to move toward an area that held large two-door cabinets, obviously for storage. They went from floor to ceiling, all of their doors securely shut, except one that was slightly ajar. You had to be searching diligently under the low lighting with a keen eye to even notice it was open a crack.

Katie kept her back close to the wall, directing her gun

forward. She inched closer. Stopping short of the cabinet, she listened intently but only heard a faint noise coming from the vents above.

Moving again, she stopped to the side of the cabinet. Pausing a moment. Focusing intently. She gripped the small door pull and jerked it wide open.

Inside was Dr. Rimini, hiding with his legs drawn up against his chest.

"Dr. Rimini?" whispered Katie, relieved that he was there and—alive.

The look of surprise that washed across his face was overwhelming as he let out a huge sigh of relief. "Detective," he managed to say. His eyes were still wide with fear as he stared at her Glock. "What are you doing here?"

"John called us."

Katie scanned the area. Goosebumps prickled up her arms and the back of her neck. She knew he was close—the intruder —the killer. The weekend campus and lab area was a perfect place for someone to wait, to pounce, to kill, and then leave without anyone encountering him. She put her finger to her lips to quiet the professor. He immediately obliged, but still had a look of confusion and fear on his face.

Katie whispered into her microphone, "I have him."

There was no response, but she could tell that the line was still open.

She guessed that he might be in a position where he spotted the intruder and couldn't talk right at the moment.

"I'm going to get him out of the building."

Katie helped Dr. Rimini to his feet, making a signal for him to stay behind her.

They were just about to leave when all the lights went out.

THIRTY

Katie and Dr. Rimini stood motionless in the dark. After ten seconds, the emergency lights went on. "Where are the light switches?" she said.

The professor steered her to a wall panel and he flipped the switches up and down. Nothing happened.

"We're going to have to make our way out, okay?" she stated.

He nodded in agreement, his eyes wide with concern.

"It's okay. We'll just move slowly, okay?"

Katie waited to see if she could hear anything around the area. She still hadn't heard from McGaven. She spoke softly. "We lost electricity. I don't know if you can hear me but we're making our way out and then to the parking lot." She waited for an answer, but it didn't come.

"What happened?" she said softly said to Dr. Rimini, still watching every corner.

"I... I... was going through some files and updating some shipping and receiving logs like I do on most Saturdays." He took a moment to compose himself. "I heard someone come in, which is weird because no one comes to lab after 3 p.m. on Saturday."

"Then what?"

"I saw him."

"Who?" she said turning to look at him.

"I don't know, a man, thin. He was dressed in black pants, I think jeans, and a cap. Goggles obscuring his face."

"Was he young or old? Race? White, Black, Hispanic?"

"I don't know... white, I guess. But... he held a semiautomatic gun and it looked like he had a silencer."

"You mean a suppressor on the end of the barrel?" she said. The man must've struck the guard on the way in and had most likely used his gun.

"Yeah. So I wasn't going to hang around after I saw the guy had a gun, but I couldn't get out... so I hid and he finally left."

"Okay." Katie watched every dark corner and kept her wits.

"Why are you here?" he said.

"John called me and said he couldn't get ahold of you." She hesitated on how much she should tell him. "There's more you need to know, but right now, let's get out of here first."

"Where's your partner?"

"I don't know, but he's coming." Katie hoped that McGaven would be coming out right behind them.

She began to retrace her steps. "Is there an outside door from here?"

He nodded and pointed to the opposite direction from where she had come in.

They turned right and made their way down the hallway, passing only a few faculty offices. The low lighting began to pulse, making it difficult to see into the darkened corners. Katie's senses were amped to the limit. She kept the professor close and behind her in case they came in contact with the intruder. She tried not to dwell on the fact that someone wanted to intimidate or possibly kill Dr. Rimini and was bold enough to enter the college campus as if he owned the place. The investigation was becoming more complex, intricate, and dangerous by the second. It was going to take the entire police department to solve this one. She hoped that security cameras caught even a glimpse of the man's identity.

Katie slowed the pace and stopped just before a turn into an adjacent hallway. She looked at the professor and pointed, indicating she needed to know if that was the correct direction. He nodded in agreement.

Just as they turned the corner, she heard a door open and close. The hollow metal sound echoed, which meant that it was an exit leading outside.

"Katie?" said McGaven's voice in her ear.

"Gav, where are you?"

"I'm just passing a lab with a ton of bones."

"There's a man dressed in black carrying a gun with a suppressor that Rimini hid from." She could hear her partner's breath in her ear and she also felt his frustration. "We'll wait for you, go north and take the first left. Use your compass app. We're in the corridor."

"See you in just a minute."

"And Gav... we just heard the exit door ahead open and close."

"I'll be there in seconds."

Katie leaned against the wall. She hated waiting, feeling like a trapped rat wanting to burst out the exit door and chase down the perp. But her first responsibility was to stay with Rimini and make sure nothing happened to him.

Soft footsteps approached, making a weird sound that coincided with the blinking lights.

She could finally see McGaven's outline. He looked taller and bigger than she remembered. But the lights going on and off overhead made him appear like a superhero. He finally reached them.

"You both okay?" he said.

"Yes, we're fine," she said.

Dr. Rimini nodded. He still looked fearful, like the monster was still after him.

"Alright, let's go," said Katie. She led, followed by Rimini, McGaven taking up the rear as they made their way toward the exit.

As Katie stood at the door, she paused. She looked to her partner. He took a cover position as Katie took point. Now that she was at the exit door, she hesitated, thinking that the killer might be waiting for whoever would depart next. The vivid memory of skeletal remains and the bodies were difficult for her to put aside when her adrenalin was surging.

Pushing the door open, with the evening light confronting them, Katie stepped out, swinging her gun in an arc motion to ensure that no one was hiding or waiting to take them out. "Clear," she said.

McGaven appeared. He took the right as Katie took the left. When both were satisfied that the black-clad perp was not around, they headed down the path with a shaken Dr. Rimini.

McGaven was immediately on his phone contacting the college campus police and the Pine Valley Sheriff's Department.

Katie walked ahead, still mindful of the surroundings. The twilight evening made everything look prettier: the trees, plants, and even the overgrown walkway. It was a path that clearly wasn't maintained on a regular basis. Weeds grew in between the cracks, dirt and leaves muddled the sides, and tree roots had uplifted a few of the sections causing odd bulges in the path.

She could hear McGaven talking on the cell phone and asking Dr. Rimini some questions to verify his story. This part of the evening would be enjoyable under most circumstances, but something felt abnormal and out of place. It was the same sensitivity that Katie got when she was working with her army team—it was when someone was watching them.

Katie looked up in the trees as a couple of birds fluttered around finding insects. The wind from earlier had died down again, leaving the cool air still and quiet around her. Then she saw it—a movement between the trees. A black shadow. Stealthy. A tall, male figure moving around as if trying to get a better vantage.

She looked back. She couldn't see her partner and the professor, but could hear McGaven talking in a low tone.

Should she do it? Could she get the upper hand in time? There was no time to lose.

The images of Jimmy's body with its dead eyes staring at her flashed across her vision—almost accusing her of not finding the killer sooner.

Katie looked back again. She quickly sent a text to McGaven: *Gone after the man in black... southeast.*

She took off at a full run heading south down the pathway, her arms pumping and her heart racing. She stayed as quiet as possible. It was obvious why no one ever took the walk, it abruptly ended and continued in softly packed dirt, mostly consisting of California sand mixed with some silt and clay. With each stride, her boots made an imprint causing a dusty cloud to swirl behind her. Zigzagging around dead uprooted bushes and old tree stumps, she kept going south until she could head east then back up north hoping to flank the perp.

Katie half expected to hear McGaven yelling at her to stop, but it was strangely quiet. The only sound she heard was her own breathing booming in her ears. She slowed her pace and gained her bearings in the forest. She moved with stealth and caution as she rounded several clustered pine trees.

There was a movement in the thick forest about twenty feet in front of her. She halted, keeping her heavy breathing as quiet as possible. There. She saw it move again. No doubt in her mind that it was a figure wearing black and it was the back of him.

She crept closer, watching her immediate surroundings. What if he'd brought a partner—was working with another person? Maybe that was why he could be all over town, following and killing anyone associated with the Maple Road arson house. Were there two killers? It would make sense with two crime scenes years apart.

Katie stopped behind the covering of a large tree trunk in both front and back. She dared to lean around and survey the area up ahead. She saw him. The tall thin figure that moved like a man had his back to her, dressed in black, combat boots, hood up, cap pulled down. She couldn't see his hands because he wore gloves; there weren't any identifying characters of the perp —no visible tattoos, couldn't see basic color of hair, race, or facial features. Her frustration mounted. She knew that McGaven was going to read her the riot act for acting without the proper backup, but they had Dr. Rimini and couldn't leave him without protection. An overwhelming gut instinct made Katie believe that this person was acting alone and she was going to get to the bottom of it. She moved closer with practiced stealth.

The man dressed in black stood still and appeared to be watching something. Katie didn't know for sure if he was watching McGaven and Dr. Rimini, but it was a good assumption.

She moved even closer, making sure her footsteps were well placed and quiet. She was about six feet from him. His hands were down at his sides and his gun was stuck in his waistband.

This was her chance... she may not get another one.

"Police! Put your hands in the air! Now!"

The man remained still; he didn't even flinch as if he knew she had been behind him all along.

"Turn around slowly!"

He didn't move.

"I said turn around with your hands in the air!"

He still didn't move.

Katie felt frozen in time as if she was in some type of computer game that had stopped. She took a step forward and her boot stuck in a small hole, making her lose her balance. By the time she caught herself, he was gone. Like a ghost.

"No, no," she said.

Katie took off running. She had nothing to base her path on but she thought he would take a route that was easy to navigate through. Losing her sense of direction, she paused a moment, when she heard a car start its engine.

"Damn..."

She ran toward the noise as she heard the vehicle accelerate its high-powered engine and leave at high speed. When she got to the lower parking lot, it was empty. The smell of exhaust was still wafting in the air. The man in black was gone. There was no way of knowing if that was the killer they were hunting and hiding from, or if he was on another criminal mission.

Katie pressed her cell phone and hit McGaven's number.

"Katie, where are you?" said McGaven, obviously angry.

"I lost him."

"Wait, what?"

"I found the intruder but he ran and got away. He had his exit route all planned out."

"Don't ever take off like that again."

She had never heard McGaven sound like that. The cold cases and the recent murders had everyone on edge. "I won't," she said softly. "How's Dr. Rimini?"

"He's fine. Still shook up. I've updated him on what's happening." He paused. "Where are you?"

Looking around, she said, "By what I can tell, behind the science building. I'm on my way back up."

"Get back here. We're behind the parking lot where we parked."

"On my way."

The connection abruptly ended.

When Katie got to the parking lot where they had started, it was full of campus police cars, security, an ambulance, and two deputy sheriff's cruisers. The daylight was fading. The outside lights along the buildings and pathways were lit up and there were more large lights set up on tripods. The parking lot was the headquarters for the officers in charge.

Katie caught up with McGaven. He was on the phone and relaying information.

"Hey," she said.

He nodded and continued with his calls.

Katie looked around and saw Dr. Rimini talking with campus police and giving a statement. She saw a large white SUV drive up and knew it was her uncle. "Oh boy," she mumbled under her breath.

McGaven completed his calls and walked back to Katie. His frown, clenched jaw, and rigid demeanor told her everything she needed to know.

She decided not to provoke him or make things worse. "How are things going?"

"They're tending to the security guard's wound, probably a mild concussion. They'll take him to the hospital. I've filled in the campus police on what's been going on and why we were here. We'll have more of an official report for them later."

"Okay," she said.

"Did you get anything about the intruder?"

"No, nothing. He was well covered and never turned to face me." Katie was frustrated, but she didn't want her anxiousness to show. It was obvious he was still mad at her.

"You know you're going to have to tell Sheriff Scott about what you did."

"I know. He'll read about it in my report."

"I'll read about what?" said the sheriff as he approached the detectives. "What did Katie do?"

"Once we exited the building with Dr. Rimini, she saw the intruder making his way down one of the overgrown paths and she took chase," said McGaven.

"I see. Is that how it went?" he asked.

"Yes."

"Were you able to identify him?" His demeanor was relaxed and calm.

"No, he was too well covered, and I never saw his face."

"We need to see the video footage," said McGaven.

"I'm releasing you both from here. A copy of the footage will be forwarded to you at the office."

"What?" Katie began to object, but then decided to remain quiet. "What about Dr. Rimini?"

"I'll make sure he has accommodations or can stay with someone. He will be safe."

Katie nodded and glanced back at the professor. He still looked shaken and his face was pale.

"Have you made any progress with Jimmy's case?" she said.

"Not at this time, but we're working it. Now I'm ordering the both of you to go back to Katie's house and *stay* there unless otherwise ordered. At least until Monday." He emphasized *stay*. "Chad and John are already there. John is updating some of your security cameras. The four of you need to watch each other's backs. Understood?"

"Yes, sir," said McGaven.

"Yes."

"How you maintain security among the four of you is your decision, but this is serious. And I expect you to treat it as extremely serious."

"What about you?" said Katie.

"I will be fine. A couple of my lieutenants will be bunking at my place for a couple of days. We're all making compromises."

"Don't worry, we'll be fine," she said.

"I expect to have your reports."

"Of course," she said. Katie wanted to hug her uncle, but it wasn't the time or place. "We'll give you an update in the morning."

"That would be fine," the sheriff said and left to talk with deputies and the campus police.

"That went well," said Katie.

"What do you expect? Have you not been paying attention? There's a killer who has already killed several people, including one of our first responders."

"Of course I understand what's at stake," she said as they walked to the sedan. "It's all I think about. This case has become personal."

McGaven turned to Katie. His face softened. "Look, I know you realize what's at stake. We all have to bunk together like we're in protective custody or something." He chose his words carefully. "You can't just run after a perp without telling me what's going on—I'm your partner. I thought we were past this."

"I know. And I'm sorry."

He opened the car door. Before he got in, he said, "I don't want anything to happen to you."

"I feel the same way about you, partner."

THIRTY-ONE

Saturday 2045 hours

Katie and McGaven rode in almost complete silence. They were both deep in thought and it was obvious that McGaven was still annoyed with Katie. They drove back to the Pine Valley Sheriff's Department so that McGaven could pick up his truck, then they caravanned back to Katie's house.

Until Katie turned up her driveway, the situation didn't completely sink in about someone stalking first responders. A Jeep and a large truck were already parked—they belonged to Chad and John. She wondered how they were getting along and if they were telling stories that would embarrass her. She would find out soon enough.

She parked the police sedan and cut the engine. Opening the driver's door, she was met by a very excited Cisco followed by Chad and John. "Hey, there they are," said Chad. He kissed Katie. Looking at her solemn expression, he said, "Everything okay?" He then looked at McGaven, raising his eyebrows.

"You'll have to ask your fiancée," he said with some of the usual humor in his voice.

"What does he mean?" said Chad to Katie.

"Nothing. I tried to run after the intruder guy and he got away. Simple as that."

"Nothing is simple with you," he said.

"Now that's the truth," said McGaven.

"Oh great. Is this how it's going to go? I want to trade in my weekend roommates."

Everyone laughed as they walked to the front door. It was a way to let off some steam.

"Wait," she said. "I don't have much to eat."

"All taken care of," said John who had been staying in the background. "Chad and I picked up some stuff at the store."

Katie was relieved and suddenly hungry. "Thank you." She saw duffel bags and an overnight bag sitting just inside the entrance. "I don't know about you guys but I'm starving. It's been a long day."

"Come in and relax," said Chad. "We just got the party started."

Cisco was running from person to person begging for food. He was so happy to have company.

Katie was immediately hit with the wonderful aroma of meat cooking on the grill outside. "What's cooking?" She saw several grocery bags, deli containers, beers, and wine.

"Steak and chicken," said Chad. "And, I have to say that John is awesome with marinades. Who would've thought?"

"It's all in the fresh ingredients," he said.

"Wow," said Katie. "Have you guys divvied up where you're going to sleep?"

"I already have my room," said McGaven stuffing part of a roll in his mouth.

"I don't mind the third bedroom with the uncomfortable roll-out bed," said John. "And all the paint supplies."

"You could also sleep on the couch," said Katie. "Cisco would love it."

"Thanks," he said. "I might do that."

Katie went to the kitchen and grabbed a beer, checking out the groceries as she did.

"How do you like your steak?" asked John, poking his head inside.

"Medium," said Katie.

"Rare," said Chad.

"Medium rare," said McGaven.

"You got it." John went back outside.

The four of them relaxed as much as was possible, chatting about anything but the cases and why they were under house arrest at Katie's house. They laughed. Joked. And ate great food together. But the investigation was never far from their minds.

An hour and a half later, everyone was full and relaxed. Katie was cleaning up the kitchen. Even Cisco was tired as he lay on the floor near McGaven.

Katie looked into the living room. She could feel the tension —the type of feeling that comes from the anxiety of the unknown. She knew it—and suffered it. After all the condiments and groceries were put away, she dried the last dish and set it in the cabinet. The entire time, her mind kept rewinding back to the man in black who entered the school and seemed to be looking for Dr. Rimini.

How would he know the professor had helped with the skeletal remains?

Did someone send him?

Who? And why?

Chad joined her and nuzzled her neck. "You know I have to go back to work in eight hours."

"You do?" She was disappointed. She had hoped they could finally get to spend some time together.

"Yep. But Gav mentioned that you needed to see the investigation on the arson. And we got our guy, but... he said that you need to see everything."

"True."

"I have the files with me, and anything else you need I can forward to you." He went back to the living room where McGaven was playing around, making them all laugh.

"That sounds great," she said but he was distracted and didn't hear it.

Katie sat down and patiently waited—it helped that she had had two beers, so she wasn't so anxious and impatient.

Finally Chad flipped a mood switch and got back into professional arson investigator mode. "Okay, I know this is a bit unusual, but I wanted to go over some main points for the arson investigation at 717 Maple Road." He retrieved several eight-by-ten photographs and passed them around.

"Why not just digital files?" said John.

"We do that too, but I use these for informational purposes. Like what Katie and Gav do in their investigation.

"First, Pine Valley Sheriff's Department served an arrest and search warrant for Stewart Fitzgerald, aka Flash."

"Score one for the good guys," said McGaven as he stared at the arrest mug shot of the dark-haired stocky man.

"I know that the arson investigation has crossed with some of your cases, namely Travis Stone's homicide. If it weren't for Detective Hamilton handling the case, we might not have found out about the man he hired to torch the house."

Katie looked at several photos of the burned home and the close-up shots of where the incendiary device had been attached. She had seen all types of bomb devices and this reminded her of what she had seen in the field. "Was this his MO? Were there others?"

"Yes, we were able to find tiny pieces that included fragments from a trigger, timer, and accelerant that were consistent with other fires that had been set in the county and two other surrounding counties. We were also able to reconstruct it by using a software program with an eighty-five percent probability."

"It looked like it was simple," said McGaven.

"Yes, that's why his work usually would burn completely without a trace of the device, but this time... it didn't." He looked around the room as everyone took their time assessing the photo. "I'm sorry that it wasn't helpful in your investigations," he said, looking at Katie.

"That's not true—it's been very helpful," she said. "Travis Stone was originally a person of interest in the Cross family homicides and now we know he didn't commit the murders."

"You sure about that?" said McGaven.

"There's nothing to connect him, at this point, to those murders," she said. "Yes, they rented from him. Yes, he was a pain in the ass and even harassed them. Yes, they were found buried on the property. But I don't believe he did it. It was clear that he was only interested in the insurance from the house—Randall Construction had probably given him too high of a bid. Stone usually had them do all the work on his investment properties."

"I don't know..." said Chad. "That's a lot of yeses."

"I'm not completely convinced," said McGaven.

"Really? Then who killed Jimmy? And went after me and Dr. Rimini and the others?" Katie paused, trying not to get anxious. Why weren't they seeing her point of view?

"I think what I meant to say is," began McGaven, "we need to make sure the killer and stalker are indeed the same person."

Katie hated not being able to use her case board. It was difficult sitting around in the living room trying to explain her view. "It's called inference. The recent homicides and attacks are related to one crime scene."

"It seems that way, but what if it's—" began McGaven.

"No coincidences. Everything started right after the arson... It brings us to here, right now."

McGaven nodded in agreement.

"That doesn't mean we don't follow every lead no matter what."

"You've been quiet," said McGaven about John.

"Just listening. I'll have forensic tests back for these cases for you in a couple of days, but it's true, it would have to be an amazing round of coincidences to not be connected."

Katie was thinking about the cases and evidence they'd found. Whether or not they somehow connected to Travis Stone, she needed to map his properties around the county and look into each of them. She didn't doubt herself, but there was one aspect that could still make Travis Stone involved.

"What's up, Katie?" said McGaven. He watched his partner.

"I agree with what you all are saying and I think that Gav and I should run down all of Stone's properties to see if we find any anomalies or situations similar to the Crosses' experiences."

McGaven knew Katie well. "And?"

"It's due diligence while we wait for information on Sara Simms and forensics." She looked at her partner. "What if the killer had a partner—and then the partner killed him—and now he is trying to clean up all loose ends—us."

THIRTY-TWO

TWENTY-FIVE YEARS AGO

Snyder Fields, Pine Valley
Summer

Sara Simms slowed her pace along the trail. The path was becoming narrow and too much of the prickly brush scraped her arms and legs. Her thoughts were that the forest was going to ruin her new outfit, but the anticipation of getting to the secret party was more important. She shivered from the dampness and darkness from the dense trees.

Sara hummed softly to herself, hoping to make the time pass.

A sharp snap cracked behind her.

She stopped and looked around. "Hello?" Her voice wavered.

Standing in partial darkness, Sara waited, but there was only the musical sound of the breeze filtering through the pine trees. Looking around, she began to move forward as fast as she could go.

Sara finally came to a clearing and the sun beamed down, warming her. No more creepy forest. She let out a sigh of relief as she closed her eyes, tilting her head toward the heat.

A rustle followed by sharp crackles came from behind her.

She turned in fear, expecting to see someone, but there was no one there. Not saying a word, she turned and hurried toward the party. The sounds crashing through the forest continued to follow her.

THIRTY-THREE

Sunday 0745 hours

Katie sat on her back deck just outside the kitchen sliding door in her much-loved patio swing—a place where she often would go to no matter the season or the time of day. It was a place where she felt safe and a place where she did most of her thinking.

The sun was just rising above the hills around her, a cascading aura of yellows and oranges preparing for a new day. It was serene and comforting.

Cisco had grown weary of checking out and marking every bush, plant, and tree on the property, so he gave up and snuggled up with his favorite person. He was calm and warm as he pushed his body up against Katie.

Katie pulled her pale yellow robe tighter over her pajamas, keeping the collar up around her neck. She sipped a steaming mug of tea and pondered on everything that had been talked about the night before. The guys were still sleeping and deserved to rest as much as they could. They had all been through so much stress and uncertainty in the past few days. It made her miserable. It felt like there was no way out of the situation that she and her colleagues had found themselves embroiled in—they were being picked off one by one by a phantom man in black.

The sliding door opened and Chad stepped out. He was already dressed in his typical firehouse clothing and his hair was still wet from the shower. His bright blue eyes were now somewhat troubled as his brows were wrinkled.

"Hey, babe," he said and kissed her. "I hate to leave, but I've got to get to the house."

"Last night was nice," she said.

He kissed her again. "Now, you're not supposed to leave today."

"I know. Don't worry."

"Katie, I know you."

She held his hand. "Don't worry about me; I have a couple bodyguards who are sleeping on the job right now."

He smiled. "You mean in addition to Cisco?"

"Be careful driving to the firehouse. Okay?"

He kissed her again. "I will. I'll be off on Tuesday."

"Okay," she said and hesitantly let his hand slip through hers.

He stopped. "I like how the painting looks. You'll be out of here in no time."

"What do you mean?" Katie became defensive. "The house has needed some fresh paint for a while now."

"I just meant... the house looks nice and should be easy to sell."

"To sell?"

"Well yeah, if we buy a new house, we can't keep this one. We talked about this."

"Actually, you've decided this. I still haven't decided if I want to sell."

"C'mon, Katie. I understand this place has memories, but we're going to begin a life together."

Katie couldn't look Chad in the eye. She turned and gazed at the property. There were too many memories flooding through her mind. They weren't like ghosts, but something real that had defined who she was. How could she sell the house and walk away?

"I can see that you're troubled. Let's just take one step at a time. But you're going to have to make a decision. When we get married, it's our life together."

"Well..." Katie couldn't finish.

Chad stood for a moment watching her. Then he quietly slipped back into the house and was gone. Katie heard the Jeep start up in the driveway and listened to the engine noise become softer as he drove away. There was silence.

She pushed away the conversation about the house. Once again her mind drifted to the crime scenes. Travis Stone was on her mind—there was something she was missing. She went back and forth with the crime scenes and her conversation with the real estate investor.

Katie heard the slider open again. Cisco raised his head to see who was there.

"Hey," said John. He looked a bit sleepy in his T-shirt, loose sweats, and bare feet.

"Morning. Did you sleep well?"

"I did. I didn't think that a roll-out cot would be comfortable, but amazingly it was."

Katie laughed. "I know, it really is."

"I was asleep when my head hit the pillow." He walked to the edge of the patio and stared out at the property. It was a crisp but beautiful morning with infinite numbers of green around them. "It's great here. Probably why I slept so well."

"I couldn't imagine being anywhere else," she said.

"But you and Chad are looking for a house together, right?"

Katie couldn't make eye contact. "We're looking. I think it's going to take a special house."

There was an awkward silence before John spoke. Katie knew John had some things on his mind, so she let him take his time without any questions.

"After Jimmy's call, something changed for me," he said. "Then when I tried to call Sal and couldn't reach him. My mind immediately went to Jimmy's apartment that night."

Heartache was something that Katie knew well.

"I've never had to deal with these types of tragedies after I got out of the Seals. My work is great, but I guess, somehow I thought it would shelter me from personal loss. You know about that..."

Katie remained quiet, slightly swinging in her chair and petting Cisco as she listened. She gazed out at the views from the property; somehow it made certain things hurt less.

"My brother and I enlisted into the military together."

"I didn't know you have a brother," said Katie. She realized suddenly there were many things she didn't know about John except his great work.

"Tom. He was my big brother even though he was barely two years older." John moved toward the edge of the patio. "I came back and he didn't. Instead, I had to bury him."

Katie felt goosebumps scuttle up her arms. No doubt loss was heavy among some of her friends and co-workers.

"I think Jimmy really brought back some well-hidden memories and I'm sorry that I pulled you in on it."

"I'm glad you did. You can't go through things like this alone. You have us, all of us. Don't forget there are all types of families—and I definitely think we're family."

John turned and smiled. He nodded in agreement.

It was difficult to tell if John was glad he opened up about his personal life, but Katie was glad he did.

"So I'd imagine that you weren't just sitting out here enjoying the scenery. You have something on your mind."

"Maybe, but I think we all need breakfast first," she said. "Is Gav up?"

"No, I could hear him snoring when I left my room."

Katie stood up and Cisco seemed ready for anything after his short nap. "Let's make breakfast. I saw there was bacon."

"That should wake him up," he said. "I'm going to jump in the shower."

"And I'll start cooking," she said.

Katie and John went back inside, followed closely by Cisco.

After the traditional large breakfast of eggs, bacon, shredded hash browns, and whole wheat toast, Katie explained to them why they needed to go back to 717 Maple Road and check out the basement—she wanted to conduct due diligence before the scene was released. She waited for McGaven and John to respond.

"I have no problem going with you as backup and recovering potential evidence," said John.

McGaven appeared to have some reservations. "Have you cleared it with the sheriff?"

"No, I haven't talked to him. He sent a text this morning to see how we were all getting along."

"We need to get that wall area where the scratches are located forensically tested," said McGaven.

"The arson property is still officially a crime scene, meaning we can go back for as long as it takes until it's released—by us," she said, trying to sound matter-of-fact. "Even the fire investigators have completed their investigation."

"It should only take about twenty minutes or so," said John.

Katie could tell that McGaven didn't like the plan. "Fine," he said. "We're all together, so that's good."

• • •

Katie and McGaven rode with John in his large truck. Before leaving Katie's house, they made sure that the property was secure, cameras tested and set, with Cisco safely indoors.

Katie's idea had sounded good to her at the time, but now, as she sat in between John and McGaven, she wondered if it was such a great idea venturing out without the sheriff's approval. This phantom man in black didn't seem to mind when he attacked or killed people—day or night.

She flashed on the memory of the four-door sedan revving its engine without lights and then turning on the high beams against the background of the forest—like he was trying to provoke or scare her. Was he watching them right now? Katie turned and scanned the cars that were within their vicinity.

When they reached the house on Maple Road and parked, Katie and McGaven got out and took a look around—everything looked the same and the chain-link fence was still upright and secured.

John reached into the back to retrieve a good-size toolbox along with some forensic containers. He also opened his glove box and took out three sets of gloves.

"Can't go in there without gloves," John said.

"Of course not," she said, donning a pair.

McGaven pulled on his gloves. "You got it."

Katie walked to the area where she had entered before since the gate was still locked. She squeezed through and waited for McGaven and John to enter.

Katie's confidence was waning a bit. She agreed with McGaven that it was imperative they come back here and check out the wall. It had bothered her the first time she saw it and now they were going to document and retrieve it for testing. It was more than being thorough. She knew there was something odd and even unsettling about that wall.

She made her way back down to the basement once again, mindful of the condition of the house. She stood in front of the dark brown painted wall. The light from the late morning made it easy to see the details—the scratches looked like someone had tried to claw their way out of somewhere.

"That's it," she said out loud.

"What?" said McGaven. He bent and looked at the wall, scrutinizing it.

"Doesn't this room look like it has been repaired or completely redone recently?"

"It does," said John as he set down his equipment. With camera in hand, he took more photographs, documenting this visit before he took a sample. "It's a dark wood underneath. It looks like dark walnut."

"So?" said McGaven.

"Wouldn't a contractor know that this doesn't meet code?"

"Maybe it was grandfathered in?"

"I don't think so," she said. "That essentially means that this would have been legal during the time it was built, but it was built about twenty-five years ago. This still wasn't legal."

"What are you getting at?"

"Well, it means something was drastically changed and whoever it was had to fix it as best as they could."

John finished the photos and waited for Katie.

She walked up to the wall and gently touched her gloves to the scratch marks—they almost perfectly lined up with her hands. "I think," she said slowly, "this wall was turned around. This surface used to be on the inside."

"On the inside?"

"There's only one way to find out," said John. He retrieved a crowbar.

Katie backed up and nodded.

John pried several places around the five-foot square of wall. It was attached extremely securely. He took the crowbar and tapped it around the wood—it sounded hollow behind it.

"Gav, could use a bit of help here. I want to keep it in one piece." He handed the detective a large claw hammer.

John and McGaven went to opposite sides and began prying the piece. The nails and secure screws squeaked. Groaned. Creaked.

The pitch of the sounds made Katie wince.

Suddenly the wall broke free. They removed the piece and carefully moved it to one of the bearing wall supports—making sure they didn't scratch or dent anything that might prove to be evidence.

Katie stood quiet, mesmerized, and didn't move a muscle. Not able to avert her gaze, she stared at what had been hidden behind the wall. She had known that there was something wrong about it and it had seemed oddly out of place, but she never expected this...

McGaven and John gawked at the space as well.

It was a solid five minutes before any of them spoke.

"I need to document this before we explore any closer," said John.

The sound of John's voice breaking the silence made Katie twitch. "It looks like... some kind of storage area," she said, examining closer, looking at every inch of the space before John photographed it.

After several overall photos, John then moved in midway, and then close-up, careful not to miss anything. He looked for areas where air from outside could enter the confined space. "I can't tell if there was some way to get air into that chamber." He looked further. "Nope, too much of the house is gone."

"'Chamber'?"

"That's what it looks like."

"This is incredibly creepy—like one of those horror films," said McGaven.

"I'm going to take samples from these areas," John said and pointed to more scratches.

The interior was like a cramped room with wooden sides, directly underneath the sturdiest part of the house. There were holes where it appeared hooks had been attached to the walls. It was difficult to tell what kind of hooks, but it still raised serious questions.

Katie and John looked at the other side of the removed piece. It was painted a different color and seemed to match the other parts of the house that still remained; the five-by-five piece of wood had been turned around and repainted—recently.

"This is big," said Katie. "It could indicate that someone was held here—especially if there's DNA matching anyone in the Cross family. If we retrace the Cross timeline, there were two days before they supposedly vacated. We know by the invoice from the cleaning company when the storage company dropped off the storage container, picked it up, when they fully cleaned out the empty house, and then... their car, belongings, everything including the Cross family disappeared."

"The big question is why?" said McGaven.

Katie knew that they were on the precipice of a breakthrough, but what did it all mean? She watched John take a small hacksaw and remove the areas with the scratches. He protected them with special paper resembling heavy tissue paper, attaching it on both sides before carefully stacking everything ready to take back to the lab.

"The family didn't seem to have enemies and they weren't involved in anything illegal like drugs that would put them in harm's way. From everything we have discovered, they were just an average family living their lives. But..."

"They saw or heard something they weren't supposed to?" said McGaven.

"What would make someone want to kill the entire family?" She studied the scratches and scanned what was left of the basement. "I think it all goes back to the beginning—Sara Simms. We find her killer, we find the Cross family killer."

"What do you want to do now?" asked McGaven to his partner.

"I think we need to go and talk to Randall Construction again," said Katie. "They may have information about someone else who had access to this house. And I think they know more about Travis Stone than just he was difficult to work with."

THIRTY-FOUR

Monday 08 10 hours

Katie and McGaven were on their way to Randall Construction. They had called ahead and made an appointment with Seth Randall at 8:30 a.m. at the office, since they had already spoken with his brother David on the previous visit. It was important to speak with them again.

McGaven drove the police sedan and left his truck at Katie's house. The group arrest for all of them was still in effect until further notice from the sheriff, so they would be roommates for a while longer.

"So is it weird having me and John bunking at your house?" said McGaven.

"Very," she said and laughed. "No, it's a little bit strange, but you both are like family. It's actually nice having someone else around besides Cisco."

"And Chad?"

"Of course. His schedule is the most difficult to manage working twenty-four hours on and then off. Then my schedule. It's been a bit crazy." She looked away.

McGaven looked at his partner when they stopped at signal. "Are you rambling?"

"Too much coffee."

"I don't think so."

"Well, I don't care what you say," she said.

"Well, you should."

"I think you're a bit stir-crazy."

"I could be, but I think that you are nervous having John around."

"What are you talking about?" This was one of those times that having a partner you worked with every day could be annoying.

"I don't need to spell it out, but I think you're nervous when there are two men in your house who have taken a fancy to you."

"Fancy? What are you, back in the Victorian era? Who even uses that word anymore?"

McGaven drove over the same set of train tracks they had previously. It rattled the interior and the undercarriage of the vehicle. "I know when I can't win with you," he said but kept a big smile.

"Now, there's one thing we can agree on."

As they drove into the parking area for Randall Construction, they saw Seth Randall arguing with another man—not his brother. The argument was heated and there was some pushing and shoving going on. They were yelling at each other.

"What do you think?" said McGaven.

"C'mon, let's break it up." Katie got out of the car and headed straight over to the men. "Okay, okay. Everybody calm down."

"Who the hell are you?" said the big man. He wore a heavy long-sleeved work shirt and jeans, making him look like someone who was in the construction trade.

"I'm a police detective. So I said stand down."

Seth Randall smiled and backed up, leaving the big man standing alone.

"I'm not going to ask you again," she said.

"Fine, but it won't be the last time you'll hear from me," he spat out and stalked away.

Katie composed herself. "I'm Detective Scott and my partner, Detective McGaven."

"I remember."

"What was all that about?"

"Just a misunderstanding."

"Happen a lot?"

"Time to time, I suppose. Look, the construction trade can be lucrative and it can also dry up without warning, so people can get angry if they think you stole one of their customers."

"I see."

Seth walked over to one of his excavators and grabbed a towel to wipe his hands. It appeared that he had been working on it. "So. What's on your mind, Detective?"

McGaven started looking around the property at all the construction equipment and scrutinizing anything that might seem suspicious or out of place. He let his partner ask the questions while he acted as backup. Sometimes when questioning a suspect or witness it was important to get a solid handle on the location—whether home, or place of business.

"We're following up on Travis Stone." Katie watched him closely when she mentioned Travis's name. She wanted to see if anything she said caused a reaction.

"I thought he was dead."

"Yes, he is."

"Then what do you want to know?"

"You said that he wanted to do a remodel on 717 Maple Road."

"Correct."

"And then he decided against it?"

"Correct."

"Did you ever do any work there?"

"Nope."

"Did he have someone else do work on that property?"

"I don't know. Maybe."

"Did you ever work on the basement?" She watched him closely.

"Look, Detective, I told you that I didn't work on that house. Just spit out what you want to say."

Katie smiled. She knew he was nervous and guarded. Often people who were worried or didn't really want to answer a question said things like "I'm being honest here" or "Just ask me what you really want to ask." "Well, Mr. Randall, did you remove a wall in the basement, secure hooks for chains, and then close the chamber up again?"

Seth looked at Katie as if he couldn't believe she just said that. "Are you high? I mean what kind of story are you telling me?"

"The truth."

"Truth or not, I told you I didn't work on that house."

"Which Travis Stone house did you work on?"

"Most of them."

"Can you give us a list?"

"Sure. David can print you out a listing." Studying the detective for the first time, he calmed his demeanor. "Did he really have a space like that? You're not just jerking my chain?"

"We're not jerking your chain. Wouldn't dream of it."

"I know he did have a freaky room at his mansion."

"What do you mean?"

"Well, you know how rich people have those panic rooms in case there's a home invasion."

"Of course."

"Well, he had one strictly for kinky sex. Lots of S&M things."

"I see. Did you renovate it for him?"

"No, but I did other work at the mansion. Two bathroom remodels and floor-to-ceiling bookcases for his study. Oh, and I fixed some things with the plumbing and drains."

"Did you grow up in Pine Valley?" she asked.

"Yep, born and raised."

"And your brother?"

"He went off to Southern California to college and stayed for a few years, but eventually came back. It's worked out well for the business."

McGaven walked up. "Do you remember a missing girl— Sara Simms?"

"Yeah, sure. When you're a kid and someone goes missing like that—it's not easy to forget." He shrugged.

Katie watched Seth's reaction. He appeared disinterested or even detached about Sara.

"Anything that stands out in your mind?" said McGaven.

"Not really. It was a long time ago." He jammed his hands into his pockets.

"I look forward to reading your job list with Travis Stone. Thank you for your time, Mr. Randall," said Katie as she left with McGaven and entered the office.

A young woman sat in the front area, sipping coffee, and stared at Katie and McGaven.

"Hi," said Katie. "Seth said you would be able to run a list by client of all the jobs done for them."

"Yes, but—"

"C'mon, Cindy, if Seth says it's okay, then it is." David Randall had appeared from an office. "What client, Detective?"

"Travis Stone."

The receptionist hit a few keys and waited for the list to print out.

McGaven looked again at the home and commercial building renderings, framed beautifully, hanging on the wall.

They were done in pastel colors, which gave them an antique feel. "Wow, these are really amazing. You guys do some great work."

"Thank you, Detective. It's all a labor of love. Creating something from nothing—it's a great feeling."

"Did you like working with Travis Stone?" she asked.

"Not one of my favorite people, but he did have vision and knew what he wanted. I respect that."

Katie thought that was an interesting answer.

Cindy grabbed the papers and stapled them together.

David took them and walked around the reception area and faced Katie. "There you go, Detective. If you need anything else, just let us know. We all care about Pine Valley and want to help in any way we can."

"Thank you."

Katie and McGaven headed to the door.

"Hope you solve your case," he said as they left.

"Interesting," said McGaven under his breath.

Katie raised her eyebrows.

Before they reached their car, Cindy came out of the office carrying some paperwork. For a moment, Katie thought that they must've forgotten something.

"Excuse me, Detectives," said Cindy waving the papers. Her brightly colored blouse made a stark contrast against the building.

"Thank you," said Katie, not knowing what else to say.

Cindy handed her the papers. "These are just duplicates of what you already have."

Katie looked puzzled.

"I wanted to talk to you both before you left."

"Okay."

"It doesn't take a genius to figure out that you're investigating Seth and David."

"We're following up on the investigation."

"Of course," said Cindy with a huge smile. "I just wanted to add my two cents. You see, I've been working for Randall Construction for six years and I know a thing or two about what goes on here."

Katie patiently waited for the receptionist to explain what it was like to work for the brothers.

"I can tell you, hands down, that Seth can be very mean, demanding, and sometimes provoking some of our clients. We've lost more than a few customers. Quite frankly, the only reason that this business stays afloat is because of David. Now we're talking a nice man. He's efficient and great at managing the company."

"I see," said Katie. "Thank you, Cindy. If you have anything else that might be helpful, please don't hesitate to contact us."

"Right. Will do," she said and hurried back into the office.

The detectives got into the car and drove away from Randall Construction.

"Interesting bit of information."

"It's not like we couldn't figure that out ourselves," he said.

"Still... I think she's telling the truth."

"I think Seth Randall is hiding some things," said McGaven.

"I agree, but I don't think it's murder. It may have to do with how they do business. And like Cindy said, he can be hotheaded and make clients leave."

"Meaning?"

"Take that angry guy just now. I have a feeling that Randall Construction might cut corners with permits and materials. That alone would make people angry. Maybe putting in low bids over competitors and using cheaper means."

"Maybe. I'll check out their license and permit records just to make sure," said McGaven as he increased speed and raced over the railroad tracks.

THIRTY-FIVE

Monday 1030 hours

Katie and McGaven hurried back to their office in the forensic division at the Pine Valley Sheriff's Department. Once inside the building, McGaven grabbed his computer and headed to the large room near the forensic examination area.

Katie shed her jacket and put her briefcase on her desk. She noticed a large packet of information and a rolled-up aerial map with a rubber band wound around it. There was a three-by-three-inch sticky note on top of the packet with a note: *This arrived by a personal courier from the Simms family. The aerial map is from the county archives. ~Denise*

"Yes! Thank you, Denise," said Katie. She grabbed her notes, the couriered packets, photographs, miscellaneous information, and her laptop and headed over to the larger room.

When she walked through the forensic examination room she found John, hovering over his scanning electron microscope. "Hi, don't mind me," she said.

"You don't have to say something every time you come through."

"Okay."

"Oh, wait. I received this text from Dr. Rimini," he said.

"Is he okay?"

"Oh yeah. He is staying with his brother and family. He's fine. But..." he said, scanning through his cell phone. "I had sent him a photo of that phalanx—the finger—that was found in the neighbor's yard on Maple Road."

"Oh," she said putting down her things. "What did he say?"

John started to laugh.

"What?"

"It's actually a proximal pedal phalanx from an American alligator, which can resemble human finger bones."

"An alligator finger?" Katie didn't see that one coming.

"I'm sorry for laughing, but I didn't examine it closely enough—it's not even bone, it's actually plaster or some form of either gypsum, lime, or cement. I don't think we need a breakdown."

"So you're saying that bone is actually from an alligator? And it's not really a bone but a replica?"

"That about covers it."

"What would that be doing in the ground and where would someone get that?" she said.

"Who knows? Maybe a kid bought it at a zoo gift shop?"

Katie grabbed her things. "Now that was something I didn't see coming. Please thank Dr. Rimini too."

"Will do," he said and continued his forensic examination.

Katie entered their temporary investigative headquarters. McGaven sat at the end of the table, working on the computer, pulling up reports from the county building and planning department.

"You'll never guess," she said, making more room for herself at the table.

"I love guessing games," he said sarcastically.

"John just told me that Dr. Rimini said that finger bone that

Cara Lewis found in her yard is actually... wait for it... a plaster alligator phalanx."

McGaven looked at his partner. "What?"

"That's what I said. An alligator finger."

"He's sure?"

"Yep."

"This case keeps getting weirder." He went back to his searches. "At least we can mark that off our list of evidence." Turning around again, "Where would that come from? A toy or souvenir?"

"It could have been used for teaching purposes and ended up in the ground, but it doesn't matter. Another dead end."

Katie opened the bundle and took the rolled-up maps first. Two were of the area near Maple Road, one from today and one from twenty-five years ago. There was also a clear map of the older version. "I love Denise," she said.

"Uh, I found her first."

"She is amazing."

"She is one of a kind—and she loves me. Figure that one out."

There was a small beige cabinet in the corner of the room—a half-size storage with two doors. Katie opened it and found a desk lamp among some other items of office supplies. She took a handful of color pens for the whiteboard, magnets, and the lamp.

After plugging in the lamp and placing it on the table, she rolled out the maps.

Both detectives bent over the table, scrutinizing the maps. Katie put the current one on top and studied it.

"Look, here's 717 Maple Road right here," she said and marked the property with a blue marker. She then indicated the basement and yard. "Okay now," she said. "Both maps are to scale but twenty-five years apart." She carefully laid the transparent map on top.

"Wow, that's interesting," said McGaven.

"That's the Snyder Subdivision before it existed. It was just a forest, like many other areas before the residential projects were built. Pine Valley and the surrounding areas have grown quite a bit as well."

"What are those notations?" he said, indicating some small square boxes.

"I think," she said, looking at the map legend with symbols, "it looks like electrical and maintenance areas. Plus, it appears there's some type of structure located near the ravine area."

"Looks like a house or cabin."

"Not sure."

"Is it still there?"

"I don't know. Something to check out."

"You think?" he said.

"Due diligence."

McGaven took a photo on his cell phone for reference.

Katie ran her finger to the nearest areas: school, church, and Sara Simms's house. She marked the girl's house location—and the area in between her house and school.

"Do you think she went where she said?" he asked.

"It was during the summer, so why would she be going to school?" Katie opened up the packet from the Simms family. There was a thin yearbook, papers, photos, and a journal.

"Looks like we have our work cut out for us."

"I'll go through this and mark things, but you should go through it as well. Two sets of eyes are better than one."

"Sounds good," he said and returned to his computer.

Katie looked at the board on which the maps were pinned up, notations marking where the bodies had been found. In addition, there were lists of victims and of persons of interest—and where they were located. She worked on the wall for about twenty minutes and realized that there was a story being uncovered.

"So everything started at the arson fire," she said. "Then it morphed into four bodies found—three recent and one from twenty-five years ago. I still think we're looking at these like separate departments, but it should be part of one big investigation."

"You think the same person killed all those victims? You said that yesterday. You still think so?"

"Don't forget Jimmy. And the attempt on Dr. Rimini," she said. "And the deputies and Hamilton, and the rogue car with me."

"That's a big what-if."

"Think about it. Who would bury an entire family in the same area next to another previous victim from twenty-five years ago?"

"For whoever killed the Cross family it was probably just the easiest thing to do. As for Sara Simms's remains... maybe the killer just happened to pick that spot?"

"Or, maybe they already knew about Sara's body being buried there." Katie updated the board. "This is what we have so far—for the entire investigation."

McGaven watched the list get longer.

Persons of Interest:

Travis Stone, real estate investor, landlord, hired an arsonist to burn down 717 Maple Road for insurance, murder victim

Simon Brady, butler

Stewart Fitzgerald, arsonist, left forensic evidence, killed TS

Seth Randall, Randall Construction, worked for Travis Stone on various properties

David Randall, Randall Construction, brother of Seth, manager

Stan Bates, Operations Manager, Thomas and Young, Architects, boss of William Cross

Tiffany Moore-Benedict, Serenity Spa manager, boss of Heather Cross

Cara Lewis, neighbor, neighborhood watcher, found finger/alligator plaster phalanx

Kent Simms, brother to Sara Simms, went to school with her, lived in area, moved to Oregon two years after Sara's disappearance

Victims:

William Cross

Heather Cross

Raven Cross

Sara Simms, 25-year-old cold case

Travis Stone, real estate entrepreneur

Simon Brady, butler to TS

Jimmy Turner

Katie read and reread the board. "This is insane." She sighed.

"You're just now realizing that?"

"No, really. Our murder list keeps growing." Katie tried not to let her frustration show, but her chest tightened and the four walls felt as if they were closing in slowly around her. "What is the killer trying to accomplish? How does everyone connect?"

"That's why they pay us the big bucks."

"These names and crime scenes keep circling around us, but—I hate to say it—the key to everything in these cases and incidents is Sara Simms."

"What makes you so sure?"

"It's the point where everything began..."

"Katie, I'm following your reasoning here, especially looking at our board. But you really think that the same person who killed Sara Simms killed the others? I know I sound like a broken record."

She nodded. "I know how it sounds. I'm not going to operate the investigation based solely on that one aspect, but we have to run every lead down."

"Okay, I'm with you one hundred percent," he said. "But..."

"What?"

"Where's your preliminary profile of the killer? I've been waiting for it."

"I know. I've been struggling with it."

"You?"

Katie studied the growing investigation board.

"The basement enclosure is a huge development, but I can't seem to put it into proper perspective."

"What's on your mind? I know you're wrestling with something."

"First, it's the timeline. Was the hidden room made specifically for the Cross family? If so, when? So I regressed back to everything I've read about killers. Maybe we're looking at this wrong." She stepped closer to the board in front of the pictures of where the graves had been excavated.

McGaven sat down and listened.

"I thought about what kind of killer, serial killer, would make torture chambers, or anything that would keep their victims captive. What caught my attention was killers who made their own homes into some type of torture chambers."

"Yikes."

"Think about it. We have killers like Jeffrey Dahmer, who lured young men into his apartment where he would rape, torture, and murder them by different means. His apartment was essentially the trap, or torture chamber. Then, what about John Gacy?"

McGaven made a sour expression. "What about him?"

"He would lure workers into his house by means of alcohol

and drugs, handcuff them, and then strangle them to death—hiding their bodies in crawl spaces. His house was a torture chamber. And there's unfortunately more, but what did they have in common?"

"Well, they were intelligent and skilled at what they did."

"Yes, but they felt comfortable killing in their own homes, in their neighborhoods, and they showed skill and were organized."

"And?"

"Everyone always says serial killers are crazy because of the despicable and heinous crimes they commit. They are not crazy, but they do have a disease of the mind. And that's what allows them to be cunning and fit into society with regular jobs and homes—but their downfall is their irresistible impulse to kill—whether it's for pleasure, a cause, revenge, or to somehow make a right where someone had done them wrong."

"Where does this come in with the Cross family and Sara Simms?"

"Someone killed young Sara Simms and I have a suspicion that it was the turning point, something that triggered their irresistible impulse."

"You mean the beginning of their killing spree? But why haven't we seen any more murders from this killer?"

"It's possible that there has been. Maybe one or more of our missing persons? Another county or state? But the strangulation seems to be up close and personal and could be a crime of passion."

There was a sound of an incoming email.

"Hey, here's something," he said, clicking icons on his screen. "It's from the campus police. They've already viewed the security video from the university around Dr. Rimini and here are the highlights from their perspective. How nice of them. What, we can't make that decision ourselves?"

"Go ahead and open those files and see what it shows," she

said, looking over McGaven's shoulder. It would give them a break if they could see anything identifiable from the man in black—she could barely breathe.

The first of five video files showed a tall, thin man entering through the exit, but his face was always facing away. Katie immediately recognized him as the same person she saw in the forest. The man in black approached the security guard who was on the phone and struck him with the butt of the gun.

The second and third videos show the same man go into Dr. Rimini's lab and this time the suppressor on the gun was visible. He walked around the lab area slowly, looking underneath tables, and in the office. Dr. Rimini must've hid when he saw him. The fourth and fifth snippets showed him running down the long hallway and exiting the building.

"We can't see his face or profile or anything except a thin guy in black who has a nine-millimeter gun."

"That was the caliber that killed Mr. Cross."

"We need the guy and his gun for comparison."

McGaven's cell phone rang. "Detective McGaven ... That would be great. See you then." He ended the call.

Katie waited.

"That was Kent Simms, Sara's brother. He wants to talk to us."

"When is he coming?"

"He's here in Pine Valley, staying at the Forest Inn."

"He's here?" Katie was surprised.

"He can talk to us at 2 p.m."

THIRTY-SIX

Monday 1355 hours

Katie drove to the Forest Inn, which was located on the edge of Pine Valley near a freeway. It was a lower-end motel, but clean and affordable for many wanting to visit the area. McGaven shuffled through the Sara Simms file, trying to find something that Kent Simms could answer for them. He quickly read a copy of his statement.

Katie's cell phone rang. She saw it was Chad and hit the speakerphone option.

"Hello."

"Hey, babe. Just wanted to say hello and that I was thinking of you," said Chad. "Sorry about this morning. We need to talk things through." His voice was tense.

"I was thinking of you too," said McGaven with a chuckle.

"Sorry, you're on speaker. We're on our way to interview someone."

"Hey, Gav. You better have my girl's back," said Chad.

"Always."

"I won't keep you. I'm off shift tomorrow 0800, but I still

have some paperwork from the arson investigation that will take another hour or so," said Chad.

"Okay," she said.

"And I'm going to my house after that to meet with an electrician to fix that weird light switch problem in the kitchen. I'll see you at your house later then?"

"See you then. Love you," she said. She knew it was crazy, the way they were going between two residences. The fact was that she didn't know how she would ever come round to selling her childhood home.

"Love you more." The connection ended.

"I like him. He's a keeper," said McGaven, still reading through material.

"I think so too," she said, smiling. The truth was, she missed him like crazy. They hadn't had much time to spend together lately and things had been a bit tension-filled, but as soon as this case was over she would make seeing Chad more her priority.

Katie watched the rearview mirror and every car around them—the ones she passed and the ones behind them. She didn't know what to expect if someone might try and run them off the road. Nothing seemed out of place. She didn't notice the same car in more than one area. Still, she gripped the steering wheel to keep her balance, not in a physical way, but mentally. It was as if she were a bystander watching a merry-go-round go by with all the evidence, victims, and locations just out of reach.

Katie took the off-ramp and then the frontage road leading to the motel. Even though it was close to the freeway and traffic, it was still a little slice of the beautiful Pine Valley forest.

She turned into the limited parking lot. The motel had only twelve rooms. It had been a small place thirty years ago and now it had been revamped for anyone wanting less busy and a more simple accommodation.

The one-story building was in the shape of an L, which

wrapped around to the back, where there were views not only of the wooded groves but also the rolling hills.

Katie parked the police sedan and turned off the engine. "Well, here we are."

"I've been here before," he said, looking around.

"Oh, really?" Katie said with some humor.

"Not like that. I was dispatched here for a domestic call."

"Oh."

"He's in room..." He looked at his notes. "Room twelve."

"Let's go."

The detectives stepped out of the car. It was automatic for Katie to give one good scan of her surroundings. She glanced at the cars already parked. It was still early and most probably hadn't checked in yet. The hum of traffic on the freeway was audible, but it was easily imagined that it was a running stream.

The motel was painted in a Southern California–style with colors of pink, turquoise, and white, which gave interest to an otherwise boring structure. There were plants framing the entrances to each room as well as the office. The walkway had been paved recently and new lights had been installed along the walk as well as across the motel's eaves.

Room 12 was all the way at the end with a small patio out front. A wrought-iron table with four chairs was surrounded by pots of colorful flowers. The view looked out over the valley and rolling hills behind.

A man sat at the table with his back to the walkway. His medium brown hair was short and his build lean. He wore a white shirt and jeans and looked to be in his late thirties. When he heard footsteps approach he stood up and turned around. He smiled and said, "Detectives?"

McGaven took lead on the interview. "Mr. Simms?"

"Yes, that's me. Please, call me Kent," he said. He appeared to be nervous. His hands moved up and down, and then he ran them down his thighs, as though he was trying to dry sweaty palms.

"I'm Detective McGaven and this is my partner Detective Scott."

The detectives each shook hands with Kent. Katie couldn't help but notice that his fingernails were stained with dark rust paint.

"Please have a seat," he said.

Katie took a look around. They seemed to have privacy. Room 11 next door didn't have anyone booked in yet. She looked through its window and saw that the maids had been there, beds made, but there was no luggage or personal items around.

Katie sat down, facing the way they came just in case someone did happen to show up. McGaven took the seat next to her where he could have a vantage of either direction.

McGaven began, "Thank you for seeing us—after I spoke with you on the phone I didn't think you wanted to talk more in person. On behalf of Pine Valley Sheriff's Department, you have our sincere condolences for the loss of your sister."

"Thank you. That means a lot to me and the family. When we received the news, and I think that I speak for all the family, our first feeling was surprise. After all this time, you found my little sister. We had given up hope quite some time ago and had had to live with that."

"I'm sorry to be the ones to bring everything up again, but we are working her case," said McGaven. "We want a few things clarified, if that's okay."

"Anything I can do, please ask."

"We wanted to get a sense of what she was like."

"Oh, well. She was a little sister and could be a pain, but she was my sister. She was smart and mostly got her way. You know, a twelve-year-old kid."

"What about the day that Sara went missing?"

Kent took a deep breath.

Katie couldn't help but notice that he had some scratches on the back of his left hand and wrist.

"It was summer and Sara was talking about some get-together or party. It was supposed to be at the lake."

"Pine Valley Lake?" said Katie.

"Yes. Sara said that there was going to be a lot of her friends there. I didn't pay much attention to what she was talking about since I was a year older and had different friends. Our parents were used to Sara always getting her way," he said, slightly clenching his jaw. "The last time I saw her was when she left out the front door and she never came home." He paused, trying to gain control of his emotions. "I'm sorry. I haven't talked about this in a very long time."

"Take your time," McGaven said.

"Uh, so my parents made some calls at first, thinking she was at a friend's house. Then as it got later, they went out looking for her. The usual places: the school, the mall, a hot dog place where many of the local kids hung out. But no one saw her. No one. How could that be possible? How could not one person in town, including her friends, have not seen her?"

"That's what we're trying to get to the bottom of..."

"Then my parents called the police and had to persuade them to open a report. And because my parents were known around town and had spoken with so many people, they started a search party. No one ever dreamed that Sara was dead or had been taken captive. No one."

"When your sister left that day, did she seem different? Angry? Upset? Acted in a way that seemed different to you?"

"No, not at all. I've relived that day thousands of times in my mind, thinking that there was some type of clue or comment that I missed. Something. Anything."

"You were only thirteen years old. You can't blame yourself for anything."

"How could I not? She was my sister." Kent's eyes welled with tears.

"Do you remember Mrs. Betty Anderson?" McGaven asked.

"Of course, she taught seventh grade. I had her when I was in seventh grade. She was Sara's teacher."

"We haven't spoken with her yet," he said.

"I... I'm not sure how much she would remember, and she's probably quite old now. But she might remember something. There's always a chance."

Katie thought that was a strange answer for someone who lost a loved one and discovered that the police had just found their remains twenty-five years later.

"Is there anyone you think we should talk to?"

"So much time has passed. I sent you everything my parents had. They've both since passed away, I'm sorry to say. I only have an aunt and two cousins left."

"Since you were a kid, can you remember anything like, say, the places the kids liked to hang out? Maybe it was secret from parents?"

He shook his head. "I don't know. I mean, we would play at some of the parks."

"Would it be around the area of Snyder Fields, which is now Snyder Subdivision?"

Kent thought about it. "Maybe. You mean like some sort of clubhouse?"

"Would Sara have any reason to be in that area?"

"I really don't know."

"That area is where we found her buried remains."

Kent looked away from McGaven's gaze and was silent for a few moments. "I'm sorry. I thought it would be easier now since so much time has passed."

"Just take your time."

"I'm really at a loss. Maybe the yearbook and her journal

might answer that?"

"We haven't been able to find anything yet. What do you do for a living?" asked McGaven.

"I restore classic cars. I have clients all along the West Coast area. I even have a specialized restoration garage here in Pine Valley—The Engine Block."

"How long have you been working on cars?"

"Most of my life, it seems, but I opened this business about ten years ago."

"Thank you for your time. Have a safe trip back."

Katie and McGaven walked back on the smooth new walkway to the parking lot. She glanced back to see Kent still sitting at the table with his back to them. He seemed to be at ease, like he had been here before.

When the detectives reached the car, McGaven said, "I'll drive."

Katie said, "Wait a minute. I'll be right back." She hurried to the motel office.

Only gone for five minutes, she returned.

"What was that about?" he said.

They got back into the car, McGaven turned over the engine and began backing out the parking place.

"Well, I had a hunch that Kent Simms had been here before. Especially with his specialty garage," she said.

"And?"

"He has."

"Okay."

"You don't understand. He's been here quite a bit, especially in the last three months."

"That's during the time of the Cross family deaths and everything else that has been going on."

"Yep."

"What would his motive be for killing his sister?"

"Who knows? He was a kid. Maybe it was revenge? Maybe

it was an accident?"

"But that doesn't mean he killed the Cross family," he said.

"No, but we still need to look at everything."

McGaven thought about it. "He did seem a bit uneasy with some of the questions. But why would he make this trip if he initially didn't want to talk about it?"

"Maybe he wanted to know what we knew and how close we were getting to finding the killer?"

THIRTY-SEVEN

Monday 1515 hours

"Where are we going?" said Katie, looking around. "Are we going back to Maple Road?" She preferred to drive, but she knew that having a partner meant that there were times of give and take. And this was one of those times.

"No, well, in a way," said McGaven.

"So now we're speaking in puzzles?" She smiled and watched the passing landscape race by the passenger window.

"Just be patient."

"Sorry. Not one of my strengths."

"In this business, you better learn fast," he said.

McGaven turned down what looked like a driveway or service road that had been covered with medium-sized gravel to keep the dirt from washing away. He slowed his speed as the tall weeds and overgrown tree branches grazed the sides of the sedan. The gravel crunched under the tires, causing some slippage. Then the narrow road, more like a wildly overrun path, slowly began to descend. More of the forest slapped the windshield, allowing little visibility.

"What in the world?" said Katie as she braced herself for impact. She leaned back in her seat holding firm to the door handle as the vehicle began to bob and weave.

"It looked better on GPS and the internet." He downshifted the automatic transmission to a lower gear. Immediately the car groaned and slowed their travel. They rode it out for another twenty-five feet or more. Once at the bottom, the forest and overgrown undergrowth seemed to open up as a way of greeting them.

Katie gritted her teeth and waited for more jolting, but the path was strangely smooth now.

McGaven put the car back into the regular automatic gear as they inched forward. He found a place good enough to stop and turned off the engine.

The car protested as the hot engine made a distinct high-pitch *ticking* sound.

"Is the car dead?" said Katie.

"I think it just needs a break."

She turned to her partner. "Where are we?"

"You know that place on the map with all those little square symbols in the legend?"

"We're at it now?"

He laughed. "C'mon, let's go take a look around." He had to force the driver's door open in order to escape the car.

Katie wasn't amused, but she trusted her partner. There was something about being in a dense area where the enemy could attack from all sides that made her anxious. She felt her pulse elevate. A few flashbacks pushed their way into her mind.

McGaven had already got out of the car and was carefully scouting the nearby areas. "C'mon," he said and waved her out of the car.

Katie slowed her breathing. There was no way someone could have known they would be here or followed them down this road without either one of them seeing. She opened her door and stepped out. Some of the weeds were almost waist high—at least for her.

Joining her partner, Katie looked around and was surprised as she began to see the landscape of what was once here. The tree line was beautiful, growing in clusters and accenting the acreage. Even though there were high weeds, it had clearly once been an open area perfect for a structure or building.

"This is the backside to the Snyder Subdivision."

"Really?" Katie looked around. Her direction bearings must have been off because she felt that she was more south, away from the town.

It was a clear day with a vivid blue sky. No clouds. Cool, comfortable air.

Katie closed her eyes for a moment, grounding herself, which enabled her to focus—things around her actually became more vivid and detailed, making it easier for her to scout whatever they were searching for. The birds in the distance were the only sound she heard. Wait. No wind. But there was a faint sound of water. She knew that McGaven kept perfectly still as she went through this practice when she was in a new place or entering a crime scene. This was definitely a place she had never been before, but it had a strangely familiar feeling.

"I take it no one has been here in a while," she said.

"Doesn't look like it."

Looking around, Katie could almost see the layout of what it must've been like in another time. "Was this the area where the small cabin or little building was?"

"I thought so, but it's probably long gone."

"I don't know. There have been quite a few old cabins and building structures pre-1900s that are still around Sequoia County—mostly up in the higher elevations. Some only have foundations but others still have sections of walls."

"True, but I think I almost blew up the engine for nothing."

"Since we're here, let's follow the sound of water."

Katie and McGaven slowly worked their way toward the sound. It was difficult pushing weeds away and stepping through them. Even though they were in a deserted unknown place, Katie didn't feel there was any danger. It was a bit creepy but the sun was out and they had each other's backs if something went wrong.

At the edge to the land where they couldn't go any farther was a cliff and below was the rushing creek.

McGaven moved around and tripped over something but regained his balance. "What the...?"

"Wait—stop." Katie leaned down to look closer. There were large roundish stones about eight to ten inches in diameter in a rectangle shape that seemed to be a foundation. "Look at this," she said, brushing dirt to the side.

"It does look like an old foundation. What is this?"

"I don't know. It's close to a creek. Maybe it's an old fishing cabin?" She scanned the area.

McGaven traced the shape. "I'd estimate it to be about fifteen by fifteen feet."

He trampled down some brush.

"Hey, there's part of a wall over here," he said.

Katie followed where McGaven had walked to see what he was talking about. There was a partial wall with the same types of rock—part of it was about three feet high and parts were closer to six feet.

Katie walked around the foundation again. Her thought was it would've made a great place for kids to hang out. "How far is it from Maple Road?" she asked.

"As the crow flies?"

"Yeah."

"Less than half a mile. This is the area that backs on to the subdivision. Who knows why they didn't keep building more streets with houses. Maybe its not stable here for construction, or maybe it was supposed to be left vacant."

"Interesting. From the map, this area is between Sara Simms's home and school. According to her brother, he said she was going to a get-together at the lake. But the lake is the opposite direction and would be a long walk."

"I've skimmed the reports," he said. "Kent was extremely active in the search for his sister. He set up groups of friends to help—amazing at that age. Some of the other statements said that he wasn't close with his sister. And, I never read anything about Sara going to the lake mentioned."

"That's troubling."

"He seemed almost indifferent when he recalled that day when she left."

Katie thought so too. "He said she was always used to getting her way. And..." she remembered, "that they never dreamed she was dead or taken captive."

"All the people we've talked to about their murdered or missing loved ones, people usually say kidnapped, but not taken captive," he said.

"I agree."

"We need to look further into Kent Simms."

Their search was interrupted by McGaven's phone ringing. "Wow, there's actually reception out here. Detective McGaven ... Yes, thank you for calling me back." He paused. "Oh, no, I didn't know. I'm so sorry to hear that. Thank you for the call." He slowly hung up and slipped the phone back into his pocket.

Katie knew that it wasn't good news.

"That was Tricia Anderson, Betty Anderson's daughter."

"Sara's seventh-grade teacher?"

He nodded. "She said her mom was attacked in a home invasion three days ago and she's now in a coma."

THIRTY-EIGHT

Monday 1715 hours

Katie was relieved that McGaven suggested they leave the department at the normal time, which would give her time to read over reports at her house. They were still officially on first responder lockdown, so it was just as well they were in a comfortable place. They were able to convince John to caravan back with them. They all had reports to write and being in a home environment made it more restful. They also all needed a good night's sleep. There were too many things that had happened in less than a week, which took a toll on the mental stress levels of all of them.

As McGaven drove his truck back to the house, he asked Katie, "So how's your Jeep doing?"

"They said they can fix it, but it would be expensive. They suggested that they total it and I could get a new one." She sighed.

"Well, that's okay, right?"

"I keep losing Jeeps, almost every year."

"Oh, that's right." McGaven kept watching the rearview mirror.

"Anything I should know about?" Katie caught him double checking all the mirrors just as she did earlier in the day.

"No, just making sure we're all safe. John's the only one tailing us."

"Oh," she said, not to him, but to the white SUV already parked in her driveway.

"The boss."

McGaven drove into Katie's driveway followed by John and they both parked.

Katie quickly grabbed her jacket, box, and briefcase and got out of McGaven's truck. She headed to the front door just as it opened and Cisco blasted out to see everyone, running in circles around them. Her uncle stood in the doorway.

"Good to see all of you are obeying orders and traveling together," said Sheriff Scott, eyeing each of them with a serious expression.

"Everything okay?" she said and entered.

"Depends on what you think is okay."

Katie dropped off her stuff on the end of the couch. She didn't like what her uncle had to say.

McGaven and John came inside and shut the door.

"Sir," said McGaven and nodded his greeting.

"Nice to see you, Sheriff," said John.

Cisco ran around the room trying to get someone to play with him.

"Detective Hamilton hasn't found any substantial leads?" she said.

"Afraid not. He's not you."

"That's for sure," chimed in McGaven as he helped himself to a beer.

"That's not fair."

"He's doing everything he can on the homicides and I've

called in Alvarez for extra help." The sheriff looked more tired than normal and his voice sounded weak.

"You sure you're okay?"

"Just tired." He changed the subject. "You and McGaven seem to be covering a lot of ground."

John walked up to them. "I wanted to let you know," he said to everyone, "that the preliminary DNA testing came back positive on the wood barricade at the house. It's a match for Mr. and Mrs. Cross. I'll have more information for you tomorrow."

"Thank you, John. I know you had to pull some strings to get those results so quickly," said Katie. "No DNA of the daughter?"

"Afraid not."

"Good to know. Thanks, John. And good work to all of you for going back to investigate that barrier. Even though you weren't supposed to leave the house on Sunday."

"I'm sorry. I did include it in our daily reports," she said.

"I'll overlook it this time due to the extreme circumstances we're facing, but you need to remember I take *all* of the safety orders seriously," the sheriff said.

"So that confirms our suspicion though—that the Crosses were held for a short period of time before their murders."

"That's great to know, but we're not any closer to finding the killer."

McGaven handed Katie a beer. "Not true—we're slowly putting together their last hours or days in a timeline. It's all important."

The sheriff walked to the front door ready to leave. "Well, I came over to check on Cisco, but I can see he's in good hands now."

"Won't you stay for dinner?"

"No thank you. I think my lieutenant is cooking up some pasta dish. I didn't know that he was such a chef—I'm going to have to diet after all this is over with." He opened the door. "Oh,

I took the liberty to order some pizzas for you. Have a good evening."

Katie went to her uncle. "Thank you for thinking about Cisco and for ordering pizzas for us." She gave him a kiss on the cheek. "When are we going to get back to our lunch dates again?"

"Soon. I promise." He took a moment to smile at her. "Night, all." He quietly shut the door and Katie made sure everything was secure after he had left.

"I'm starving. Can't wait for that pizza," said McGaven.

Katie still thought about her uncle. He didn't seem like his usual self. These cases and recent murder of Jimmy had everyone on edge.

After devouring the pizza and working on another beer, Katie made herself comfortable on the couch with Cisco curled up at her side. She began to carefully read through the information that Kent Simms passed on to them.

McGaven joined Katie with files and his laptop, sitting down in an overstuffed chair. Drinking another beer, he began to sort through lists.

"Where's John?" said Katie.

"He's crashed out. I think he's exhausted."

"I know the feeling."

"What are you working on?" he asked.

Katie flipped through photos of Sara and family. "Just photos and newspaper clippings about Sara's disappearance."

There were numerous newspaper articles from the time of the disappearance. As time went on the stories became shorter. There were obituaries of the parents. The mother, Mrs. Simms, died from complications of a stroke five years after Sara disappeared, and Mr. Simms was killed in a car accident almost ten years after Sara's disappearance. There was a photo of a heavyset young man with a notation on the back that said Mick. A newspaper clipping referred to Mick Simms as the cousin of the missing girl, Sara Simms. The article said that he died three days after a bar fight where he was shot—the date was almost five years after Sara's disappearance. "Take a look at these," she said, handing the packet over to McGaven.

Reading, he said, "Interesting, but nothing stands out."

"Except that family had more than their fair share of tragedies." She petted Cisco and pulled a blanket over her lap. "And I've been reading through Sara's journal."

"And?"

"Well, it reads like a typical twelve-year-old girl's life. What girl liked who, what boy was cute, clothes, but..."

"But what?"

"I've read the statements from friends and family and it seems that they paint a very different picture of her. She seemed to be such a sweet girl, but there was also a dark side to her. Maybe it was what attracted the killer to her?"

"I got that feeling, the way her brother talked about her. It was like he was reading a script when he was describing her. It seemed that he was being careful what he said."

"Maybe he didn't want to speak ill of her now that she's gone?"

"It's possible. But he seemed a bit shifty to me."

"Okay, here's an example." Katie flipped to an entry two weeks before she disappeared. "She says, 'Everyone knows A. is such a loser, and he will get what he deserves.'"

"Wow. Harsh."

"You have to take it from the source, but there are other entries that talk about A. and 'he' should just leave, or go away, and he doesn't matter."

"Who do you think she's referring to? Her brother? Someone at school?"

"It's difficult to tell. I've read through everything she's

written in here and the only identification has been A. I'm skimming through again to see if I've missed something."

"It might be a name, not a given name, but a nasty name she's calling the person and didn't want to spell it out," he said.

Katie leaned back to think about it some more.

"Katie, there's too much information and too many crime scenes. I know I say this a lot."

"I still believe that Sara Simms is the key to unlocking all of this—all the cases."

"Whoever killed Sara would be twenty-five years older now and they've been on a crime spree to cover up the original murder. Wouldn't they be too old?"

"Not if Sara's killer was a kid."

"It would have to be someone who grew up here and would have the opportunity to come back and clean up anyone working on the case." He thought a moment. "That would only leave a few people who would be late thirties."

"Like," she said, "Kent Simms or someone he knew in school." She pulled out the small yearbook and began thumbing through the pages.

"You find the killer?"

"Very funny. No, there's been some kind of water damage and half of the pages are unreadable."

"Let me see that," he said. Katie handed him the yearbook. He smelled the cover and then the pages.

"What are you doing?"

"It doesn't smell like mold or mildew, something that would cause this damage. It should stink. You know, like something that got wet in a garage or basement." He carefully turned the pages and tried to unstick them.

"You're right. You think it was damaged on purpose?"

"What was done on purpose?" said John as he entered the living room looking like he just woke up. He scratched his scalp.

"We didn't wake you, did we?" said Katie.

"No, I just needed to crash out for an hour."

"Here's the forensic guy we need. Smell this?" said McGaven as he stretched out his arm with the book in hand.

"What?"

"Tell us if you smell anything on this yearbook."

John hesitated but then took the yearbook from McGaven.

Katie and McGaven watched with interest.

John looked at the cover and the back and gave it a sniff. Then he opened the book and judiciously examined the pages stuck together. He smelled them. "Okay."

"Well?" said McGaven. "Was the water damage caused from storage or was it done on purpose?"

"I'm my opinion, but I wouldn't swear to it in court. This damage has no odor. It has been damaged recently." He handed the yearbook back to McGaven.

"Yeah, see. Is there something Kent Simms doesn't want us to see?"

"Maybe," she said.

"I'm going to get some fresh air," said John as he headed to the sliding doors.

"Take Cisco with you," she said.

At the sound of his name, the black German shepherd bolted to the door.

"Is that for protection or just because the dog needs to relieve himself?"

"Both." She laughed.

McGaven began looking at the yearbook again. "I wonder if there's a way to enhance these pages? Maybe if I scan them into a computer and then use different light sources?" He began reading some of the student signatures that were visible in the front and back. "Wow."

"What?"

"There are some nasty things written in here on the inside cover." He began to read: "'You think you're better than us' and

'Do us a favor and die' and 'You're not going to make it to the eighth grade.'"

"Let me see that," she said and looked inside where students sign and make the usual comment of "have a nice summer" and "see you next year." "Did you notice that it's written by the same person? Different slants but look how the word 'us' is formed."

McGaven moved to the couch and sat down next to Katie. "You're right. I'm not a handwriting expert, but it looks like they tried to change the writing to make it look like it's from different people, but it's not."

"Do you think this person made good on their threats?" Katie frowned. "Great, now the entire student body is under suspicion."

"Consider where we got this. You know he read his sister's diary, so if there was anything in it she wrote about him, it would be gone."

"Okay, let's look at this another way," she said, adjusting her pillow behind her back. "If the person who killed Sara Simms was someone she went to school with and then grew up here, why would they also kill the Cross family years later?"

"Maybe they found Sara's body?"

"Possibly. But who would have contact with both the Crosses and the property?"

"Besides Travis Stone?" he asked. "Randall Construction."

"Wait a minute," said Katie as she popped up the lid of the box, thumbing through household invoices from the Cross family. "I didn't realize this when we were talking to Kent until he said the name of his business. What was that? The Engine Block?"

"Yeah, I think so."

"Here," she said, holding up an invoice.

"The Cross family used services by The Engine Block?"

"Yes, from a year and half ago," she said, reading it. "It was for a carburetor rebuild on a 1966 Mustang."

"Nice ride."

"It states something about rebuilding the carburetor for premixing vaporized fuel and air in proper proportions supplying the mixture to an internal combustion engine—sixteen hundred dollars."

"Ouch. That seems high."

"You know what this means? That connects Kent Simms to Mr. Cross."

"Coincidence?"

"We need to find out."

THIRTY-NINE

Monday 2355 hours

Katie fell asleep as soon as her head hit the pillow. So many theories had echoed through her mind, she had thought she might have some trouble quieting her thoughts and drifting into sleep. That didn't happen. The only sound was the old antique clock that hung on the wall in the living room—it gave an almost melancholy tick-tock that helped to calm and lull into slumber. The entire house was quiet and everyone slept.

Cisco took his place in the corner stuffed chair in Katie's bedroom. He tucked his tail, curled up his long body and fell fast asleep.

Katie's dreams were uneventful and thankfully not about killers and crime scenes. She drifted into a deep sleep and her heart rate, temperature, and blood pressure dipped. Her body was healing itself both mentally and physically.

A noise jolted her awake.

Cisco emitted a low growl.

Katie sat up now, wide awake. She turned to look at her bedroom window.

Outside the window a dark shadow moved along the back of the house. The shape was reminiscent of the lean man dressed in black.

Her first thought was that either McGaven or John was taking a security round or maybe they heard something and were searching. She swung her legs out of bed, put her feet to the floor. Quickly pulling on a pair of sweats and sneakers, she retrieved her gun from the nightstand.

Cisco was wide awake and on the bed.

"No, Cisco. *Bleib,*" she said, to make him stay. He grumbled and sat down obediently.

Katie went to her bedroom door, listening for a moment. It was silent. She quickly opened the door and peered out, looking up and down the hallway. The two other bedroom doors were closed. Slipping out, she closed her door behind her. Still quiet in the house. She waited for a moment for anything that was out of the ordinary. It didn't come.

Keeping all lights off, she decided to go to the security laptop that had all the cameras loaded from outdoors. Still with her Glock in her right hand down at her side, she moved cautiously. At the end of the kitchen bar counter, the laptop sat open.

She stepped up to it and saw that on the east side of her property was a figure, which looked like a tall thin man. She couldn't see his face, but knew by the man's build and movement, it wasn't McGaven or John.

A door opened down the hallway.

Katie waited and saw McGaven coming towards her. For a tall guy, he could move stealthily. Once he was closer, she whispered, "You heard it too?"

"Yeah," he said quietly. He had his shoes on with sweats and T-shirt. His Glock was in his right hand as well.

"Look," she said and gestured to the screen.

"Who is that?"

Katie shook her head.

"It looks like he's scoping out the property."

"He's staying away from the house so that the cameras won't capture his face. So he knows where the cameras are and he's probably been here before," said Katie grimly.

"But what's he doing? Did he follow us?"

"Not hard to find someone these days."

Katie stepped back, thinking.

"What do you want to do?"

"Find out who it is and why they are on private property. If we call this in, they'll be gone before the first patrol gets here. We're cops, let's go."

"I thought you'd never ask," he said.

Katie grabbed a sweatshirt that was lying on the couch and quickly put it on. She disengaged the security to the house so that they could enter the backyard without setting off the alarm.

"Do you want to deploy Cisco?"

"No, we don't know what we're getting into. I don't want to take the chance of him getting shot. The last time we saw a man dressed in black he had a nine millimeter with a suppressor." She double checked her weapon, securing the magazine once again. "I think stealth is better and on our side."

"I agree. Let's go, partner."

Katie steadied her nerves, grabbed a flashlight, and quietly opened the sliding door. It made a quiet *whoosh* that didn't sound like a door or window. It was like a breeze that just blew by.

Katie stepped outside. It was colder than she had thought and she was glad she had put the sweatshirt over her thin pajama top.

They heard a strange thumping racket coming from the east side of the property. It almost sounded like someone pounding a nail into wood.

Katie kept her back against the side of her house and slowly moved along. There was no bright shining moon, only dim lighting cascading strange shadows around and through the trees. Glancing back, she saw McGaven hang back slightly and keeping watch behind them.

Katie kept her focus. At that exact moment, a gusty wind kicked up and then settled back down. It blew in her face and ruffled her hair, but she kept a vigilant watch up ahead. She knew that there was an old gate at the end of the property. It wasn't used anymore, but she had been meaning to have it taken out and secured. She knew that was how the intruder had entered and that the video security didn't reach that distance. It could only record if someone came into view near the house.

At the corner of the farmhouse, Katie inched her way to the edge so she could quickly peek around the corner. She scanned the area—it was clear. Everything appeared like it should be. The landscape was rural with trees, bushes, and various California annuals. She hedged back and turned to McGaven who was steadily approaching. She nodded and slowly moved forward, wanting to see the area next to her bedroom window.

There were fresh footprints of a work boot, approximately size ten. She would have John take impressions just in case there was ever a boot to compare it. She turned back to McGaven and whispered, "Boot print."

He nodded and then motioned toward the back fence line.

Katie agreed. He must've heard the hammering noise earlier.

They split apart by eight feet and covertly moved forward.

At this point, Katie turned on the flashlight. The beam lit up most of the bushes and trees revealing that there wasn't anyone hiding, but the partners still moved with caution.

They continued to check the entire area until they reached the small, outdated gate covered in dried vines and weeds.

Katie stepped closer and could see that the gate wasn't

closed. The single gate latch, old and flimsy, had been opened recently and wasn't closed properly.

She turned the light to a fence post a few feet to the right. Sticking into the wood was a hunting knife.

"I take it that doesn't belong here," said McGaven.

"Look closer," she said and directed the beam so that he could see it.

"What the...?"

"It's a warning."

The large hunting knife with a deadly serrated edge had impaled a business card, attaching it securely to the fence. It wasn't just any business card—it belonged to Detective Katie Scott.

FORTY

Katie rode with McGaven to work. John had already left for the forensic lab a half hour before them. He wanted to get the shoe impression evidence from Katie's yard along with the knife and Katie's business card back to the lab for examination as soon as possible.

Katie didn't want to hear anyone ask her again if she was okay. When she first saw the blade that had pinned her business card on the fence in her own yard, she was taken aback. Fear had run through her body. But after she had thought about it more, she became angry. This killer, one who seemed to have killed for more than two decades and who was now going after the people trying to solve the case, had made her more determined than ever to find.

"I can't believe we don't have any surveillance evidence showing who this guy is," said McGaven as he turned into the Pine Valley Sheriff's Department and parked in the usual employee area.

"Yeah well, the killer better enjoy his time free because if I have anything to say about it—his day is coming." Katie unhooked her seat belt, grabbed her things, and got out of McGaven's truck.

McGaven didn't respond. He followed his partner into the building and into the forensic lab.

It never ceased to amaze Katie when she entered the forensic division that being there always actually calmed her. It was a phenomenon that she couldn't explain. She hadn't slept well under the circumstances, but she still had enough energy to face the day, and more. Missing Chad was an understatement; she would be relieved and fortunate to have him home tonight.

She turned the corner and passed the forensic examination room.

"Hey," said John from the doorway. "Good morning. I've got fresh coffee and some information for you."

"Sounds great. Let me put my things down and I'll be right there." Katie walked to the cold-case office and unlocked the door.

"Ooh, coffee," said McGaven, going straight to John's office to pour himself a fresh cup.

Katie hung up her jacket and put her briefcase down on the desk. She took a moment, looking at the wall showing where the murder sites were located. Thinking of that knife spearing her card to the post on her property got under her skin—it was as if to say "you'll never catch me, no matter how hard you try." "We'll just see about that," she said under her breath.

Katie grabbed her notebook and walked to the forensic examination room, where McGaven and John were joking around. It made her feel good to see them getting along. They had been through so much—they *all* had been through too much.

"Hi," she said, trying to keep her emotions even.

"You ready to get started?" said John.

"You bet. What do you have?"

"First, I want to reiterate that the DNA on the wood enclosure in the basement definitely matched William and Heather Cross."

Katie appreciated that, but she needed more.

"Next," he said, "I've combed through the children's clothing that was buried in the yard and there were some fibers and DNA. There were two pairs of jeans, one sweater, two T-shirts, one pair of socks, one pair of underwear, and the backpack." John went to one of the workstations and keyed up some forensic graphs. "Raven Cross's DNA was found on all of the clothes and they appear to be the appropriate size for an eight-year-old girl."

Katie's hopes were falling by the second.

"But, there was a stray hair found on the sweater. It didn't match the victims, so I ran preliminary tests. It belongs to a Caucasian male."

Both detectives watched the screen as the test results came up.

"I know this isn't what you want to hear, and that you need more information," said John.

"It's still confirming who we're looking for and that we're on the right track," said McGaven, keeping an upbeat attitude.

John looked at Katie. Her demeanor showed how disappointed she was. "The friendship bracelet from Sara Simms is interesting, but I don't know if it will help with the investigation." He turned to another screen, where a photograph had been magnified twenty times. "Usually friendship bracelets are made of thread or material woven into a braid or another type of macramé design, but this one was made with thin silver and colored wires. It seemed strange because that wouldn't be comfortable on your wrist." He showed different views of the bracelet. Normally, this type of silver wire is used in jewelry-making, between eighteen- and twenty-two-gauge thickness."

"Sara Simms had her hyoid bone broken, suggesting she was strangled," said Katie. "Could it be possible that she was strangled with this type of jewelry wire?"

"That's a great assumption, but unfortunately, without any skin or muscle, it's impossible to tell if that theory is relevant. This type of jewelry wire can be found at any craft store."

"Of course."

"I'm sorry, but to go back to Raven Cross, was there anything found in the pockets of the clothing?" said McGaven.

"No, just the usual pieces of fuzz and material fray."

Katie read over her evidence notes regarding the buried clothes at the arson house. "Anything with the keychain?"

"Yes."

"Really?" she said.

"I found trace amounts of toluene and methylene chloride on the key chain and the key."

"What is that?" said Katie.

"It's a paint thinner," said McGaven.

"Close. It's a brush and tool cleaner. And it's quite toxic." He clicked on a few computer icons. "I did some digging and this particular combination is found in one specific product called BANE and it's used for cleaning synthetic-bristle brushes, artist brushes, roller covers, trays, and equipment after a project. It removes hardened latex and oil-based paint, enamel, varnish, shellac, lacquer, and polyurethane."

"What's the significance of this BANE?" said Katie.

"Well for one, it's toxic and deadly to adults, children, animals, and the environment. It can cause autoimmune disease, cancer, and even death. Nasty stuff. It must be used with caution and with the appropriate gloves, et cetera."

"Why isn't it off the market?" said McGaven.

"There have been numerous lawsuits filed and they usually settle to the complainant."

"Who would use this type of cleaner? Painters? Artists? Mechanics?"

"Just to name a few," he said.

Katie thought about it. "It seems that many of these things could be used in construction."

"And automotive," said McGaven.

"Absolutely. The more I read about it—people who have a tendency to use this type of cleaner use it for everything."

"And this compound was on a little girl's keychain? Would it transfer from, say, someone's hands onto the key ring?"

"No, because it's very caustic to bare skin. It would have to have been on something like clothing or a pair of gloves."

"Was there any trace of it on the clothes?"

"No, nothing like that."

"What about the backpack?"

"No, that was clean as well. The backpack was too clean."

"What do you mean?" said Katie.

"You know, kids carry backpacks around, set them on the ground, spill stuff on them, things like that. But this backpack was squeaky clean, which would be impossible even if it was just purchased from a store. There still would be some type of residue of something."

John watched the detectives as they processed this information, waiting for more questions.

"Thank you, John. I'm sure that you found more evidence in Detective Hamilton's cases." Katie realized that she had brought up Jimmy's case in a roundabout way. She tried to backpedal. "I'm sorry, I shouldn't be talking about other people's cases."

John stood up. "No, it's okay."

"John. I'm so sorry. I've been fixated on our cases but that was truly insensitive."

"It's okay—really. Just so you know, we have found viable evidence but haven't found any matches in AFIS yet. Until we have a suspect to compare prints and blood to—we'll just have to wait."

Katie felt bad she had sounded so flippant about the other cases. She was venting her own frustrations. "I think that's all for now. Thank you, John."

"My pleasure. Oh, and let me know when we all have to caravan home."

The detectives went into the large room where there were more maps and photos of persons of interest on the wall than there ever had been before.

"It's always interesting when we talk to John about our cases," said McGaven, taking a seat and opening his laptop.

Katie didn't answer right away. She looked at the photos of every victim—directly in the eyes. "So the trace evidence belonging to a toxic cleaner could come from Kent Simms or even Randall Construction, right?"

"Yes. I did a background on Kent Simms and his record is clean—nothing unusual. I also did a few other backgrounds, including Seth and David Randall, they're also clean. And yes, I know that doesn't mean anything. It just means that if they committed a crime or two they haven't been caught yet."

"And there could be other people who have used the cleaner," she said.

"Even the neighbor, Cara Lewis."

"For?"

"Her backyard was tidy, and did you see those pavers around the flowerbeds—pristine. Maybe she used that cleaner to make it look so nice?"

"Let's look at the thirteen properties that Travis Stone owns —until his will is read I assume they are still accessible—and the project list from Randall Construction for Stone," she said.

McGaven pulled out the paperwork and Katie scooted her

chair next to him. "Stone has thirteen properties: three houses on Maple Road, eight other houses around Pine Valley, and two commercial properties." He studied the project list. "It looks like Randall Construction worked on seven of the properties and 717 Maple Road would have been number eight."

Katie looked at the estimates, budgets, and billing records. "Nothing seems unusual. The billing records are very detailed and most of the projects came in on budget—two were over by five percent." She looked over the commercial properties. "Wow."

"What?"

"Did you know he bought the old lumber mill up on Sierra Skyline?"

"I didn't know that was still around. Didn't they demolish that?" he said.

"I don't know if they've demolished it, but that mill was closed down by the state. Why would Travis Stone want that property?"

"Maybe a write-off? Investment for development?"

"Maybe. It sure wouldn't be a good area to build condos."

"What's the other commercial property?"

"Looks like a storage facility. No, actually, it's a public storage."

"That's right, I remember that."

"What's the deal with it?" she said.

"Some developer built public storage facilities all around California, but he never finished this one. It was something to do with endangered wildlife on the property. I'm not sure what happened, but building just stopped. Everything was frozen."

"It must've not been in litigation when he bought it. What's the year he purchased it?"

McGaven shuffled through several sheets of paper. "Looks like a year ago."

"Was Randall Construction going to work on the job?"

"Doesn't look like it. But there's some initials: R.C.—Randall Construction? There are no permits requested or pulled for that the job."

Katie looked at the huge investigation board that was now filling two walls in the room. Then she took a red marker and began making a list on the whiteboard.

Preliminary Killer Profile:

Organized: the Cross family were methodically murdered and buried with little or no evidence. It appears to have been thought out. The level of decomposition makes it difficult to obtain clues, which the killer counted on. Shows organization and planning. Knowledge of police forensics and evidence?

Strategic (killer patterns): intelligent, thinks he's smarter than police, obsessive-compulsive—the murders were considered. Killer taunts the police (killing and harassing people connected to Cross crime scene), has no issue confronting police, showing arrogance and boldness. Knows firearms (Dr. Rimini, road rage with Katie, Katie's business card).

Killer's skill: might own a business. Independent, potential to excel, supervisor, some college, some life of normalcy, married/divorced, bold, high-minded, supervisor position.

Reactionary: mission oriented, power control (killing entire family, made holding area, buried with another murder), making situations work his way.

Trauma/defining moment in childhood? Could contribute to retaliatory, taunting police, escalating and adapting to situations by using different means of murder: shooting, knife, strangulation. Accomplice?

Signature: heavy level of force for killing his victims with shooting, strangulation, and stabbing. More force than necessary to obtain results.

Katie stepped back, rereading her list.

"This paperwork inspired all that?" he said.

"No. All the crime scenes motivated it. The victims. The killer. Coming after us and letting us know he can get to us anytime. You, me, the patrol working the arson site, John, and who knows who else is on the killer's list." Katie's tone was flat. It concerned her that everyone at the arson scene might be a risk. "I think we've reached the point to become proactive now. This killer is escalating and still coming after us... He was issuing a strong warning with my card on the fence in my yard. I've handed out cards to everyone we've interviewed."

"Yes, I agree, but to what extent?" he asked.

"We can't just sit back and wait for another murder—we just can't."

"Katie, I know that incident last night has you rattled, but we can..."

"Can what?"

"Well, what do you suggest?"

"Since Seth Randall is on our radar, let's shadow him and see what shakes out. And I want to check out Kent Simms's activity as well."

McGaven nodded. "Okay, that sounds good."

"We need a different car."

"I'll see what I can rustle up."

FORTY-ONE

TWENTY-FIVE YEARS AGO

Snyder Fields, Pine Valley
Summer

The low-hanging branches of the forest encroached onto the trail and sounds crashed behind Sara Simms as she made her way down the path. The sunlight peeked through the trees and gave fast flickers of brightness as she hurried.

In her mind, the sounds became louder and louder behind her. She ran. Falling twice, she managed to get to her feet again, readjusted her backpack, and ran faster. Her mind played tricks. Every darkened corner and tree trunk seemed to have someone hiding. Waiting.

Sara finally came to a clearing and, by her handwritten map, she was close. It brightened her spirit and she felt silly thinking that there was something or someone in the forest that was coming after her.

Looking at the trail, she saw there was a well-worn path leading to where she was going.

"Finally," she said, a bit winded.

Sara let down her guard and continued onward. As she

walked, she tried to hear if there were voices because that would mean she was close to the party. There was nothing. Only the sounds in the forest.

Her skin prickled with a rush of heat and she felt as if someone was behind her. She stopped and turned suddenly, almost colliding into him.

"What are you doing here?" she said, annoyed.

There was no answer.

"Well?" She grew frustrated.

He stared at her.

"Fine," she said and went to walk around him.

Sara was grabbed and thrown down. Her head flopped backward, striking the ground. The pain was excruciating and caused her to become dazed. She looked upward and only saw the forest canopy above her. Sleep entered her mind as she closed her eyes.

Sara was jerked to her feet and her arms were pinned behind her as she felt the restriction against her throat, pressing hard against her windpipe, making it impossible to speak. She tried to gasp. Opening her eyes, she stared at her attacker. His eyes were fixed on her like a predatory animal. There was only hatred staring back. Slowly the sounds faded and the forest view dulled, turning to complete darkness. But her attacker remained in her memory. Sara Simms could still hear a faint pulse in her head, which finally surrendered to silence. Everything went dark.

FORTY-TWO

Tuesday 1145 hours

Katie waited next to McGaven's truck in the police parking lot for him to return with a car. She could feel her anxiety rise the more she thought about this killer taunting police and killing anyone associated with working the crime scene at Maple Road.

Katie sent a text message for Chad.

Love you. Hope you've had a great day. Stay safe. See you tonight.

She thought it was strange that he hadn't called or text-messaged back to her—maybe he was still upset with her about their conversation about selling her house. He did say that he was meeting an electrician so he was probably busy with that. She would try him later.

Glancing at her watch, she saw it wasn't quite noon yet. She still felt time moving forward at warp speed. Time was running out.

Taking deep controlled breaths, Katie braced for the next

wave of potential symptoms of panic. She didn't wait long. Her mouth went dry. Her chest felt heavy, making it difficult to breathe in a normal relaxed manner. She tried to focus her vision on her surroundings, but a weird dizziness attacked her perception, making things look skewed. But she wasn't going to let anxiety win or a panic attack worm its way into her concentration on this case. Her body buzzed with a strange energy. She focused intently on being in the moment.

Suddenly a white four-door car pulled up and the window rolled down, "Hop in," said McGaven.

Katie picked up a duffel bag and got into the small sedan. "This is perfect. White cars blend in."

"Thought you'd like it," he said and smiled. "What's in the bag?"

"Just some stuff I thought we might need. Binoculars, digital camera, extra magazines, and some clothes."

"Hmm," he said. "No lunch, by chance?"

"Nope."

"Pity."

"Whose car is this?"

"No one's."

"It has to belong to someone. There's a license plate."

"Well, it did belong to someone, but it was confiscated because of them being a drug dealer."

"With this car?" she said.

"Why not? Oh, you think all drug dealers drive BMWs and Mercedes."

"Well?"

"Misconceptions... and like us, they didn't want to be recognized."

"Okay," she said. "Then the luxury cars are in the garage."

"Let's get some coffee and sandwiches."

"Deal."

. . .

Katie drank one and half cups of coffee and felt better, even though the caffeine raised her pulse. She ate half a sandwich, just enough to keep her stomach from growling. She was more interested in seeing what Seth Randall was up to in his day.

McGaven had studied his local maps and decided on a route that led to an elevated view of Randall Construction. He drove up the back road and then stopped at an acreage that was for sale, driving on the land to its edge. The main viewing point peered down on the industrial area and so they had an optimum view of Randall Construction's yard.

Katie kept quiet and went over the packet of information about Sara Simms in her mind as well as the interview with her brother Kent.

"You okay?" said McGaven.

Katie flashed him an annoyed look.

"You know me, I'm a worrier, but you seemed really stressed back at the office."

Katie couldn't be indifferent to McGaven, given their experiences together since they had been partnered. "You know when we first met?"

He laughed. "I thought it was the worst assignment and I was being punished."

"I thought I was being punished."

"When the sheriff said that I had to watch you, I thought my career was over because I was considered a babysitter and not a cop. I knew you were his niece too. I took quite a bit of grief from the other deputies... But you set me straight and now I'm a detective."

"The sheriff knew what he was doing and I wouldn't have had it any other way."

"Ditto," he said. "So if I ask if you're okay... I mean *are* you okay?"

"I'm fine."

McGaven peered through his binoculars and scanned the area. "They have a lot of stuff in their yard."

Katie joined him and scrutinized the area. She agreed the yard was filled with equipment. "Really a lot of stuff." She saw Seth drive up in his large black truck, pulling a trailer. "What's he doing?"

"Maybe a new job?"

"Maybe."

There was an unidentified man driving one of the front loaders to the trailer. They watched until four pieces of equipment were loaded and chained down. Then Seth filled the back of his truck with lumber.

"You're probably right. They are starting a new job." She continued to scrutinize his movements. He had a stiff gait and when he turned to his employee it appeared that he was yelling at him, arms in the air. He was almost to the point of pushing the man over. "Seems Seth has an anger problem."

"Maybe he's just passionate about his work?"

"Oh yeah, and misunderstood."

"Hey, wait a minute," he said. "Check out the last of the lumber."

Seth and his employee had moved a large piece of wood resembling the same wood that had enclosed the place in the Maple Road basement.

"I see it," she said. "But that could be standard—any construction company would have these pieces of wood."

"That size doesn't seem to be standard off the shelf."

"Still."

Katie moved her binoculars to the building and saw Seth's brother come out with a small, zippered satchel. He got into his black SUV and left.

"What do you think? Should we follow the brother? Seth doesn't seem to be doing anything criminal."

"Let's see where—what's his name, David, that's right—where he goes."

McGaven turned on the engine and drove out of the property, heading down to the main road in hopes of catching the black vehicle.

"That was a nice piece of land back there," she said.

"Maybe a place where you and Chad could build your dream house?"

"Build our own house? Great idea, but kind of expensive. We would have to sell both our houses and then live in motels."

"No way, you could rent a cabin or something," he said. "That would be cool and Cisco would love it."

"First, don't ever say the word 'cool' again," she chuckled. "You sound like an aging surfer."

"And how cool is that? You promised me that you would teach me how to surf."

"Yes, but we need to go to the coast."

McGaven watched his mirrors and the road—back and forth. They were able to intercept David's SUV seamlessly on the main road and get into position to follow him without being detected.

The black SUV drove barely over the speed limit and finally turned into the parking lot of a bank. McGaven followed and then parked with a view of David as he entered the bank.

"Must be checks to deposit," said McGaven.

Katie sported the binoculars again to try and see more detail of David. They didn't have to wait long until he reappeared. This time, he was on his cell phone, and it looked like he was having an argument. He walked out of the bank but stayed on the sidewalk and turned to his right.

"He's really mad," said McGaven.

"Try to watch his lips to see what he's saying."

It was clear that he was angry, saying things like "You're going to do what I say" and "That's not good enough."

Katie said in a low tone, "It's not good enough... no way... no... that's not the way... something..."

"He could be arguing about a bid or a bill. Anger seems to run in that family," he said.

Eventually David Randall got off the call and back in his car. McGaven and Katie continued to follow him as he stopped at various locations. He was obviously running errands for the next couple of hours. He went to the dry cleaners, a sandwich shop, and a real estate office to drop off paperwork.

"Well, we can't get back those couple of hours," said McGaven.

"Don't look at it that way. We've witnessed his attitude problems and anger. That's something. What were we expecting to see? We need to keep Randall Construction on our radar, that's all."

"And we need to find out what Kent Simms is up to as well."

"Absolutely."

"And," McGaven said, "I did background checks on the Crosses' places of employment and Stan Bates of Thomas and Young has a few skeletons in his closet. Sorry, bad use of words. But he has been in trouble for harassing another employee at his previous employment and he was once arrested for disorderly conduct at a bar."

"Interesting," she said.

"Just doing our due diligence. Someone really *cool* told me that once."

FORTY-THREE

Tuesday 1545 hours

Katie drove past The Engine Block, located on Locust Lane. It was an area that led to a rural part of the county. Older homes had been mostly turned into businesses, but there were still a few houses that remained residential. Each property was situated on more than an acre, which made it enticing for anyone who wanted some space just outside of town.

"I think that's it," said Katie, reading the sign and address numbers.

"Yep. There's no official sign, just a banner along the top of the building," said McGaven. "I can see high-end cars in the garage area. Looks like there's one with a cover on it."

His phone rang. "Detective McGaven." He listened. "Yes, thank you so much for calling back. Can you hold for a moment? Thanks." He put the call on hold.

"What's up?"

"Pull up here and park for a moment," he said.

Katie parked in the driveway of a closed business. She turned to her partner.

"Thomas Rhodes is on the phone with his girlfriend Sadie Myers. They were the tenants before the Cross family."

"Excellent. Put him on speaker."

McGaven picked up the line again. "Mr. Rhodes, I'm here with my partner, Detective Scott. I'm going to put you on speaker. Is that okay? Great." He pressed the speaker button. "You there, Mr. Rhodes?"

"Yes, I'm here."

"We appreciate the callback. We won't keep you long, but we just wanted to know what your experience was renting the house on 717 Maple Road from Mr. Travis Stone."

Katie and McGaven heard a big sigh.

"Well," Rhodes began, "it started out okay. Sadie and I were excited to live there, but Mr. Stone kept pressuring us with questions. They weren't just regular questions but possible scenario questions."

"Like?"

"For instance, we were thinking about getting a dog and at first he said that was fine and said he was going to ask for a five-hundred-dollar deposit. But then... then he said we would have to get rid of the dog if the blinds ever got fur on them or if the dog vomited on the rug."

"I see."

"Thinking back, we probably shouldn't have rented the place, but... he kept getting more aggressive. That's the only word that I can think of to describe it. He badgered us about rent before it was due. Showed up at Sadie's office unannounced. Stuff like that."

Katie listened intently, realizing that Stone seemed to stick to the same script with his tenants.

"Did he ever threaten you or assault you?"

"After we gave notice, he became more threatening, but never laid a hand on either one of us. He said stuff like we were never going to get another rental and we didn't deserve to live in a house."

"What happened after you gave notice?"

"He ranted at us every other day. But it was weird, in the end he gave us back all of our deposit. We had pretty much figured that money was gone."

"Was any construction or repairs done on the house when you were there?"

"Before we moved in, Mr. Stone told us that the stairs to the basement were being repaired. But the thing is... when we had walked through the house before we decided to rent it, the stairs had seemed fine."

Katie remembered that when she walked down them, they were stable underneath her feet, as if they had been constructed recently.

"Did Mr. Stone say anything more about them?" said McGaven.

"Just that he would have someone come over and check them out."

"Did someone come by?"

"A guy."

"Randall Construction Company?"

"No, I don't think he was a contractor. He seemed odd."

"Odd how?"

"I don't know. He just didn't act like someone in the trade. Didn't seem to know basic things. He went out in the yard for part of the time."

"What did he look like?"

"Dark hair, baseball cap, tall, thin. I'm sorry but it was a while ago."

"Did you ever see Mr. Stone's assistant?"

"Yeah, kinda creepy. No, that wasn't the guy who came by to check out the stairs."

"If I send you some photos would you take a look?" said McGaven.

"Sure."

"We're at a location right now. I'll send you them when we get back to the office."

"No problem, Detective."

"Thank you for taking the time."

The phone call ended.

Katie looked at her partner. "That was interesting. More questions than answers, I'm afraid, but I think a picture is beginning to form."

"One thing's for sure."

"What's that?"

"Travis Stone was one weird, obsessive-compulsive guy."

"You forgot arrogant and creepy."

"No, actually I didn't. I just thought those were enough adjectives for now."

"But the real question is: was he a killer? Or did he hire a killer?" she said. The detectives were silent for a moment. "Let's go see what Kent Simms is up to and what his business is all about."

Katie and McGaven decided to leave the car parked where it was and walk to the classic car restoration garage. It was several businesses away from The Engine Block.

Katie hung back a bit and studied the area. It wasn't what she had expected. When Kent Simms said he restored classic cars and had clients all over the state and up the West Coast, she had thought he would have an upscale garage.

The road was in desperate need of grading and repaving. It was part gravel and what had been a blacktop street. Now it was full of chuckholes and was severely uneven—caused by a gradual washout from rain and settling of the road.

One of the businesses was an upholstery shop—it looked to

be a family business. Katie could see a "Closed" sign, but inside, she saw rolled-up fabric on large tubes and bags of foam.

The next building was empty. There was a "For Sale" sign in the window, Meadows Real Estate, and a faded local phone number. The windows and doors were intact, but the front yard was sadly overgrown and looked as if it had been abandoned.

Katie considered her initial thought: that Kent Simms's business wasn't as successful as he wanted people to believe. She thought that maybe it had been a shrewd business plan and he had managed to negotiate a great deal on a building in this area. It was quiet and out of town. Maybe that was the way he had planned it.

As Katie and McGaven neared The Engine Block, Katie's thoughts about a smart business lease soon dwindled. The building was old, several torn screens were lying on the ground beneath the windows, and the white paint was peeling, showing remnants of a darker color underneath.

The sound of voices arguing and becoming heated could be heard.

McGaven looked at Katie. "Do we wait or intervene?"

Katie sighed. "Let's go see what's going on."

The detectives hurried to the open garage, where Kent Simms and another man were arguing. Kent had a crowbar in his hand. The calm demeanor he had at the meeting with them was replaced with a very angry man.

"Hey, hey," said McGaven as he entered the garage first. "What's the problem here?"

Katie joined her partner. "Kent, put down the crowbar now."

Kent seemed confused when he saw the detectives. "What? How'd you get here?"

"Put down the crowbar," she repeated again.

"Of course, Detectives," he said, gritting his teeth. He

slowly turned and put the crowbar on the workbench and raised his hands.

"About time, psycho," said the unknown man.

"Shut up," said Kent.

"What's going on?" said McGaven as he moved closer.

"Well, he's ripping me off, that's what's going on."

"What's your name?" said Katie to the other man.

"Mike, Mike Patterson."

"Okay, Mr. Patterson, tell us what happened."

"He gave me an estimate for my 1972 Mercury Cougar to rebuild the top part of the engine. And it's exceeded the estimate. I call that BS."

The sleek black vehicle was in the middle of the garage with the hood up.

Katie turned to Kent. "Is that what happened?"

"Look, an estimate is just that—an estimate. Parts were more than expected by about twenty percent, so that's reflected in the bottom line. But I explained this to him before I ordered the parts. Everything was fine until it was time to pay the bill."

McGaven looked at Mike. "Is this true?"

"Well, I guess."

"Can you work this out?" she said.

"Well, I can give him a discount on the interior work," said Kent.

"Is this something you're willing to work with?"

Mike looked down and seemed to contemplate the new arrangement. "I guess. As long as he keeps to his word."

Kent nodded.

"Okay."

"We're good?" said Kent.

"We're good," said Mike as he left the garage.

"I'm sorry that you both had to witness that, but things have been... up and down in the business." Kent absently straightened some tools and rags on the work area.

Katie looked around briefly and took a mental inventory, not sure of what she was looking for—if anything. Then in the far corner she saw it—a dark amber glass bottle with the name BANE on the label. She blinked twice, remembering what John had to say about it—traces were found on the keychain belonging to Raven Cross. She wondered how many people used the product.

"We just wanted to stop by and see if you could remember anything else that was going on in Sara's life before she disappeared," said McGaven. He seemed to be aware that Katie was looking around the garage.

"She did mention a bully once," said Kent.

Katie watched him, finding it interesting that he hadn't mentioned this before.

"What happened?"

"Not sure, but she was complaining about some bully calling her names in front of her friends."

"How long before she disappeared?"

"Maybe a month or so. I'm not sure," he said.

"Do you remember a name? A first name? Maybe a nickname?"

Kent paused as if he was trying to remember. To Katie it appeared to be a tactic for effect. "No, I don't know. It was so long ago—being kids and all."

"Okay. The more information we know about the time before she disappeared the better," said McGaven.

"I'll think about it."

Katie watched Kent become agitated again. He paced and kept picking up the same wrench and setting it back down again.

"Everything okay?" said Katie.

"Sure. Just trying to keep the budget together on these jobs —one of my guys quit last week. You know how it goes…"

McGaven glanced at the car. "Nice ride," he said, referring to the 1972 Cougar.

"Yeah, it is."

Katie looked at her partner.

"Call us if you think of anything."

He nodded.

"We are working on your sister's case and we take these types of cases very seriously."

"I... we appreciate that."

McGaven and Katie left the garage and returned to their car.

Katie drove back down the road and left the area. "What do you think?"

"What I thought about Kent Simms when we met with him first is completely different to what I think of him now."

"I saw a large glass bottle of BANE in the corner of the garage. It could just mean that he cleans tools and equipment with it or it could..."

"Or, it could mean that he's connected to the Cross family deaths."

"Or at least 717 Maple Road."

FORTY-FOUR

Tuesday 1730 hours

Katie drove the white sedan back to the empty lot above Randall Construction that they had visited previously. She cut the engine. She contemplated her decision for a moment, but still had the sense that they needed to be more proactive in the murder cases.

"Well? Are you going to tell me what's going on?" said McGaven.

"Have you ever heard of finders keepers, losers weepers?"

He laughed. "Of course."

"Well, I want to search Randall Construction."

"You do realize that we don't have a warrant."

"I thought we'd go old-school."

"Meaning?"

"You can learn quite a bit about people from their... trash."

McGaven lit up and smiled. "I see where my partner is going with this."

"You in?"

"Did you happen to check the pickup days?"

"Yep, it's tomorrow morning. It should be full of stuff."

The detectives got out of the car and opened the trunk. They grabbed gloves and an empty garbage bag.

McGaven stood at the top of the hillside looking down. "It looks like their vehicles are gone and since it's after five—the receptionist is also gone."

Kate joined him now, wearing a sweatshirt instead of her nice jacket. "See that back alley? That's where the trash dumpster is located. So... technically that's not their property."

"Wouldn't it be easier to drive up?" he said.

"Yes. But we don't need to draw attention."

Katie led the way.

Since there wasn't a path or roadway, they had to carefully scale the hillside until they reached the alley. The dirt was loose and made it slippery as they descended. The weeds and tree roots helped to slow them down.

Katie struggled a little and was relieved when she reached the bottom.

McGaven didn't have any trouble following his partner down. "That was fun," he said.

"All part of the job."

Katie looked around and made sure that there wasn't anyone around who might ask questions or report back to Seth Randall.

There were two dumpsters. One was specifically for leftover items from construction jobs, such as lumber, cut pieces of granite from bathrooms and kitchens, and drywall portions. This trash container was allotted a maximum weight of eight thousand to twelve thousand pounds. They didn't need to search it.

The other one was for basic trash from the building and yard. It was dark brown and was twenty-two feet long, eight feet wide, and six feet tall. There were two lids. Katie flipped up both of them and was ready to jump inside.

"Wait," said McGaven.

Katie stopped and looked at him. "You are just going to jump in there?" He seemed concerned.

"How else are we going to find out what's in the trash?"

"Well, I didn't think you were going to get in."

"Uh, I'm not the only one. It will go faster if we both search."

McGaven stared at his partner.

"Don't tell me I've found what Detective Sean McGaven fears the most."

"Well no, but..."

Katie laughed as she pulled on her gloves. "Give me a boost."

McGaven helped her up to the top and she easily swung her leg over and jumped down inside the dumpster. "You coming?"

McGaven wasn't pleased but he followed his partner and climbed in. He covered his nose. "It stinks in here."

"What did you expect?" It was true; it smelled like old garbage that had been in the sun for weeks.

"What are we looking for?"

"Anything that might provide us with more information about Seth Randall. Notes, bills, printouts of emails. Anything."

McGaven pulled out a coffee cup from a local coffee house. "There's a lot of these. I better not find a human finger or ear in here."

Katie kept her head down and began to systematically open garbage bags and search the contents. There were typical things like lunch throwaways, shredded paperwork, and broken dishes. She continued to search until she found a small wastebasket plastic bag, which had notes from a yellow steno pad and other various office paperwork. "Bingo."

"Found something?" he said, frowning.

"Some paperwork that hadn't been shredded yet. There are

handwritten notes, names, and places. Also some pink phone message sheets." She put the entire plastic bag into the empty bag she brought.

"What are you expecting to find?"

"I don't know, but we need to find out if they had ties to Travis Stone's house or the Cross family. Anything that might prove to be useful."

The detectives spent another fifteen minutes searching but found nothing of worth to the investigation.

After Katie and McGaven climbed back out, they looked around to make sure no one had been watching. It was all clear and no one had come back to the construction site yet.

Katie walked toward the construction yard and looked through the chain-link fence. She walked along the property line, systematically scanning the area, not sure what she was looking for.

"See anything?" said McGaven joining her.

"I don't know, there's so much stuff back here. I'm assuming it's supplies from previous jobs. Maybe waiting to be taken to the dump?"

"Looks like typical construction stuff."

Katie came across an opening at the back corner fencing that appeared to be loose and wide enough to squeeze through.

"No, you can't do that. We aren't authorized to enter the property without permission."

"We have permission. We were here the other day."

"You know what I mean."

"I just want to look in the back shed. I can see the lock is dangling and the storage is open."

"No."

Katie kept looking around the area. She needed to make sure that there wasn't anything suspicious or incriminating. "Give me two minutes." She squeezed through the fencing and was out of sight before McGaven could object again.

Once inside Katie checked for video cameras up high but saw none in her immediate area, so she went directly to the medium-sized metal building where the lock hadn't been engaged. Still with her gloves on, she quietly removed the lock and opened the door and went inside.

Katie didn't want to turn on the light, so she retrieved her cell phone and used the flashlight mode. She swept the light back and forth, but there was nothing of interest, just the usual construction supplies. She looked for any type of wood that would resemble the piece taken from the basement at 717 Maple Road, but there was nothing.

Walking to the right near a worktable, she saw all types of saws, electric screwdrivers and hammers, vises, hand tools, pipe fittings, joists, boxes of screws and nails, and many types of miscellaneous tools.

She was about to turn around and leave when she saw several buckets and containers. Directing the light on the bottles, she saw a familiar name—BANE—with several warnings. With her phone, she took a photo of the industrial cleaning product.

Looking down at the floor, she saw faint boot prints in the sawdust. Her instinct kicked in and she took several photos of the impression with a dollar bill as scale.

Without wasting any more time, Katie left the building, leaving it the way she found it. She made her way back outside and the detectives climbed back up the hillside to the car.

"You have to stop doing that," he said, hoisting the full garbage bag from the dumpster.

"What?"

"You know what. You can't just run off or jump into an area that's off limits. Even if you find something, it would be thrown out in court—because the proper channels haven't been taken."

"Gav," she said trying to catch her breath, "I know that. But it still gives us the potential right direction or helps prove our instincts are right."

She showed him her phone where there was a photo of the BANE bottle.

"Good to know. I thought that this cleaning solution wasn't used very often."

"That's what John said, but now we have two people of interest with a nice big bottle—Kent Simms and Seth Randall."

FORTY-FIVE

Tuesday 1845 hours

Once back at the office, Katie stood in front of the wall looking at the investigation from beginning to end. She was growing tired and knew that they needed to go home, but something was nagging at her. She read the names of all the victims, persons of interest, and those giving statements. Kent Simms, Seth Randall, David Randall, Dr. Sal Rimini, Stan Bates, Tiffany Moore-Benedict, Cara Lewis, and Travis Stone all grew up in the Pine Valley area, still lived here, and were around before the Snyder Subdivision was built.

Was this connection between these people important?

How could all these people be connected to the arson house in some way and have these three things in common with one another?

Katie stared at the photos of the Cross family posted on their investigative wall. The smiling faces and closeness of the family even came through in photos and it tugged at her heart. The short videos weren't far from her thoughts. She knew personally what it was like when she had been about Raven's age, being with her mom and dad. She loved those memories and they'd become a part of who she was today. The senseless murder of the Cross family pushed her hard to get to the truth. One of the people on the case board was the killer. She didn't just know it—she felt it.

Katie picked up the phone and dialed John.

"Hey, I was just on my way out," he said.

"We're going to be leaving soon. But, I wanted to ask you if you found anything in the dirt that Jimmy sifted from the arson site." When she mentioned Jimmy's name it made her wince.

"No. Just some recent coins, a quarter and two pennies, and an old beer bottle."

"Oh, okay. Thank you for checking. Oh, one more question. You know that cleaner, BANE?"

"Of course."

"About how many bottles are sold every year—here in Sequoia County?"

"Let me do some checking and I'll text it back to you, okay?"

"Thanks, John, appreciate it."

"See you later at your house."

"Bye," she said and ended the call. Her hopes were slightly dashed. She had still hoped there might have been something in the dirt from the Crosses or from the killer.

Katie dialed Chad's cell phone and it went directly to voicemail. She hesitated but then hung up. He would know that she had called a couple of times and would return her call when he was available.

McGaven was searching databases and checking emails. "Check this out. I was cross-referencing the list from Travis Stone on rentals and houses. Guess who owns a house on Maple Road just down the street from the arson house?"

That piqued Katie's interest after her disappointment over the sifted dirt, and she joined her partner. "Who?"

"Stan Bates from Thomas and Young."

"Mr. Cross's boss? Does he live there?"

"I'm not sure. With this information, it doesn't say if he resides there himself or has a tenant."

"Wait a minute." Katie went back to the table and began looking down the list of projects from Randall Construction. "What's the address?"

"729 Maple Road."

"That was one of Randall Construction's jobs—from about two years ago. Looks like they had a kitchen renovation with new cabinets and granite countertops."

"That's interesting."

"Maybe, maybe not. It could just be an innocent situation, like Stan Bates saw the construction trucks at a neighbor's house and then called them."

"You mean he had a neighbor who was also one of his employees who ended up murdered—and he happened to use the same contractor that was used on their house?"

Katie sat down. "I have to say that this is one of the most frustrating cases."

"Two cases."

"Exactly." She moved paperwork around on the table. "I'm going to go through these again."

"Maybe we should come back early tomorrow morning with fresher eyes? Not to mention, I need a shower to get the smell of dumpster off me."

"My mind is still active and I want to go through these again."

"What are you looking for?"

"Not quite sure, but seeing if anything coincides with the same addresses or Travis Stone's properties."

"Need help?"

"No, keep doing what you're doing, searching through the names and properties. Could you run anything on Stone's properties?"

"You got it." McGaven went back to work searching through police and county databases, cross-indexing with lists they had acquired.

Katie organized notes and receipts from Randall Construction's dumpster and discarded everything else garbage-related back in the trash bag. She found innocuous things, which included appointments, estimates of costs and labor, rental companies for construction equipment, and receipts from suppliers. There were also invoices from lumber, miscellaneous items, drywall, doors, windows, tile, and flooring companies.

Katie went through the suppliers again looking at the addresses notated on the receipts. They seemed to be legitimate invoices from local suppliers for authentic construction jobs in the area. The copies were faint and were obviously either triplicate or quadruplicate pages, which had been thrown in the trash. They obviously didn't need more paperwork and most likely entered everything into the computer with one copy of the invoices.

Pulling three invoices from the pile and smoothing the paper flat, Katie stared at the job site listed and the amounts at the bottom of the page. Two different companies were recorded; one was a rental company, Jack's Rental, which was located near the freeway, and the other was ACE Construction Supplies and Equipment located farther out of town.

The invoices seemed out of place for the types of jobs Randall Construction worked. They had rented a large water truck a week ago and it was open-ended, indicating they still had it in their possession. Where? It was the kind of truck that carried between two thousand and four thousand gallons of water.

"What's up?" said McGaven. "You look like you're wrestling with something."

"There are two invoices from Randall Construction that seem out of place."

"Like?"

"Well, renting a water truck, for one. Why would you need that? Swimming pool?"

"It's possible. Or maybe a well. But I think they're typically used in places that don't have access to a large amount of water all at one time."

Katie clicked in a few search words on her laptop. "It says that the average swimming pool holds between eighteen and twenty thousand gallons of water."

"That would take several truckloads."

"I haven't seen any jobs listed with a swimming pool or including one," she said.

"What's the other invoice?"

"Well, you saw all the equipment they had on their property—some really big stuff. So why would they rent a large excavator if they already have one?"

"Again, there could be many reasons why. Maybe the one they have wasn't working? Or, they didn't want the wear and tear on their own equipment?"

"True. But something bothers me. There's no evidence, just a hunch. A hunch for what—I don't know." She leaned back, rubbing her forehead. "Can you cross-check these addresses and names with what we have?" She gave him the invoices.

"No problem." He began pecking away at the keyboard.

Katie couldn't keep her eyes from the Cross family—their faces, their eyes, and how they related to one another. They had been a happy family with a bright future ahead of them.

She then turned her attention to Sara Simms—her bright smile and blonde curls were unforgettable. Both cases were connected by a killer—she knew it—but the problem was finding him.

Looking at the forensic and autopsy reports as well as the crime scenes made her reconsider the signature behaviors of the killer at the crime scenes, as well as "disease of the mind" and "irresistible impulse." The weight of the investigations weighed heavily on her conscience.

"Okay," said McGaven, interrupting her rundown of the investigation. "I've cross-referenced with the persons of interest, properties, Randall Construction, and the victims."

"Anything?"

"Nothing."

Katie sighed.

"That's where we are at right now. C'mon, let's get some rest. Tomorrow we'll pick up right where we left off."

Staring at the wall with everything they had learned so far, Katie said, "You're right." Her mind still rehashed everything over and over and she probably wouldn't get much sleep that night.

FORTY-SIX

Tuesday 1945 hours

McGaven drove out of the police department parking lot with Katie. They were still under orders from the sheriff to stay together until further notice. John was already at Katie's house and was checking the security system before dark.

"Hey, babe, it's me again. Haven't heard from you. Give me a call," she said and hung up.

"What's going on?" McGaven asked.

Katie was getting upset. It wasn't like Chad to not call her back. "I don't know. The firehouse said Chad left this morning to meet up with the electrician to fix a problem in the kitchen, but I haven't heard from all day and now it's after 7 p.m."

"Let's go by his house."

"I think that's a good idea," said Katie. "Thank you."

"Of course. What's the address?"

"It's a small cottage at 1188 Spreckles Lane."

McGaven programed the address into his truck's GPS. "Got it. Don't worry, maybe he lost his phone or something."

Katie tried to force a smile. "I hope that's it."

McGaven made it to Chad's house in less than fifteen minutes. "Cool little place," he said as they pulled up the cobblestone driveway and parked behind Chad's big Jeep. "See, there's his car."

Katie jumped out of the truck and rushed to the front entrance. She stopped short of the entry. There was a piece of paper taped to the door with a quick note from Antonio's Electrical. It said: *Stopped by but you weren't home. Call if you still need the job done.*

McGaven walked up behind her. "What's wrong?"

"There's a note from the electrician," she said then turned the doorknob and pushed the door open. "Chad? You here?" She looked down at her hand and saw it was covered in blood. "No, NO!"

McGaven stayed close and scanned the interior. "Wait. Katie, wait!"

It was too late. Katie had run into the kitchen to find it had been smashed up, kitchen cabinets were broken and hanging from their hinges, dishes were scattered on the floor, and there were blood streaks across the counter. "NO! Chad!"

Katie ran and looked in the two bedrooms and bathroom, but Chad wasn't there. She made her way back to the front door. Her legs were weak and she began to hyperventilate, not able to get enough breath into her lungs. "No, not Chad," she whispered.

McGaven came to her aid. His face was ashen. "Take a breath, slowly. Okay."

Katie's eyes welled up with tears. "They killed him..." She couldn't believe her ears when she spoke those words. Her fear was working overtime.

"No," he said. "Listen to me, Katie. Listen. He's not here, that's a good sign."

"What?"

"Think about it. Jimmy was killed inside his house and left

there. But Chad isn't here. Looks like he fought like hell but for some reason someone took him."

"Who? And where? We shouldn't have separated." She leaned against the doorway to steady herself, fighting the urge to faint. Her heart sank. She couldn't imagine living without Chad.

"Let's figure it out. I'll call the sheriff, okay?" He stepped into the small living room and made the call.

Katie began pacing the room as she heard McGaven talking with her uncle; her partner's words were muffled as she fought hard to figure out where Chad could be. Her mind raced almost out of control. With every step, her anger rose. She recalled the investigations. The people. The statements. The crime scenes. The forensic evidence. She kept berating herself.

Where?

Who?

How could she have not seen the potential for this?

She stopped and stared at a photo of her and Chad when they went camping last year. It made her think... where would be the best place to hold someone against their will? Somewhere remote and quiet. It had to be connected with their investigation—connected to the arson house. She had never thought that the killer would go after Chad just because he had investigated the arson—not the murders.

"Katie," said McGaven, who had kept calm but was deeply worried. "Your uncle is putting together a task force."

"For what? We don't know *who* or *where*."

"He's getting backup ready and a task force for anything and..."

Katie went to the kitchen and opened one of the drawers where the spare keys were kept. She grabbed the one for the Jeep and ran out the door.

"Katie! Where are you going?"

"I'm not sure, but I can't just sit around and wait for the call... the call... that he's..."

"Katie," said McGaven. He held his partner. "Take a breath. We don't know anything yet. We can figure this out, okay?" He let her go but held on to her arms.

"I..."

"We can figure this out, okay?" he said again.

She nodded, holding back the flood of tears that wanted to surge. Knowing that she had to be strong and focused, she caught her emotions before she let them take over and wouldn't be able to make them stop. "Don't you see? The killer is hunting us. Chad was taken because he was connected to the arson investigation and it's also as a way to get back at me. Think about it. Why would the killer leave my card stabbed on my fence? He could come after me anytime, but he didn't. He could have killed me on that road, but he didn't. He's taunting us. He's looking for a way to get rid of all of us and then, in his mind, this case goes cold. He doesn't have to worry anymore."

"Katie, please just take a moment here and think about this."

"We don't know when he was taken and I'm not going to waste any more time."

"When was the electrician supposed to be here?" he said.

"I don't know, I think about eleven this morning. And that's my point, too much time has passed."

"I don't think that you're in a good place right now. Let's wait for the sheriff and re-evaluate."

Shaking her head, Katie said, "No. I'm not going to wait. We do know that the killer kept the Cross family detained before they were killed in the basement. It was no more than a day or so, so that means that Chad's time is running out. Or it may already be..." Katie couldn't finish.

"Katie, you're not alone. We can find him together. Chad is

a smart and very capable guy; he's going to do whatever he has to."

"Did you not see the kitchen? He fought like hell and they still took him." Katie struggled to keep back the tears but it was now impossible.

"We will find him," said McGaven.

"You don't understand."

"What?"

"The last time we were together we fought about me selling the farmhouse. I had reservations, but he thought we needed a fresh start for when we get married. But... now it doesn't matter and it's not important."

McGaven hugged his partner as she shuddered and cried, letting out her frustration and sadness—not only about finding Chad—but for the Cross family and Sara Simms.

After a couple of minutes Katie composed herself. "I'm sorry."

"You never had to apologize for this."

"I'm going back to the house," she said.

"Okay, I'll drive you."

"No. I'm taking Chad's Jeep."

"Why?"

"Mine is in the shop and we don't know where this will take us. I think that it's possible Chad is still being held, for whatever reason in the killer's mind, somewhere rural. I know that in my gut."

"Where?"

"I don't know, but if we believe that Seth Randall or Kent Simms could be the killer, then it would be somewhere remote. We have to look at properties and areas where they might take Chad. It has to be in our information on the cases—there's no other explanation."

"We don't know for sure."

"I know, but it's the only thing we have."

"Okay, but you're not going anywhere without backup, understand? I'm not backing down on this. You're not going to talk me out of it."

Katie took a deep slow breath, slowing her rattled mind, and stared at her partner. They had been through some harrowing incidents, but he knew her moves and she trusted him. "Of course. But we'll only report back to the sheriff when we find something."

"Okay, let's get back to your house and gear up."

FORTY-SEVEN

Tuesday 1850 hours

Katie pulled out a copy of an aerial map and laid it on her kitchen counter along with the list of real estate owned by Travis Stone. Her hands slightly shook as she smoothed the map so that they could see it clearly. The situation was becoming more intense by the minute. She kept her mind in the mode she had used when she was in the army. Strong. Focused. Ready for battle.

"If we want to keep Travis Stone's properties as the point of origin of where everything began to unravel, basically where everything began with the arson, then we need to figure out where someone might take a hostage." She could barely say the word "hostage" when referring to Chad, but she made an effort and kept her focus and determination front and center.

"That basically leaves us with only one house that isn't occupied, Travis Stone's estate, both businesses of Randall Construction and The Engine Block, and the industrial properties of the shut-down timber mill, and the industrial storage," said McGaven.

"It would have to be remote. The killer is smart but he thinks he's too smart."

"But also accessible."

"Have you ever been to the old lumber mill?" she said.

"A long time ago when it was still a working mill, but I couldn't tell you anything about the property."

"You think it would be a place to keep someone hostage without anyone knowing?"

"I do." He scanned the map, studying areas of entry and escape. "We should enter here," McGaven said and pointed to an area just north of the property. "We can easily conceal the Jeep here and go in."

Katie agreed. "You ready?" She didn't want to waste any more time before getting on the road. They had to stay proactive and keep moving.

"You bet."

The daylight was already dwindling and it was taking a chance to try and find Chad in the dark when they didn't know exactly where they were going to search. The task wouldn't be on their side. Katie and McGaven worked diligently and quickly to get everything together they might need. Luckily, McGaven already had a large plastic container with his police vest, extra magazines, hunting knife, and appropriate camouflage gear. What he didn't have, Katie did.

"Are you sure you want to bring Cisco?" asked McGaven securing his gear.

"It's not about wanting... We need his nose, especially since it will be dark. We can cover much more ground and dismiss areas that he has no interest in."

Cisco was already geared up with his military vest, which had reinforced areas on it that were knife- and bulletproof. The black dog was calm as he watched Katie. He knew that something big was going on.

McGaven nodded in agreement.

"You don't need backup?" said John.

"We need you here, but we'll be in contact," she said.

"If you need me, I can be there in record time."

Katie secured her second gun in an ankle holster. "Thanks, John." She stood for a moment. "It really means a lot."

"I have two vest cameras for you, so I can see everything you do," said John. He helped Katie and McGaven insert them. "And state-of-the-art earpieces and microphones, so you can communicate with each other."

"Thank you."

He smiled and lightly squeezed Katie's arm before he left the room to continue to check security.

"You ready?" said McGaven.

"Yes."

"Remember it's not if *you* can do this—it's that *we* can do this."

Katie nodded. She was scared and worried about what Chad was going through—if he was still alive. Anything else, she pushed from her mind. She could barely wait until Chad was home safe and with her.

"Oh, here," he said and gave her a knife in a sheath.

"I don't usually carry a knife."

"This isn't usual circumstances."

She complied and attached it to the side of her belt.

Katie looked at her home and then picked up her duffel bag and left. Cisco followed behind her. McGaven paused and locked the front door. John was still there and ready to help with any information they needed.

The detectives loaded the Jeep as Cisco obediently jumped inside and took a seat in the back.

Thoughts flooded through Katie, both of memories and the current events, helping to fuel what she had to do next. Not knowing exactly what to expect, she pushed forward with a mission of life or death. She had never dreamed that this mission could possibly mean death of her fiancé. It was something that she wasn't prepared for—and something she would prevent at all costs. They had known each other since they were kids and almost every childhood memory had Chad in it. She wasn't going to lose him.

She climbed into the front seat, securing the safety belt across the front of her. There was a slight smell of Chad's usual soap, making Katie hesitate as she put the key in the ignition. He had been in the seat only hours earlier when he left the firehouse to go home.

The Jeep roared to life.

Katie pulled out of her driveway and they headed toward the old lumber mill up on Sierra Skyline. She drove in silence, but it wasn't awkward. They needed the quiet before they met with whatever they were going to confront.

The more they drove, the higher they climbed. Katie couldn't shake the feeling of her many memories. In her two tours in Afghanistan, whenever her team had prepared for a mission, no matter what it entailed, she had had the same feelings of trepidation. All the worries of "are we going to make it through?" and "what if I screw up and someone gets killed?" These same thoughts were tormenting Katie now.

"I think we're close to the area we need to be in," said McGaven. His face was solemn and there were no fun or light-mood comments from him. He was ready and alert.

Katie turned down an area that wasn't a road or even a trail. The Jeep bounced and bobbed and weaved its way onward. She pulled the SUV into a space where there was an arch of trees, which made a perfect place to stash it. The sky was clear, but the light was disappearing quickly.

"Okay," said Katie. "I'm going to put Cisco in tracking mode. We'll have a good view up here to see if anyone is here or has been here recently."

"Why would Travis Stone even want to buy this place?" McGaven said.

"It's a nice piece of property. Maybe he was looking for investors to make it into a resort or luxury housing."

Katie opened the back door and Cisco easily jumped out. She attached a long lead to him, but decided to retract it to about ten feet.

McGaven rechecked his gear. He had decided back at the house to have a shotgun in addition to his sidearm.

Katie checked Cisco's gear as well as her own. "Let's get going." She had a regular flashlight and a small penlight, but for now the natural evening light would have to do.

"Ready?" said McGaven. He checked his small compass, which was secured on a leather strap around his neck.

Katie nodded. She let out Cisco's lead and they trudged forward. She watched the dog move at a moderate pace, tail and head down. Occasionally he would raise his head with his ears perked forward but then go back to moving at a moderate speed. He almost blended into the evening light with his black coat.

They came to a ridge with several large boulders and stopped. The old lumber mill was visible below. It felt as if they were catapulted back in time. Once the trees were selected and cut down, they were then cut to the appropriate length, branches were cut off, and then the logs were loaded onto trucks. The long wooden structures on the property could easily accommodate huge trees, which would have been brought in by semi-trucks.

Now the place seemed more appropriate to the backdrop of a horror movie. The sides of the old wooden building were missing boards and the roof looked weak and as if it would cave in soon. Pine needles were everywhere and had piled up several inches high on the roof. It wasn't clear if anyone had been there recently, but an SUV or heavy-duty truck could access the property without much difficulty.

Since there were no cars in sight, Katie and McGaven headed down a side trail. Katie watched Cisco, but he acted as if they were on an evening hike rather than a recon. Nothing made the dog stop or sniff the air for familiar or live scents. The forest was quiet except for their footsteps crunching the leaves and needles. The group continued until they reached the main area, where at one time semi-trucks had unloaded their bundles of newly fallen trees.

They were out in the open and that was when Katie felt the prickly feelings up and down her arms. If someone was looking, they would see them quite easily. She moved faster, keeping to the darkened trees and sides of the buildings.

They moved into the main cutting area. There were still some huge chains hanging and rollers that had been used to push the tree trunks along. The ravages of time had hit the lumber mill hard. The structure had once had high ceilings and rafters with symmetrical windows across the back, which were now missing their glass panes. Many heavy winds had trans-ported much of the outdoors in, with needles, leaves, branches, weeds, and dirt swept inside the structure.

Katie was the first to speak in a low tone. "I don't think anyone has been here in quite some time." She looked at the areas where someone could park and there were no footprints.

"Let's look around a few minutes before we call it quits."

She knew he was right, but the longer they took searching an area on the wrong property, the more likely Chad could be dead. She knew his time could be running out and it made her heart break.

Chad, where are you?

They walked around the main building and several other structures that must have mostly been used for equipment and supplies. There was no indication anyone had been there recently. No footprints. No clean areas where someone would have touched. Nothing designating current technology like extension cords, generators, or hidden supplies.

Cisco was calm and curious about certain things, but he showed no alerts or concerns.

Katie and McGaven hiked back up to where the Jeep was parked. It was almost completely dark now. The search was uneventful and frustrating. Maybe they were grasping at something that wasn't going to pan out and in the meantime, Chad needed them.

Once back at the Jeep, Katie said, "Maybe my instincts were off?"

"I don't think so."

"This place is like a ghost town. My emotions may have impeded my judgment." Katie vented her disappointment.

"C'mon, were not done yet. We're not giving up now."

She loaded Cisco into the SUV. "I hope you're right. We need to check out the industrial storage area."

"Even if the industrial storage area is deserted like it is here, we'll step back and re-evaluate the situation before we move forward. In the meantime, your uncle is working on tactical backup."

Katie appreciated the levelheadedness of her partner. She needed to keep it together and move forward. If Chad was at the other location, his time may have already run out.

FORTY-EIGHT

Tuesday 2345 hours

As Katie drove to Beaver Creek Road, located high up near the mountains, McGaven took the opportunity to search his phone for areas around the commercial storage property. The area was still somewhat remote and property was cheaper than in lower elevations.

A text message came in on his phone. "It's John. He's checking in and says that there's nothing new on his end. He's in waiting mode." McGaven quickly sent a text back as to their situation.

"If we don't find something soon, Cisco's going to fall asleep," she said.

McGaven turned around to look at Cisco in the back seat. The dog was sitting on the right side, alert and watching through the front windshield to the side windows. "Nope. He's not snoozing anytime soon."

"Do you think it was a mistake to assume that the killer is using one of Travis Stone's properties?" she said. Her question hung in the air, making her want to cringe.

"To be honest, it's as good as any place."

"Meaning?"

"You feel strongly about the cases all being a part of one big case. One killer? Right?"

She slightly nodded, still watching the road and slowing a bit.

"I know you, Katie. You stick to your guns when you're on a case. The only reason you doubt yourself now is that Chad has been thrown in the scenario. What would you think if he weren't part of this?"

"I don't know." She drove off the main road that paralleled Beaver Creek Road. "Look," she said and stopped the Jeep.

From their view above, the surveyed the massive property that had been under construction for two years and was now sitting abandoned. There were hundreds if not thousands of metal storage areas. Each unit was the size of a small house. It wasn't a public storage like the ones most people were used to seeing. These were supersized locked containers to store industrial equipment and heavy-duty tools. Semi-trucks could also store their trailers. It was a huge area with many places to hide and to keep someone hostage. There could be a dozen semi-trucks on the other side of the property that they couldn't see. It was going to be a huge undertaking, but they had to approach it quickly and efficiently to get through most of the area in record time.

"Wow," said McGaven. "That's going to be quite the search. It's a super storage ghost town."

"That's why we have our ace—Cisco," she said slowly.

"Wait a minute," he said, looking through his infrared binoculars at an area near one of the large storage containers with recently opened paint cans and cleaning solutions along with fresh litter. "It looks like someone has been here recently. When did it say the last of the construction was done?"

"It's been more than two years. And we know that no one

else owns it except for Stone, so no one should be here or have access until his estate and properties are settled."

"So who has been here?"

"That's what we're going to find out," said Katie. A surge of energy was pushing her forward. She drove the car farther away so that they could stay hidden. She wanted to check out the property without being seen. "Surprise is still the best offense."

She wove the Jeep in behind some trees in one of the densest parts of the forest. She wasn't worried about getting stuck; the Jeep could maneuver its way out of most terrains. She cut the engine and lights and they sat in darkness. The world around them was silent. The wildlife was hiding.

"We can't wait any longer," she said. "Time isn't on our side." Her heart ached to see Chad again—to be home with him where he was safe.

They got out of the SUV with Cisco, who was watchful and ready to get started on the search. The dog was their alert system and scent detector. At first Katie had hesitated over bringing him in for safety reasons, but now, as the huge compound of industrial storage units awaited them, she was relieved that her K9 partner was with them.

Katie took a precious moment and bent down to face Cisco. She hugged the dog. They had been through a tremendous number of battles, gunfire, and witnessing the loss of life together. She looked into the dog's golden wolf eyes and knew that he understood what was at stake. "We need to find Chad," she whispered to the dog.

"C'mon," said McGaven. He pulled out his phone. The light from the small screen lit up the area around them, giving a weird dreamlike atmosphere. "Here's the basic layout of the place, but we don't know what's been built and what areas are still under construction." His face had an amber glow from the phone.

Katie memorized the layout.

"It would be easier to have an entire team to search this property."

"We have to be in stealth mode, so no one knows we're here," she said. "We don't know if this is even the place, but we don't get another chance for the surprise element. It could mean the difference between life and death." She knew the same was true for their lives as well—but it didn't need to be said.

McGaven reached back into the Jeep and retrieved two black baseball caps with lights attached to the brims. "Here, this will help you see, and it's easy to extinguish if necessary."

Cisco trotted over to a tree and sniffed around, coming right back to Katie's side.

Both detectives made sure their communication earpieces were operating correctly. Now they were ready to go.

"Gav," she said. "I know you're not going to like this, but—"

"We should split up to cover more ground faster." His expression was intense.

"How do you do that?"

"You're my partner," he said smiling. "I always know what you're going to say."

It was a nice quick moment of encouragement and strength that Katie needed. "Wouldn't want it any other way—partner."

"Okay, the way I see it," he said. "You take the southern areas and I'll take the northern—we work our way back to the middle."

Studying the map again, she said, "Okay, got it."

"Stay in contact at all times. I don't want more than five minutes to pass without hearing your voice."

"Got it." This time she kept the leash hooked to her vest and let Cisco freely stay by her side. Since she was alone in her search, it would be easier and safer to not worry about the leash. She flipped on her light and it helped to keep her path lit.

Katie moved into the trees heading down to her area. She

could hear McGaven's footsteps go in the other direction—and then silence.

She was alone.

She kept her wits, trying not to think that every shadow was someone hiding in wait with a gun pointed at her head. Moving at a brisk continuous pace, she finally came to a chain-link fence, which, by the looks of it, was set up years ago. It curled from the bottom and the "Keep Out" signs were now rusted. This was as good a place as any to enter the compound.

"Any luck?" said the hushed voice of McGaven.

"I'm entering through the area about a hundred feet away from the targeted area."

Katie manipulated the fencing in between the twelve feet sections—torquing it back and forth. She finally was able to make a space to slip through. First, she held it for Cisco and then she managed to push her body through.

The little light that shined from the night sky reflected off the cement foundations, making them glow a bit and giving more illumination. She didn't need her cap flashlight on. Her boots moved almost silently across the ground. She hedged around areas with piles of forest debris and scattered construction pieces.

Once she was inside the area, Katie could see the layout more clearly. It was desolate. Isolated. The construction designer had made the entire compound like infinite figure eights. It would be easy for semi-trucks to drive in and out with supplies or equipment to store.

Katie decided to work in the manner of searching a crime scene but on a much larger scale. She opted for a strip method of search—moving in a straight line turning around and moving another straight line. It was the most comfortable and efficient under the circumstances. The metal buildings varied in square footage and heights. There were buildings that could house a fleet of airplanes while others would hold a couple of work trucks.

As she and Cisco took moments to clear each building they came to, her thoughts weren't far from Chad and what he must be going through and thinking about. She fought back the tears as she watched Cisco's behavior.

Katie still believed that every crime scene was connected to Sara Simms. That twelve-year-old girl was ground zero, along with 717 Maple Road. Her killer could just have been a kid himself who had grown up into a man who wasn't going to let his secrets be revealed.

Kent Simms...

Seth Randall...

Stan Bates...

Someone not on their radar yet... from the school... neighbor... who?

"You still awake?" said McGaven.

"Barely. Are you seeing the size of these storage containers?"

"Yep. Over here they are still in the process of being assembled. Tons of construction supplies lying around. It looks like they've been here for quite some time."

"Creepy."

"Ditto."

Katie trudged on, realizing that this might be a waste of time. They were never going to be able to search everything in a timely manner, so she decided that she would stick to the containers and buildings that would be accessible by trucks and SUVs—and easily hide them.

More than an hour passed and her anxieties levels rose significantly. Another hour. More precious time. She had to push past the strange sensations in her body and the slight dizzying of her vision. She pressed herself harder and hurried— Cisco rushed along, keeping up with her pace.

Chad where are you?

"I don't know, Gav, there's nothing—" Just then Katie spotted tire tracks in the dirt on the cement. "Wait," she said. "I think we have new tire tracks." Her breathing heightened and she began to sound winded, like she had been running. Her hope skyrocketed. It was a sign that someone had accessed the commercial property. "It looks like a passenger truck or SUV tire tracks."

"Any more?" said McGaven.

"I don't know," she said, following the tracks. "There are some large industrial impressions—like a semi or another type of tractor trailer."

Cisco became interested in the tires' impressions. There appeared to be dirt, dried mud, and some type of oil left behind. His nose pushed down on the ground as he moved along, cataloging all the ingredients to the scent he followed.

"Where did they come in?" said McGaven.

"It looks like from the main entrance." She directed light at the gate. "New lock too." The large lock still shined.

"Randall Construction?"

"Possibly, but Stone had other associates too. Maybe it was one of them? He might've wanted to get this construction going again. And Randall Construction was more residential stuff." She followed the tire impressions to another area, where there weren't any containers. "Looks like the trucks stopped here." She took a photo of the area with her phone and sent it to McGaven.

"Got it," he said. "Maybe it has to do with utilities?"

"Maybe." She walked the trail of tire tracks, but the only thing she saw within a reasonable distance was part of the drainage area.

Katie stood in the darkness staring at the immense commercial storage area and thinking about the killer—who and why. Who would have access to this place? Who would want to cover up the murders? Why would they use this place? There still was a nagging in the back of her mind—what if she was wrong?

The same name kept coming back—Seth Randall of Randall Construction. He was the right age, had the right background, had access, and had all the right equipment. Katie theorized that when he was a boy he had killed Sara Simms and left her body to decompose in the Snyder Parks, but when the land was being developed for homes he had to move her bones if he didn't want to be found out. That would have been ten years or more after her death. He had the means and opportunity to move her. He would have done anything not to get caught—and that might have proved deadly for others.

Was Seth Randall the killer?

"You okay?" said McGaven.

"Yeah, why?"

"I can hear you breathing hard."

"Just putting pieces together, trying to get events, times, and opportunities to fit."

"When were you going to let me in on it?"

"When I know," she said.

Cisco began circling the area. He was anxious and trying to tell Katie something. The dog turned away from her and barked.

"What is it, Cisco?" She unhooked his lead.

"What's going on?" said McGaven.

"I'm not sure."

Katie walked over to Cisco. He seemed extremely interested in the large drainage grate. The black metal ran along part of the property and out the back, most likely to a drain at that location. There was nothing else around that he could have caught wind of except something wafting in the slight breeze. One thing she knew for sure—the scent was something that the dog recognized.

"What is it?" she said, lowering down on her knees.

Cisco ran circles around her, panting and grumbling—his behavior and agitation was consistent with times when he had found tripwires and insurgents. She had to take his tracking seriously.

Katie switched on her light and peered down in the hole. It was deep and must take the major drainage for the entire property's runoff throughout the year. Putting her hands on the metal grate, she saw it was secured and would take a special tool or equipment to remove. She leaned closer and couldn't see anything unusual in the piping running downward, but it was big.

Cisco came up to her and pushed her arm as he turned and ran.

"Hang on," she said. "Cisco is on the scent of something and is moving to the back part of the property—northwest."

"I'm making my way to you—ETA ten minutes. Stay alert," said McGaven. Katie could hear his breathing become rapid as he ran.

"Ten-four," she said.

Katie started running to keep up with Cisco. She didn't want to yell to slow him down and let their presence be known, but she didn't know if he was running straight into danger—or worse. She sprinted behind the dark shadow of the German shepherd as he zigzagged around the large containers. It was obvious Cisco was on the scent of something important.

FORTY-NINE

Wednesday 0145 hours

Katie's mind was spinning with all sorts of scenarios as she kept up with Cisco, hoping that the trained K9 was going to lead her to Chad. As she sprinted, she kept a watchful eye on darkened areas as she ran past. Her main focus was on finding Chad alive, but her training still kept her alert for any vulnerability.

She dismissed McGaven's questions in her ear until she knew what Cisco was chasing.

Cisco rounded a large storage container which had three sets of roll-up doors. When Katie got to the corner of the container, she didn't immediately see the dog. Her fears overwhelmed her as she berated herself that she should've kept him on a long leash. Panic began to set in.

Cisco...

Katie stopped to gain her bearings and reset her objective. Running back and forth past different-sized storage containers made her dizzy and disoriented her. She forced herself to close her eyes and listen, slow her breathing, and to concentrate on ridding herself of fear. It was one of the times that her army training in extreme circumstances helped her overcome obstacles and frightening situations. She began to count backward in her head. Twenty... nineteen... eighteen... seventeen... sixteen...

Then she heard the familiar whine with a low guttural bark. *Cisco...*

Katie snapped her eyes open and ran in the direction around the corner in between two containers where Cisco stood —his dark outline was that of a perfect standing German shepherd, head high, ears forward and alert, his tail low and brushing back and forth. He whined again and poked his nose forward into a square cement outlet.

Katie took several steps forward and her boots sank ankle-deep. She realized that it was an area where the water drainage was located for the entire property. She watched Cisco catch a whiff of what he was chasing and wouldn't leave the drainage area. There was still a breeze, but it was unclear to her what the dog had been trailing.

"Katie! Katie!" yelled McGaven in her earpiece.

"I'm here," she said calmly. "Cisco tracked a scent to the back of the property at the water drainage outlet."

Clearly relieved, he said, "You don't know what you're getting yourself into. Wait for me."

"I'm not waiting—I'm following Cisco. I'll be talking to you every step of the way."

She heard McGaven sigh and knew that he was annoyed with her, but she had to get to Chad if he was in there.

"You don't know if Chad is anywhere near that water drainage system. You could be walking into a trap. Wait for backup."

"I know Cisco."

As Katie approached the entrance, she could hear McGaven talking with her uncle, making plans on how backup could get to the property. It would take more than an hour and a half by the time the sheriff rounded up a crew and made their way up here. It wasn't an easy drive, even with a four-wheel-drive vehicle.

Katie finally made her way to the water drainage pipe, which was several feet down the ravine. The cement pipe was easily five feet in diameter. There was a metal closure resembling a door, which hadn't been locked yet, most likely due to still being under construction.

"Okay, Cisco," she said. "We're going in..."

Katie opened the metal door and walked carefully inside. Cisco headed in with her. She had to hunch over, keeping her head down, and work to keep her balance as the pipe wasn't a flat surface. It sloped upward. The smell of sour moldy water like that of a pond drifted into her face. It was strangely warmer inside the pipe than it was outside, but there wasn't anything comforting about it. There was no wind, just stagnant air, but she kept moving deeper into the cavern.

The sound of Cisco's toenails echoed through the chamber. He stayed either at her left side or slightly behind her. It was clear that he was uncomfortable but his amazing sense of smell guided them.

The underground pipe opened into a middle chamber, which was large, square in shape, and had horizontal steps leading down to a lower level. There were steps on the other side. Katie hurried and moved up the other side. She fought her balance as she felt funky and there was a claustrophobic feel even though there was sufficient space around her. It was as if she had stumbled into an underground funhouse. She thought her mind was playing tricks, but it was her anxiety attempting to take over.

Katie's only thoughts were finding Chad safe.

She rounded another chamber. She said, "Chad?" Her voice strangely echoed around her.

"Katie? Everything okay?" said McGaven.

"I'm almost to the end."

"I'm about five or six minutes away."

"Ten-four."

Katie rounded another corner and noticed there was some light and a slight breeze, which must have been coming from outside. She inched forward to the area, where she gulped in air. Suddenly, with a mixture of relief and horror, she saw the figure of Chad lying on the ground. He wasn't moving and appeared to be unconscious.

"Chad?" she whispered, barely forming the words.

No...

Katie moved toward him. It was a tight squeeze with cement surrounding her like a cocoon. In her mind, she was suddenly transported to the battlefield. The sound of large-caliber ammunition boomed in her ears. She saw casualties. Blood. Gaping wounds. She heard yelling in several languages. The sensation of smoke filtering through the air almost overwhelmed her, but she snapped back into present day in the drainage tunnel.

She moved as quickly as she could to Chad and knelt down. His face was bloodied around his nose and mouth. There was dried blood on the left side of his head as if he had been bludgeoned. She gently put her hands on his face. "Chad?" she said. "Oh, Chad." Katie stifled a cry.

He remained unresponsive and ghostly pale. His jaw was lax and his head flopped to the side. Katie bit her lip. "Chad, can you hear me?" She looked down at his right leg. There was quite a bit of blood staining his pants and she recognized, from seeing it many times on the battlefield, that his leg was broken. He needed medical attention immediately, but she also knew that it would take time for the ambulance and emergency vehicles to arrive.

Cisco squeezed through the opening and pushed his way to them to check out Chad and began licking his face as his way of resuscitating him.

Chad murmured a few words. Katie leaned closer to listen but couldn't make out what he was saying.

"Chad," she said. "I'm here." She suppressed the urge to cry and break down. "I'm so sorry..." she said, repeating it over and over as if it would change anything.

Without warning, Chad opened his eyes and stared directly at Katie. "I... knew... I would see you again." He forced a smile but it was clear that he was in excruciating pain.

"Take it easy and rest. We're going to get you out of here." She looked up and could see an opening, possibly the one she had peered down from, but they weren't able to get up to it or even pry it open. The only other way was to retrace her steps.

Cisco stayed next to them and stood guard. He panted lightly but remained on high alert.

"Gav," she said, barely above a whisper. "I found Chad. He's alive."

"Oh, Katie," he said with relief in his voice. "That's fantastic."

"He's in bad shape and has a broken leg and other injuries."

"I'm almost there."

"He's fading in and out of consciousness. I don't want to move him, but there's no other choice to get him out of here. It's going to take me a bit. I need help."

"Katie," McGaven said suddenly. She knew by the sound of his voice it wasn't good news. "He's coming."

"What?" she said and could hear the sound of a large truck engine overhead.

"He's coming in through the gate."

"Who?"

"I don't know. And, Katie?" McGaven said. "The person is driving a water tanker."

FIFTY

Wednesday 0315 hours

Katie couldn't have imagined a more gruesome worst-case scenario, but when McGaven said a water tanker was coming it was obvious what the killer wanted to do and how he was going to get rid of the body so no one would ever find it, or her—except maybe after they had turned to skeletons.

Her memory fixated on the remains of the Cross family and Sara Simms. If Seth Randall or Kent Simms had indeed killed the Cross family, there was no reasoning with them because they killed indiscriminately and they didn't care who it was as long as it fit their needs.

Katie heard the truck enter the property and what she assumed was the tanker stopping next to the opening. The airbrakes took hold as the big engine idled.

"Katie, you have to get out of there now!" said McGaven.

"I can't leave Chad because he can't walk out of here." Katie heard her own frantic voice as Cisco pressed up against her.

"I'm close, but I'm not there yet." said McGaven winded. "The sheriff and his posse are more than forty minutes away."

She heard a truck door slam and footsteps as a large hose was shoved through the above opening. Within minutes, more than four thousand gallons of water would come barreling down on them—it would be like having boulders falling on your head.

She stood and looked up toward the opening as the lights from the truck flickered from the headlights and the brake lights.

"I'm going to get Chad to a safer place," she whispered, inching closer to the opening.

"Ten-four. I'll be there to meet you in minutes."

Katie knew that they might not have that much time.

Cisco pushed at Katie. He didn't want to leave her. "Cisco, *voraus*," she commanded for him to go. The dog hesitated, sensing the dangerous situation. "Go!" The dog turned and left the area, knowing that he would wait for his partner.

Katie gained as much strength she could and turned to her fiancé. "Okay, fireman, on your feet." She pulled him to his feet as he cried out in extreme pain. "We're moving now."

The roar of the tanker was deafening and the sound rattled strangely all around them. It was like being a lion's den and they were going to be prey any second.

"There's no way... I can do this, Katie," said Chad, trying to stay awake. His arms were floppy and his leg was useless. "I can't..."

"If you can pass a firefighter's physical test, you can do this." She put his left arm over her shoulder and they began to walk together slowly. "We army vets never leave anyone behind. That's a promise." She tried to persuade him to move faster, but they only inched a little bit at a time.

From above, rumbling like a runaway earthquake, the truck engine revved and water began to pour into the drainage pipe chamber.

FIFTY-ONE

Wednesday 0345 hours

"Katie!" yelled McGaven in her earpiece. It was the last thing she heard before several cracking rounds of gunfire erupted.

The water was filling up quickly—faster than the average tunnel flow. They weren't going to make it to the outside before the entire tunnel was raging with water. There would be no way to fight against the gravity force. It was their only way getting out swiftly.

"Okay, this is what we're going to do," she yelled.

Chad was weakening by the second. He kept closing his eyes and then suddenly opening them again. Katie felt his body go limp against hers. Her worst fear was the repercussions from his head injury causing blood to build up against his brain. "Stay with me," she said.

Chad made eye contact with her, but he faded in and out. He was too weak to speak.

Katie knew that she couldn't carry him out. She was going to have to improvise and use what she had to get them out —alive.

"Katie!" yelled McGaven in her earpiece.

"We're on our way," she said.

The water flooded the area and was thigh high.

"Okay," she said to Chad. "I know you can hear me, we're going to wait until there's more water so that it can carry us out. Okay?"

He nodded.

She pressed up against the side, holding tightly to Chad and securing him to her by wrapping Cisco's long lead around his torso and shoulders. The water was ice cold and she began to shiver. Her arms were burning, shoulder blades on fire, and she was finding it difficult to breathe in between her teeth chattering.

The water flow was deafening now as the tunnel was almost three-quarters full, with a strong flow that carried out to the exit.

She had to wait longer.

Not yet.

Just a little bit longer.

With luck, they could float and swim out easily.

Katie couldn't hear McGaven anymore. She tried not to think about it now—one problem at a time.

Now!

Katie gently pushed away from the side as the cold rushing water pushed them immediately. The force and the extra weight of Chad first pulled her under. She made the mistake of initially panicking and gulped a mouthful of water. Regaining her control, she popped up to the surface with Chad. His eyes were closed. She made sure she kept his mouth and nose above the water.

Something caught them on the side. Katie couldn't pull Chad away as the water bashed their bodies and faces.

"No..." She tried harder but Chad was hooked on something. Diving under the moving water, she tore at his shirt, trying desperately to free him.

Katie resurfaced, and was gasping for air and strength when Cisco's nose touched her. He had somehow paddled against the rushing current to assist her. He grabbed hold of Chad's shirt and pulled. His teeth held tight. His ears folded back against his head, keeping as much water as he could out of them.

Together, Katie and Cisco managed to free Chad, who was now unconscious. Katie held tightly to him, and Cisco kept his head above the water and managed to stay with the couple.

Nothing mattered at that moment except Chad. Katie pushed her endurance as hard as she could as they made their way toward the exit.

The less she fought the water, the easier the ride. They floated along, waves slapping against them and the water pushing them hard from behind. It seemed like an eternity to her but, in fact, it was barely thirty seconds until they reached the end and she could smell the fresh air of the forest. There was a moment of silence before they hit the uneven ground and rolled. It was heavy and awkward having an unconscious body like a one-hundred-eighty-pound ragdoll hooked to you, but she tried to get control. They awkwardly landed in the mud. It was cold and hard against their bodies, but it was a relief not having thousands of gallons of water beating down.

Katie's lungs were burning as she coughed out excess water, still with Chad roped to her and Cisco at her side. When she opened her eyes she couldn't see anything except for stars up in the heavens. She noticed one star, the North Star, in particular —that was the brightest. It was glimmering. Unhooking the leash from Chad, she clawed at the muddy ground to gain her bearings. The nighttime sky enveloped them and under any other circumstances it would have been picturesque. Her ears rang. For a moment, the dark forest spun upside-down as she desperately caught her breath.

Katie turned to Chad, leaning over him. "Chad?" He was unresponsive. She checked for a pulse and was relieved that it was strong. After making sure that his airway was clear, she had no other choice but to go on alone until she knew that the area was secure and the danger had been terminated. It was the most difficult decision she ever had to make in her career. She had to leave him behind.

Cisco nuzzled her face.

"*Bleib*," she ordered him to stay with Chad.

Two shots rang out.

FIFTY-TWO

Wednesday 0415 hours

Katie was in a strange dreamlike state. When she got up she felt like she carried a lead weight on her back and her legs because she was soaking wet. Her core shivered, but she pushed forward. There was no contact from McGaven, most likely due to water in the earpiece.

Katie moved toward the sounds, keeping her presence hidden in the shadows of the large metal buildings. She pulled her weapon from her secure holster. She could hear voices and crept closer, daring to peer around a corner. McGaven had taken cover by a nearby container, his gun drawn and directed toward the main area.

She saw a figure standing near the tanker with his hands up. The light was shining from behind him, making it difficult to see his identity.

Katie decided to move forward and close the gap.

As she quietly crept closer in the shadows, she saw the man. His face pallid, eyes wide. It was Seth Randall. It was no surprise, but she was perplexed by his giving up so easily.

Everything about the crime scenes had indicated that the killer was driven to do what he did: intelligent, organized, and not slowing down just because the cops were closing in. He had overstepped, even for a killer, by murdering one of the Pine Valley Sheriff's Department's own. This didn't seem like the man who had accomplished all those things.

She caught McGaven's attention. His face was pale in the lighting, his eyes dark, intense, and he gave a slight nod.

Katie kept moving forward. She was barely twenty feet from Seth Randall. "Get on your knees!" she yelled and kept advancing.

Seth did as he was ordered as he dropped to his knees with his hands behind his head. "Detective Scott," he said. "You don't understand."

"Tell that to the judge." Katie was exhausted and wanted this to be over. Justice for the Cross family and finally for Sara Simms.

"I didn't do this."

"You're pathetic."

"I could never kill anyone."

"Evidence says otherwise."

"Look, Detective," he said, his pleading eyes fixed on her.

Katie felt unnerved by his nervous demeanor and state-ments. He didn't strike her as the killer, but that was surely ridiculous now. It was merely psychopathic behavior.

"I didn't kill that family. There's no reason for me to."

"Just one of your classmates. What? Did she made fun of you?"

"You mean Sara Simms? I liked her. I liked her ever since kindergarten. I could never have hurt her—ever." He looked down at the ground and appeared to have remorse—even a tear. His sentiments seemed honest—and his voice was much softer than it had been at Randall Construction. Either he was telling the truth or was the best psychopathic actor ever.

Katie glanced to her right as McGaven slowly moved to join her. "Stay where you are." She slowly approached him, still not convinced that he was honest or that he didn't have ulterior motives. "You tried to kill us, so don't be offended if we don't trust you."

"I didn't want to. I'm not a killer!" he yelled and stood up. "I just had to—"

"Get on your knees!" yelled both Katie and McGaven.

A single shot from another area hit Seth Randall directly in the chest.

Katie and McGaven took immediate cover, trying to decipher where the shooter was positioned.

"Where did that come from?" whispered Katie.

McGaven pointed up toward one of the container roofs.

There was a quick flash of reflection coming from the area McGaven had identified.

She nodded.

Looking back, Katie saw Seth Randall splayed out on the ground, on his back, with his arms straight out from his sides. His pleas still resonated in her head.

I could never hurt her—ever.

Several bullets ricocheted off the metal buildings around them. There was a pause and then more.

"I'll go around and we can flank him," she whispered.

"No. We need to wait."

"We don't know what's going to happen. I can't take the chance that this person is going to find Chad and Cisco. I'm going now; otherwise, we're going to get picked off one at a time before backup arrives," she said and started to make her way toward the shooter.

"Katie..." whispered McGaven as he watched her leave in the darkness. He was angry, but kept his wits and made his move toward the shooter from the other angle.

Katie sprinted around several containers. Staying in the

darkness, she cautiously crept closer and could finally see a man on the roof. It was unclear at first who it was, but as the evening light changed slightly, she saw his face. It now made complete sense to her and the profile. And why the crime scenes seemed to have conflicting behaviors—there were two people involved. Of course. The brothers. The man shooting at them was David Randall, Seth's brother. The quiet, helpful brother who seemed to be cooperating with them, but instead was calculating his next moves.

Anger welled up inside Katie. Her hands shook and she forgot about how cold and wet she was. This man had killed an innocent girl twenty-five years ago, and a family, and one of the department's own. She wanted him dead, but she knew they had to tread lightly and strategically.

Looking around, she saw a large loader with the bucket held high. Moving closer, she saw it had been there awhile, but would help her to climb onto the roof. It was the only way to get the upper hand and take him down—dead or alive. It was his choice.

Katie readjusted her vest. Her clothes were soaked but she didn't have time to wring them out. Her boots were full of water and made a slight squishing sound when she walked. It was barely audible, but she adapted her step to make her approach silent.

She secured her gun and began to climb the loader. Finding footholds and handholds as she climbed the piece of equipment, she kept an eye around her so as to not get ambushed. It was slipperier than she first thought. Moving slowly, she managed to hoist herself onto the roof silently.

It was dark, as if she were going to fall into an abyss, but she knew that the roof was sound underneath her body. She moved in an army-crawl movement until she saw David Randall looking down. He was at a forty-five degree angle from her just across the roof.

"Stay right there and drop your weapon!" said McGaven.

Katie couldn't see him but she guessed he had taken cover behind a large stack of bricks.

"Give it up, you're surrounded," he continued.

"Really?" said David. His voice had a strange tone. He didn't sound like he did when they visited him at the Randall Construction office.

"Drop your gun!"

"I see," he laughed. "I know how this goes... my reign has finally come to an end."

"Why?" said McGaven. "What motive did you have to kill a little girl in your school?"

Katie knew that her partner was trying to keep David talking as she skirted closer. She could see David's face. Contorted. Frustrated. And wasn't going to let anyone take him in.

"Why? Really? Haven't you ever known what it's like to be bullied, hassled, and constantly berated? It wouldn't stop. It. Wouldn't. Stop. So I stepped up and stopped it. But the thing that was... shocking to me... was I liked it. I really liked it. I strangled her, watching her life dwindle in my hands. What a rush. But then it started not long after her death." He hit the side of his head several times with the gun. "It wouldn't stop... it just wouldn't stop. I had to continue."

"You could've stopped after killing Sara Simms. Why kill the Cross family? And the holding area?"

"Because that family was going to tell. I had to improvise. It's what I'm good at. They found her body when we were working on the basement stairs. Don't you get it? Aren't you a cop?" David's hand began to tremble. "Twenty-five years... and they ruined everything... everything... the planning... the perfect grave... everything..."

"You killed the Cross family and a forensic tech?"

"I wasn't done yet!" He waved the gun in frustration.

"*Everyone* that had *anything* to do with the Cross family had to die! Don't you get it? You don't see it?"

Katie inched closer too. She could barely believe that the David Randall they had spoken to at the office was this same man ranting about killing people.

"I wasn't done yet!"

"You used Travis Stone?" said McGaven.

"He was a means, a tool, to get what I needed, but in the end he was weak like all the rest. I'm glad he was murdered. So I had to do what I had to do. Otherwise the Crosses were going to the police. And I couldn't have that."

"C'mon, David, drop the gun. You're completely surrounded."

He laughed. "Where's that perky partner of yours? I know you're out here, Detective Scott. I knew it was a matter of time before we met again. This time, it's on my terms. Pity for your boyfriend." He made a dramatic sigh.

Katie kept inching toward him, hoping that the darkness of the night would be her cover. She kept her weapon directed at him.

"Come down! You're surrounded and there's no escape!" said McGaven, keeping David's attention on him. "Why did you kill your brother?"

"Why not?" He readjusted himself from lying on his stomach to a kneeling position. "He was weak and I could tell he was going to confess everything one of these days."

Katie kept moving, she was barely five feet from him. He seemed to be focused on McGaven. Her breath quiet and shallow. "Drop it! I'll give you two seconds!"

"Nice work, Detective."

"Put the gun down now!"

"Of course," he said and dramatically spun the gun and then slowly lowered it to the roof.

Katie took her opportunity and rushed him just as he grabbed for his gun.

David was strong and in shape; he was able to get the gun and aim it in Katie's direction. A shot went off, barely missing her left ear.

She heard it whiz by, momentarily leaving her hearing muddled.

"Katie!" yelled McGaven from below.

Katie tackled David, struggling to maintain her position as they moved dangerously close to the edge of the roof. They grappled. She turned her gun into his body and fired—twice. David looked stunned as he kept eye contact with her before he flopped backward, sliding off the roof. He hit the pavement, landing on his back, eerily in the same position as his brother staring up at the night sky.

Katie took a moment to look down at David's body. The bullets had hit him directly in the chest.

"You okay?" McGaven called up.

"Fine. I have to get to Chad."

McGaven alerted the sheriff as to the situation and that it had been de-escalated—safe to enter. He also requested an ambulance immediately.

Climbing down in a hurry, her only thought was Chad. The Randall brothers didn't matter anymore.

Katie ran back to where Chad and Cisco were waiting. Cisco had laid down next to him with his head on his chest. She dropped to her knees next to Chad and in horror saw that he wasn't breathing. "No, no, no." She felt for a pulse—there was none. She immediately began chest compressions, counting, "One, two, three, four..." Then she covered his mouth with hers and blew air into his lungs. She kept repeating this sequence.

McGaven jogged up and saw the scene. "We need a paramedics and an ambulance now! We have firefighter Chad

Ferguson unresponsive—Katie is giving CPR." He listened to the sheriff. "Katie, they'll be here in less than five minutes."

Katie kept up with the CPR and didn't hear her partner; she couldn't hear anything except her own breath in her ears. She had seen too many soldiers die in her two tours and she wasn't going to let it happen here—not Chad—not ever. She kept counting...

FIFTY-THREE

Wednesday 0450 hours

Katie's exhaustion took over her body and her hands trembled. She felt as if she would hyperventilate at any time and pass out, but she wouldn't stop until her last breath. She didn't know how long she had been giving CPR, but she heard the emergency vehicles enter the industrial compound. McGaven's voice yelled for emergency personnel to come this way.

Just when she thought she couldn't breathe another breath, Chad opened his eyes.

"Oh, Chad," she cried hugging him tightly. "I love you..."

His chest moved slowly, but he was breathing on his own. "Love you more," he barely mouthed.

The paramedics arrived and began tending to him before loading him into the ambulance.

Katie stood up and let them do their work.

Sheriff Scott hurried to Katie and hugged her tightly. "You okay?"

"I think so," she whispered.

"I'll take Cisco with me and you can go to the hospital with

Chad," said McGaven as he wrapped a blanket around Katie as she shivered.

Katie was relieved and handed him the Jeep keys. "Thank you."

"No problem," he said. McGaven got Cisco and walked out.

The paramedics put Chad on a gurney and Katie followed, getting into the ambulance with him. The ambulance sped away with lights flashing.

Sheriff Scott stood at the industrial storage compound near the entrance staring at the bodies of Seth and David Randall, a water tanker semi-truck parked, and a number of shell casings scattered around, waiting for the crime scene investigation to begin.

FIFTY-FOUR

TWO WEEKS LATER...

Katie patiently waited on a bench in front of the medical building on an overcast day. Her mind reflected on the funeral for forensic technician Jimmy Turner only a week ago. An amazing number of people came from all over the area as well as from the state. The respect and professionalism that was conveyed made her proud to be a police detective.

She fidgeted with her hands and observed people come and go. She knew all the crime scenes and having to watch Chad suffer and then quit breathing at the industrial storage facility would forever be etched in her mind. She carried with her all the recent incidents she experienced like a badge of honor. She was reminded so often how fragile life was in the world today and how important family and friends were to her.

The double sliding doors opened and Chad exited using his crutches. He had suffered a broken leg in two places, bruised ribs, a broken nose, and a deep laceration on the left side of his head that took twenty-seven stitches. He had been to see the doctor as a follow-up visit after his five-day stay at the hospital. His recovery prognosis was excellent.

Katie met him and kissed him several times.

"What is that for?"

"Just because..."

"That's good enough for me," he said smiling.

"What did the doctor say?"

"Everything looks good and is healing well. I should be back on the job in about eight to ten weeks."

Katie helped him out to the parking lot where his Jeep was waiting.

McGaven jumped out along with John and they helped Chad get into the SUV.

"Thanks, Gav, for picking me up in my own car."

"Of course."

"You look good, Chad," said John.

"Glad we're not on lockdown anymore?" said Chad chuckling.

"It wasn't so bad," said McGaven. "But you're not going to get rid of us that easily."

Katie climbed in next to Chad in the back seat.

"Love you," she whispered in his ear.

"Love you more," he said.

A LETTER FROM JENNIFER CHASE

I want to say a huge thank you for choosing to read *Three Small Bones* (Book 8). If you did enjoy it, and want to keep up to date with all my latest releases, just sign up at the following link. Your email address will never be shared and you can unsubscribe at any time.

www.bookouture.com/jennifer-chase

This has continued to be a special project and series for me. Forensics, K9 training, and criminal profiling have been subjects that I've studied considerably and to be able to incorporate them into crime-fiction novels has been a thrilling experience for me. I have wanted to write this series for a while and it has been a truly wonderful experience to bring it to life.

One of my favorite activities, outside of writing, has been dog training. I'm a dog lover, if you couldn't tell by reading this book, and I loved creating a supporting canine character, Cisco, for my cold-case police detective. I hope you enjoyed it as well.

I hope you enjoyed *Three Small Bones* (Book 8) and if you did, I would be very grateful if you could write a review. I'd love to hear what you think, and it makes such a difference helping new readers to discover one of my books for the first time.

I love hearing from my readers—you can get in touch on my Facebook page, through Twitter, Goodreads, Instagram, or my website.

Thank you,

Jennifer Chase

www.authorjenniferchase.com

 facebook.com/AuthorJenniferChase

 twitter.com/JChaseNovelist

 instagram.com/jenchaseauthor

ACKNOWLEDGMENTS

I want to thank my husband Mark for his steadfast support and for being my rock even when I had self-doubt. It's not always easy living with a writer and you've made it look effortless.

A very special thank you goes out to all my law enforcement friends—police detectives, deputies, police K9, forensic units, forensic anthropologists, and first responders—there's too many to list. Your friendships have meant the world to me. It has opened a whole new writing world filled with inspiration. I wouldn't be able to bring my crime-fiction stories to life if it wasn't for all of you. Thank you for your service and dedication to keep the rest of us safe.

Writing this series continues to be a truly amazing experience. I would like to thank my publisher, Bookouture, for the opportunity, and the fantastic staff for continuing to help me to bring this book and the entire Detective Katie Scott series to life. Thank you, Kim, Sarah, and Noelle for your relentless promotion for us authors. A very special thank you to my editor Jessie Botterill and her editorial team—your incredible support and insight has helped me to work harder to write more adventures for Detective Katie Scott.

Printed in Great Britain
by Amazon

13470712R00205